# WICKED
# EXPOSURE

## Also by Katana Collins

**THE WICKED EXPOSURE SERIES**

*Wicked Shots* (novella)
*Wicked Exposure*

**THE SOUL STRIPPER SERIES**

*Soul Stripper*
*Soul Survivor*
*Soul Surrender*

Published by Kensington Publishing Corporation

# WICKED EXPOSURE

## KATANA COLLINS

KENSINGTON BOOKS
www.kensingtonbooks.com

KENSINGTON BOOKS are published by

Kensington Publishing Corp.
119 West 40th Street
New York, NY 10018

ISBN-13: 978-1-61773-637-7
ISBN-10: 1-61773-637-6
First Kensington Trade Paperback Printing: May 2015

eISBN-13: 978-1-61773-638-4
eISBN-10: 1-61773-638-4
First Kensington Electronic Edition: May 2015

10 9 8 7 6 5 4 3 2 1

Printed in the United States of America

*To Heather Dune Macadam.*
*For laying the foundation, thank you.*

# Acknowledgments

When they said "it takes a village," they weren't joking! Though as an author, much of my time is spent alone, never once in the process of creating this book did I feel lonely.

Thank you to my agent, Louise Fury, Jenny Bent, and the entire Team Fury who work tirelessly day after day—particularly, Kristin Smith, Kaitlyn Jeffries, and Kasey Poserina. You are all rock stars! Go Team Fury!

To my critique partners and fellow authors, Krista Amigone, Derek Bishop, and Alyssa Cole—thank you for being my sounding boards and my pillars. Without you three, I'm pretty certain most of my books would just be structureless run-on sentences.

Many, many thanks to Martin Biro, my editor extraordinaire, for helping make this book more amazing than I ever thought it could be! Vida, for her endless hours of marketing and out-of-the-box thinking. And the entire Kensington team for doing all the little things that go into book publishing that I can't even begin to fathom!

As always, so much gratitude to my family—Mom, Dad, Bridget, Bo, Adam, Adelynn, Harrison, and my husband, Sean, for their love and support through the years. Thank you for never turning the music down while I danced to my own tune.

A special thanks to the Maine Historical Society and particularly Portland's very own Victoria Mansion, Longfellow House, and the Westin Harborview Hotel for their tutorials about Portland's underground tunnels among other hidden gems about this amazing city. And lastly, thank you to my Maine real estate agent for helping two freelancers get the brightly colored home of their dreams in Portland!

# PROLOGUE

I pressed the binoculars to my eyes, watching from the other end of the street as she moved gracefully up the front steps despite the bulky luggage dragging behind her. Her sunglasses, shifted to the top of her head, pulled her silky brown hair back from her forehead, acting as a headband. She craned her neck back and looked up at the house.

Cassandra's house. The house that I needed more than anything. Using the binoculars, I scanned Jessica's body. A camera bag was strapped over one shoulder and bounced off the small of her back as she cocked a hip, examining the stoop. A wry grin crossed my lips and the weight of my own Nikon pressed into my lap. I lifted it, dropping the binoculars down, and with several swift clicks, I captured the moment in time. A moment that was seemingly uneventful. A moment that within Jessica Walters's life probably wasn't even a blip on her radar.

But that's the thing with photography. It takes nothing moments and immortalizes them, suddenly creating more than there ever was before. When—and if—Jessica ever sees this photograph, she'll be thrust back into the smells, the thoughts, the emotions of today . . . right now. Even though in the moment, it meant nothing to her.

If Jessica was a good girl—if she did exactly as she should—these photos would never need to see the light of day. She'd never need to know just how close I've been all this time. Just how close she is to falling into the same fate as her sister. But in case she decides to be a hero, I'd be here . . . watching. And waiting. Because if there's one thing I had to guess that the Walters sisters had in common, it was martyrdom.

A shudder rolled through my body. The weight of my gun pressed into the clip at my ankle, its warm steel an easy reminder of how simple it would be to end this right here and now. Kill Jessica and the house would go into an estate auction, easily swept up by me. A thrill rushed through my body; an excitement at the memory of pulling the trigger. The feeling of a gun pulsing in your hands as a bullet careens toward your victim. There was no feeling quite like taking a life. But no. I had to remain under the radar until Cass's death had blown over.

Sweat gathered at the nape of my neck and rolled down my spine, getting caught in a musky puddle between my shoulder blades. I cracked the driver's-side window, and orange light sprang through the split, illuminating the otherwise dark, tinted sedan.

I sucked in a breath of the crisp afternoon air. This had to be a clean kill. Shooting in cold blood right now defeated the purpose of how carefully we had murdered Cass. Last minute? Yes. But calculated and tidy. The way I liked things in life. Organized. Clean. We had the plan in place for that night and were ready to kill, if needed. And oh, how it was needed.

But still, a small part of me trembled, excitement pulsing in my veins. Would Jessica run? Fight back like Cass? Or would she beg for her life, falling to her knees in tears? I closed my eyes imagining Jessica submitting to me—to death—while I stood above her. Powerful. What would her screams sound like? A breeze rushed through the open window and across my dampened brow. The screams were the best part.

My heart hammered as I jerked the camera back to my face and zoomed in as closely as I could to her neck.

*Click.*

Strong, lean shoulders tensed from beneath her shirt and I nibbled the inside of my cheek as she pulled out a set of keys, opening the door.

I shouldn't want to kill her as much as I did. But death was the ultimate form of control.

# 1

Leaves crunched as Jess Walters dropped her bags to the ground before the bright pink door. *Pink.* Her least favorite color ever. She groaned, looking up at the three-story home. What had Cass been thinking, buying this atrocity of a house? Sure, it reminded Jess of the house they had grown up in together—in a cracked-out Barbie-meets-suburbia sort of way.

Jess rooted around inside her bottomless purse until she felt the familiar chilled metal of jagged keys. Placing a hand to her camera bag, she inhaled deeply. The feel of the soft leather beneath her palm was calming. The camera was as much a part of her as her own hand. The key slid into the lock easily and with a click the deadbolt turned. After a steely breath, she gave the door a gentle push and, gathering her bags, walked across the threshold. Light flooded the entryway and spilled into the living room. Tears choked the back of her throat, but Jess quickly swallowed them down.

Nothing was out of place—typical of Cass. There were no books strewn about like in Jess's own home in Brooklyn. No piles of dirty laundry and bras flung over the couch. Jess dropped her bags by the stairs, closing the door behind her. The foyer had a vase filled with pinecones and some sort of branch-like plant sprouting out the top.

The dining room opened into a quaint kitchen and Jess dragged her hand across the polished dining room table as she wandered through the first floor. Again—spotless. Except for one almost empty coffee cup which sat uncleaned in the sink. Red lipstick rimmed the edge.

*Red?* Jess thought as a jagged breath expelled through trembling lips. The lip color was so unlike Cass. Jess lifted the glass, grasping it in two hands. God, she would have hated that this dirty cup was left here for a couple of weeks, Jess thought as the tiniest smile tugged on her lips.

Leaning against the counter, Jess fumbled for her cell, dialing her Kings County precinct. It rang twice before a nasally accented voice answered. "NYPD, Seventy-sixth precinct, how may I help you?"

Jess recognized Deb's voice almost immediately. "Deb, hey, it's Jess. I just wanted to make sure you had my temporary address to mail my most recent paychecks."

There was a pause on the other end of the phone. "Jess . . . ?"

A heavy sigh stifled in Jess's chest and she caught it before she let it escape into the phone. "Yes. Jessica Walters . . . Seventy-sixth precinct's forensic photographer?"

Silence hummed on the other end but then Jess heard the click of computer keys.

"Jesus Christ, Deb, we've worked together for four years. I talked to you last week—remember? I'm in Portland for a few weeks to get my sister's—"

"Oh, right, right, Jessica!" And yet, despite the exclamation, there was still a vacancy in Deb's voice. That lack of warmth, of connection. Yeah, sure, NYPD was a huge department, but come *on.* "Where should I send your check to?"

Jess gave Deb her sister's address and hung up quickly; the

familiar hollow feeling carved out into her chest as she looked around the three-story home. Lifting the coffee cup in her hands once more, she turned it over, examining it. The porcelain was smooth and the edging was gilded with a pewter design.

Never in her life had she felt so alone. Their parents died when Jess was a freshman in high school—a car crash. A fucking hit and run, to be exact. One that left her parents caged under their crumpled car. A shiver tumbled down her spine. She was alone now. Totally and completely alone. She had no grandparents, no cousins, no aunts, no uncles. Her sister was the only family she'd had left. It was depressing how quickly Jess had been able to pack up her belongings and come to Maine. There was no one she needed to call; no one she needed to check in with.

For a while, that had seemed freeing, having zero ties to any place. Being able to pick up and travel whenever she wanted. But now? Now it just felt damn lonely.

Jess sighed and turned the water on, soaping up a sponge. "When I get home, I need to get a dog or something," she muttered to herself. "Something that will miss me when I'm gone."

"Dogs are a lot of work, you know," a voice behind her said.

Jess screamed, spinning to find a man standing there. The soapy mug slipped through her wet fingers, shattering across the linoleum floor with a deafening crash.

The man eyed the broken cup for all of a moment before bending to clean up the pieces of shattered ceramic.

"Wh-who are you? Why are you in Cass's house?" Jess trembled, pressing herself against the counter and feeling behind her for a weapon. Her fingers grazed a knife's handle and she wrapped her palm around it, sliding it behind her.

The man looked up at her from his crouched position. He had light brown hair and striking blue eyes. The smallest hint of an amused grin flashed across his face as he stretched to a standing position, dropping the broken glass into the trash can. "I'm sorry." He brushed his palms on his jeans and extended a hand. "I'm Dane."

Jess eyed his outstretched hand, still clutching the knife behind her. "Hello, Dane" she said, and paused. "You didn't answer my question."

He gave a light chuckle and dropped his hand back to his sides. "Well, since your first question was 'who are you?' I actually did answer you. And you—wait a minute." His eyes narrowed and scanned her face before the smirk spread to a full-on grin. "You're Jess, right? Cass's sister?"

Jess relaxed her shoulders, giving a little nod, but didn't let go of the knife yet.

"I've heard a lot about you. It's nice to finally meet you."

"And yet, I still know nothing about you and why you're here." Fear trembled at the base of her belly. The guy seemed okay; nice, even. But that didn't change the fact that he was a stranger lurking in her sister's home.

"Cass set up an appointment for me to have a look at some leaky pipes upstairs."

"She must've done it weeks ago." Jess narrowed her eyes, studying the man up and down.

"Yeah, it was a couple weeks ago. I was called out of town for a job in Boston and Cass didn't seem to mind the extra wait."

He walked over to the far right cabinet, grabbed a pint glass from the top shelf, and filled it with water. Her eyes wandered over his shoulder to the thin bookshelf on the other side of the room. A framed photograph of her sister and this man— Dane—rested on the top shelf. The two of them in front of Cass's bright pink house, each holding a hammer and grinning from ear to ear.

"You seem awfully comfortable in her home." It was an observation as well as a question. Jess loosened her grip on the knife and slid her hand away from it. She took a few kickboxing classes at her gym. In a worst-case scenario, she could deposit a quick kick to the groin and run like hell.

"Ayuh," he said, his Maine accent becoming more and more prominent as Jess spoke to him. "Cass and I have been friends since she bought this place. Needed quite a bit of work at first." He looked around as though remembering an old friend. "Wouldn't be able to tell it now, huh?"

"Yeah. Except for that awful color outside."

Dane laughed. "Now, that's true. Cass was never about to change that, though. It was one of the reasons she bought the damn place to begin with."

"So, you and Cass were . . . friends?"

Dane nodded. "Absolutely. I taught her how to boil a lobstah."

Jess snorted. Her sister damn well knew how to boil lobster. They were raised here in Portland. Which meant Cass used the excuse as a way of getting closer to this guy. The thought brought a warmth in Jess's chest. "Well, how hard can it be to throw a lobster in a pot?"

"You'd be surprised. It's more humane to kill them first, anyway." From his pocket, he pulled a little orange bottle and tossed a pill into his mouth, swallowing. He drank the rest of the water with a glug and wiped his mouth with the back of his hand.

Jess wasn't sure exactly why she was warming up to the guy, especially considering the hellish week she'd had—but she was nonetheless. And her instincts were usually spot-on.

"So, where's Cass, anyway?" he asked, glancing at his watch. "Still at work probably, huh?"

Sorrow frosted over in her gut. "Oh God," Jess whispered, covering her mouth. "You don't know."

Dane tilted his head. "Know what?" His chest hitched. "Is Cass okay?"

Jess inhaled slowly through her nose. She'd had to make a few of these calls already and they ripped her heart out every time.

"Dane, I'm so sorry . . . Cass died."

# 2

Dane's face drained of all color and he set the empty water glass onto the counter with a *thunk*. "What?" The words were barely a whisper. "She's . . . she's dead?" His grip on the counter was so strong that the tips of his fingers were white. He pushed off, shaking his head and clamping those hands onto his hips instead. "No. No, she can't be. I was gone for only a little over a week! How . . . ?" The question choked on his tongue and he dropped his head, his mouth pressing into a firm line as though a thought flashed into his mind.

Jess swallowed the lump that had taken up residency at the base of her throat. "I'm sorry. I didn't know many of her friends to call . . . I-I sort of relied on her local friends and colleagues to spread the word."

He nodded, bringing his gaze back up and swiping a hand across one escaped tear. "How? When?" he whispered again.

"The police said they suspect it was a robbery gone bad. She was down by the water, on Wright's Wharf. Shot and thrown in. We were lucky that there was a fisherman checking his lobster traps; he saw the whole thing. Otherwise, she may have disappeared and we never would have known. . . ." Jess faded off, letting the silence settle in between them. *Lucky*. Right. It was laughable to use that word to describe this situation. Even as she recounted the story, it sounded off in her head. For starters, what the hell was her sister doing down by the wharf at one in the morning? "Were you two . . . well, were you more than just friends?" she asked after a few seconds.

"Yeah . . . no . . . I-I . . ." Dane shook his head as though trying to clear out the fog. "No," he answered sharply. "We were just friends." His gaze seared Jess and she shivered as he stared at her. "But *good* friends," he emphasized, the muscles around his throat tightening.

Jess nodded. "Why didn't any of her other friends call you? Or tell *me* to call you?"

Dane's jaw jumped at the question. "That's a damn good question."

He pushed off the counter, hands balled into fists, and paced the kitchen, growing angrier with each step. "Your sister's a private person. I've never seen a person compartmentalize so many facets of their life before. She had work friends, college friends, family friends . . . and she was careful that the different paths never crossed." He met Jess's eyes with a sad smile. "It's why I'm not surprised that she never mentioned me to you. But still—there was one or two people that could have called me—" His voice broke. "I'm surprised they didn't."

Jess also knew that Cass didn't *have* many friends in the first place. A couple from college who had moved on and now lived in other parts of the country. A few colleagues Jess had heard about here and there from happy hour outings after a long day. But that was pretty much it. But for a girl who never talked about having friends or boyfriends, there were a ton of people Jess had never seen before at Cass's funeral.

Why Cass hadn't actually been dating Dane was a mystery . . . he was clearly crazy about her. And Jess could totally see why

Cass would be into him, too. He was a large man with bulging muscles and a kind smile. The kind of man who could cook you a soufflé with one hand and bench-press you with the other.

"So, did I miss . . . did I miss the funeral?" His eyes pinched at the corners and his mouth tightened into a firm line.

All Jess could do was nod. After a moment, she cleared her throat and choked out, "It was two days ago. I can take you to her grave if you want."

Dane muttered a curse and dropped his head, shaking it back and forth. "I just arrived back into town yesterday. Maybe, if I had gotten here sooner—" He tilted his head, meeting Jess's eyes. "Sorry. I'd appreciate that. Knowing where her grave is, I mean. Some other time, though?"

"Of course."

He carried the pint glass to the sink, turning the water on and starting to clean it. "I can do that," Jess said, gently reaching for the glass.

"I've got it," Dane responded gruffly. Then he added with a small smile, "Can't have you breaking any more dishes." After another moment of painful silence, he dried his hands on the dish towel. "If the funeral was a couple days ago, why weren't you staying here before?"

*Good question,* Jess thought. It seemed too pathetic to say she couldn't bear the thought of staying here while her sister sat on ice at the morgue. Between the investigation and the autopsy, it took longer than usual to arrange the funeral. Even though she had only been in the water for a few hours, her body was bloated and beyond recognition. Jess couldn't even recognize her face. She had to be confirmed using dental records. "Legalities," she finally managed. "The will just came through this morning and this is now all mine." She glanced around with a heavy sigh.

Dane nodded, his eyes drooping in a way that suggested he knew what she was going through. "If you need anything, call me anytime." He handed her a card, picked up his toolbox, and headed for the door. "Hey, Jess," he said over his shoulder.

She looked up in time to catch the glint of moisture in the corner of his eyes. "I'm so sorry for your loss," he finished.

"You too, Dane," she answered. And with that, he slipped out the door. "You too." She sighed once more.

Unzipping her camera bag, Jess pulled out her Canon and wide-angle lens. She had no idea what to do with this house. On one hand, it was one of the few connections to her sister she had left. On the other, her life, her home was back in Brooklyn. It had been years since Jess had called Portland home . . . and she wasn't about to start now.

Lifting the camera, she wrapped the strap several times around her wrist and climbed the stairs. No matter what she did with this home, she'd need photographs of it; whether selling, renting, or using it as a summer place, documentation of the space was a must. Besides, life seemed clearer to Jess when she was looking at it through the lens.

As with any real estate property, Jess began at the top floor, climbing the stairs into what was likely once an attic, but had been renovated into an office and an extra bedroom. Wood paneling adorned the room in a throwback to the seventies, but not nearly as cheap looking as some places Jess had seen. It had a rustic log cabin charm to it in that way New England was well-known for.

There wasn't much to the top room—a beautiful skylight, a twin bed, a desk and chair. That was about it. Down on the second floor was another guest room, a bathroom, and the master bedroom. A tightness caught in Jess's throat as she peeked into Cass's bedroom. It held a cottage-style charm to it and Jess inhaled deeply; it even smelled like Cass in there. Her throat closed and there was a burning at the back of her eyes. One single tear escaped, gliding a salty path down the side of her nose and over her lips. She couldn't go in there. Not yet. Not without a little alcohol and a lot more preparation.

Creeping back, she bumped into a table resting next to the entrance to the guest bedroom and gasped as the corner slammed into the small of her back.

The pain, though sharp, was exactly the distraction she needed. There was always time to photograph her sister's bedroom later. So instead she ducked into the guest room, finishing quickly and moving down to the living room.

The design of the home was exquisite. Though she and Cass had completely different styles, her sister's decor was simple and classic. The L-shaped leather sectional added sleekness to the otherwise historical home. Jess stepped back, pressing herself against the staircase in order to get the entire room into the frame.

*Click.*

She refocused onto the fireplace and snapped another shot. A glistening light caught her attention from under the couch and Jess paused, narrowing her gaze.

Setting the camera down, she knelt in front of the couch, and lifted a small mask with pearls sewn onto the edging. "What the hell?" She turned the weird mask over in her hands and pushed off her knees, moving to the ornate mirror in the foyer. It wasn't the sort of mask you found in a shitty costume shop next to cheap Raggedy Ann wigs. No—this was the real deal. Heavy. Detailed. And ornate.

Jess swallowed hard as an icy chill descended down to her toes. Why the hell did a simple mask unsettle her so much? Tilting her head, she lifted it to her face, peering at her reflection in the mirror. Goose bumps surged down her arms, raising the hairs in sequence. Her nipples hardened and Jess turned, looking at herself from over her shoulder. She had to admit . . . she looked pretty sexy in a mask.

The sound of a door slamming came from below her feet

and Jess froze. Was there even a basement in this house? She didn't see a door down there from the outside, but that didn't mean it wasn't in the back of the house. She tossed the mask onto the kitchen table, grabbing her camera out of instinct, and as she made her way carefully toward the basement door, the doorbell rang from the other end of the house.

Glancing between the two doors, Jess hiked the camera strap around a shoulder and yanked open the front door. Standing on her stoop was a short, curvy girl with dark hair that came just below her chin in a layered bob. Black plastic frames sat on the bridge of her dainty nose and scarlet lips turned up in a sad sort of smile. The girl held out a plate of something that smelled sugary and delicious.

"Hi . . . you're Jess, right?"

Jess angled her chin and even though she had never considered herself tall, she stood several inches over the girl. "Yeah . . ."

The girl's already fair skin paled of any remaining color, turning whiter than the stack of simple porcelain she gripped in her hands. Her smile wobbled and there, glistening in those dark brown eyes, was the thing Jess most hated . . . pity.

"My name is Zooey," she finally said. "I worked with your sister. I just—I wanted to bring you some cookies." Zooey swallowed hard, nibbling the inside of her cheek. "That's what people do in situations like this, right? They bring food."

Memories of a freezer stuffed full of prepared casseroles after her parents' death flooded Jess's mind. "Typically, yeah. That seems to be the standard." Taking the plate, Jess lifted it to her nose, inhaling. "Oh my God, they smell amazing."

Zooey stood a little taller with the compliment. "Thanks. They're my grandmother's recipe—the only thing she ever learned to bake, actually. She hardly ever stepped into a kitchen. That's what the 'help' is for, she used to tell me." She rolled her eyes and pushed her glasses higher onto her nose with her middle finger.

"Wow," Jess chuckled. It felt good to smile. *Really* smile. And for the first time in almost two weeks, she could feel the tension melting from her shoulders. "You had 'help' growing up? Like, what? Butlers and shit?"

Zooey matched her chuckle, shaking her head. She shrugged with a good-natured eye roll. "Eh, something like that. We had a live-in nanny who also cooked. And my dad had an 'assistant' who was essentially a glorified butler."

"Damn, you must be loaded!" Zooey's smile faltered and heat burned across Jess's cheeks. "Oh, shit. Sorry . . . that was a stupid thing to say. I just met you and already I'm sticking my foot in my mouth." Jess swallowed hard. "If you couldn't tell, Cass was the eloquent one in the family."

Zooey waved the comment away with a shrug. "Nah, don't worry about it. You probably don't remember, but we met at the funeral, briefly." The apples of her cheeks rose with a sad sort of smile, causing her glasses to prop up as well. "Cass actually trained me in my position at Holtz's." The crinkles around her eyes deepened as the cadence of her voice turned raspy within a fond memory Jess was not privy to.

Before Jess could answer, Zooey was flicking a finger beneath each eye, rolling them in spite of herself. "Sorry. The last thing you need is some stranger coming over and blubbering on your doorstep."

"It's okay." In some ways, Zooey was probably closer to Cass than Jess had been. "Do you want to come in?"

"No, no, I don't want to intrude. I just wanted to introduce myself and offer any help while you're in town. Even if it's just to grab a drink or a coffee and . . . reminisce."

"Thanks. I really appreciate it." Her own friends in Brooklyn pooled together to send a bouquet of daisies, but yet, not one of them had offered to come to the funeral. What good were flowers, anyway? In a week, they were dead and you were reminded all over again how fleeting life was. And yet here was a woman she'd never met offering Jess the thing she most needed right now—a shoulder to lean on. The back of her throat swelled with that same familiar tightness she was growing to know so well.

"Anyway, here's my card. Call me sometime." Zooey backed down the steps with a little wave.

Closing the door behind her, Jess set the plate down, nibbling on the edge of a cookie. Flavor exploded on her tongue . . . vanilla and sugar and butter and gooey chocolate. Holy hell. That was a damn good cookie. Thank you, Zooey's grandma.

Jess's muscles bunched around her ears as another bump from the basement froze her midbite. "Dane?" she said quietly. But something in her gut told her it wasn't Dane down there. She'd seen the guy leave. Watched as he got into his truck parked outside and drove away. Clutching her camera, she crept to the back of the kitchen where there were two doors— one leading outside to a small back courtyard and the other opening into a spiral staircase to a dark basement. The musty smell flooded her nose. She gulped and, as quietly as she could, pressed herself against the top of the stairs, listening. There was a quiet shuffling.

Each breath came out in a sharp exhalation, her heart jack-hammering against her ribs.

Leaning forward, she saw that the stairs had only one rickety railing and the rest was wide open. Another bit of rustling and when Jess strained to listen closer, she heard what sounded like footsteps. She pressed flat against the wall beside the top of the stairs—the only barrier between her and the intruder. Pressing a hand to her pocket, she silently cursed to herself. Her phone was sitting in her purse on top of the kitchen table. Turning on her camera, she set the dial for a long exposure and crouched, setting it on the top step. The click of the shutter, though essentially quiet, was like a booming clap of thunder in the silence of the house and Jess cringed as the camera did the work, taking the five-second exposure. She heard another clatter, and then there was a final slam. Jess was met with silence.

The lack of sound was somehow more disturbing than the sounds of the intruder. Shifting her camera to safety at the top of the steps, she descended down, stopping a few steps shy of the base. With her right hand, she felt around the wall at the bottom until she slid across a light switch. Wincing, she flipped it on, half expecting something to come running at her. But there was nothing but more silence.

Scanning the basement from one end to the other, she sighed. This was ridiculous. She was letting her imagination get the best of her again. This was Maine. The land of critters and woodland creatures. It was probably just a mouse or something.

Wow. This basement—it was so not Cass. Dirty. Moldy. A layer of dust and dirt covered the cement floors at least a half inch thick. The washer and dryer were the only area that looked like it had been kept clean, but even that area was significantly dirtier than the rest of the house.

Jess walked the perimeter of the basement. There were absolutely zero windows down there. And the brick walls were solid, she thought, placing a hand to the cool stone. At the other end of the basement was a bunch of boxes and a large safe.

There was literally no way for an intruder to get in or out of here without using the steps. She caught her lip between her teeth as fear sent an icy chill through her body and awareness buzzed around her like an annoying bug. It was irrational, she knew, this fear of someone being here. And yet . . . she couldn't shake that feeling of someone watching her.

She needed to get out of this basement. Now. A tremble crept low in her belly and was seizing her whole body. And despite the screams inside her head, she could not will her feet to move. It was as if they were cemented to the floor.

And just as she thought she was going to be frozen there all night, a bat lurched from under the stairs fluttering wildly toward her head. Jess screamed and darted up the steps. Her pounding heart throbbed in her head and she could feel the quickened pulse fluttering below her jaw as well. She threw open the back door as the bat flew outside and slammed it shut behind him.

Falling into the kitchen chair, she pressed a cool palm to her forehead and with shaky fingers grabbed another cookie. Cookies helped with everything.

# 3

---

The sun dipped below the horizon and streaked orange across the sky as Jess opened a bottle of wine and poured herself a glass. She was typically more of a tequila and cocktail kind of girl, but as she suspected, Cass had nothing like that in the house. And hell, Jess certainly wasn't gonna whine about wine.

Jess trailed her hands along the banister as she made her way up the creaking stairs to her sister's bedroom, with her camera slung around one shoulder. The master suite was large and decorated with fresh yellows and bits of gray peppered in. Sheer white curtains draped from ceiling to floor on tracks around her bed like a canopy. The room was spotless; the sort of place you paid a lot of money to stay in at a bed-and-breakfast.

Jess's job here at the house was going to be easy. There was very little to go through. Very little to get rid of. Where her own apartment in Brooklyn was a hoarder's dream, her sister was a minimalist.

She inhaled deeply, circling the room and running her hands along the silky drapes.

So much was left up in the air. Should Jess sell the house?

She could sure as hell use the money. Maybe buy her own little place in Brooklyn instead of renting. Then again, maybe she should keep it. Rent it out to students or as a vacation house. It would be nice to have a place to escape to when she needed a break from the city.

Jess sank to the floor and lay on her back. The hardwood planks were cool despite the last bit of summer fighting to stick around.

*"Jessica, c'mon. You haven't been here to visit once since I bought the place."*

*"I know, I know, I'm sorry."* Jess pinched the phone between her shoulder and ear as she uploaded her recent case to the server. *"It's just really crazy right now. You know Brooklyn— the murders don't stop just because my sister's housewarming party is this weekend."*

*"It's not a party."* Jess heard her sister's sigh on the other end of the phone. *"Just a small get-together. But I'd still like for you to come."*

*Guilt trips, Jess thought. Her sister's greatest tool.* *"You're in the frame, Cass,"* Jess said with an eye roll. *It was their code term for whenever Cass was being too demanding.*

*There was a pause from her sister. "I know, Jessie. There was just something I wanted to talk to you about. . . ."* Cass's voice broke and something stilled inside Jess.

*"Well, we can talk now."* Jess pushed off her love seat and for the first time in the entire conversation, she gave her sister all of her attention. *"Are you okay?"*

*Cass cleared her throat. "Yeah, yeah. No, I'm fine. It's nothing. I just haven't seen you in a while. Can you come home for Christmas?"*

*"Of course! What kind of miser misses Christmas?"*

Only she hadn't made it back for Christmas. And here she was, almost a year later, burying her sister. "God, I'm an asshole," Jess whispered. She reached for the wineglass that rested beside her at arm's length. She felt the glass stem and as she wrapped her fingers around it, it tipped toward the hardwood floor. The glass burst with a shattering explosion.

"Shit! Sorry, Cass. Two hours and two glasses down." The wine ran across the floor, edging its way to the crack under the walk-in closet door. Jess ran for some paper towels and cleaning fluid. She mopped up the mess with the towels, picking up the pieces of glass as well. She followed the drip, opened the closet door, and sopped up the spill, spraying the all-purpose cleaner.

As she wiped in circles, her sleeve caught on a raised plank, ripping the seam open. A weary breath escaped from Jess as she fell back and let her head fall against the wall. Was there nothing she could do right? What the hell was that anyway?

Tossing the soiled towels to the side, she felt around for the plank until the raised wood caught her fingertip. With a tug, she lifted the loose board and a smirk played at Jess's lips. "Oh, Cass. You're such a creature of habit." It was like high school all over again, when Jess read Cass's diary. The hiding spots were trickier and trickier each time, too. Starting initially under her pillow and eventually coming up with a similar gem of a hiding spot, inside the air vents.

Jess set the plank aside and pulled out an iPad and a large velvet satchel with a gold-cord pull string from the floor. "What'd you leave for me?"

Flipping the iPad cover open, Jess hit the button and the screen lit with a number pad and *Enter Passcode.* Damn. She should have known her sister would have been ultra prepared. What do people usually use as passwords? Birthdays, right? Jess punched in 1019, her sister's birthday and grunted as the screen trembled, coming up with *Invalid Password.* "Dammit," she mumbled, trying again with her own birthday. Nothing. *Holy shit, this could be hopeless,* she thought, setting the iPad down next to her.

She reached into the velvet satchel, her fingers brushing chilled metal. An old skeleton key was on top of a Canadian passport with Cass's picture, but with the name *Cynthia Owens* inside. The fake passport fell from her grasp, hitting the floor next to where she crouched. Cursing her shaky hands, Jess dove for it once more and blinked away that burning sensation in her eyes. "What the hell, Cassandra?" Jess whispered to no one, flipping the passport open. Stamps, mostly from Canada, adorned the inner pages. The same numbness when she got the call about her parents' death took hold. It was Jess's best and only tool for survival; to push those terrible feelings to the pit of her stomach and avoid allowing them to surface.

A wave of sickness threatened the back of Jess's throat, but right along with her sorrow, she swallowed that down, too. From somewhere, she managed to pull the last bit of courage she had and reached into the satchel to see what other secrets her sister had been hiding all this time. At the bottom of the bag was a stack of money.

A *very* large stack of money. Entirely made up of one hundred dollar bills.

Her racing heart was felt in all parts of her body. Denial would not make this go away. And on a whim, Jess pressed her hand into the open hole in the floor. One by one, she pulled out more and more stacks of money until the pile could have filled several suitcases. "Holy shit," she gasped. "What the hell did you get yourself into, Cass?"

From across the room, her Canon caught her eye on the floor next to Cass's bed. Dropping Cass's items back into the floor and placing the plank over the top, Jess crept over to the camera and flipped it on. The image she had taken earlier in the basement illuminated the small viewing screen. The long exposure made the image plenty light enough to see without a flash, but was unable to stop motion.

A rush of anxiety chased down her arms as she zoomed in

on the long exposure. A blur of motion in the center of the image. A *large,* black blur . . . far too large to be a bat.

Jess clamped her eyes shut, flipping the camera off. With so many uncertainties in her life; with so much up in the air, there was one thing she was sure of. She needed to get the hell out of this house.

# 4

Jess sat on her sister's couch, clutching her laptop as the officers finished their search. The male cop made his way down the stairs, boots clomping heavily with each step. "All's clear on the top two floors," he said. His cropped reddish hair stuck up just enough in the back to bounce with every movement and a spray of freckles highlighted his cheeks.

"The basement and courtyard are clear, too, Donelly," the female officer sighed as she entered the foyer. Her eyes slid over to her partner's with an annoyed glance before she looked to Jess. "Whatever was down there is long gone."

Jess's jaw clenched and she pushed off the couch, turning the laptop toward Officer Donelly and Officer Rodriguez. "It wasn't a 'whatever.' It was a *who*ever. Look. This image—that black blurred spot is a human. If you look closely, you can see the sleeve of a black jacket."

Jess raised her brows and waited as the officers leaned in closely, eyes narrowing.

After a moment, the two exchanged another glance as Jess's heart dropped. The woman pressed her red lips together, her black layered bob blowing as a breeze brushed by her jaw. Zooey's same dark bob flashed in Jess's mind and she did a mental eye roll. Was there only one hairdresser in this damn town?

"Ma'am," Officer Rodriguez started, "is there any chance that blur is . . . I dunno . . . an animal? A raccoon maybe?"

Jess sent her a dagger-filled glare. "Do *you* know any raccoons who wear black coats?"

"Or . . . or what about a shadow? Could it be your own shadow reflecting off something?" Officer Donelly chimed in with a shrug.

Jess didn't bother qualifying that with a response. Instead she shut the laptop, placing it back onto the coffee table. Clearly, they didn't believe her. If there was anything Jess learned from her years with the NYPD it was that you rarely convinced the police of anything different once they made up their minds. At least not without presenting new evidence.

"But, the house is definitely clear now. Absolutely no one is in here other than the three of us." Rodriguez smiled, bright brown eyes softening as she made her way to the front door.

Jess opened it and propped it open for them with her hip. "Thanks for coming," she said politely. She knew someone had been down there. Whether or not they believed her.

"Of course," Donelly said, smiling and giving Jess a final nod before he walked through the door.

Rodriguez paused, looking over her shoulder before handing Jess her card. "If you hear anything or see anything else suspicious, don't hesitate to call. It's a big house for one person." She offered Jess a fleeting smile before hooking her thumbs into her belt and following her partner to their squad car.

The whole night, Jess trembled inside the guest bedroom. Was she totally losing it? Did she imagine a human figure from that blur because she was scared? And what the hell was her sister doing with that much cash in her floorboards? Cass was a molecular biologist working for a small pharmaceutical company in Portland. Pharmaceuticals—at least to Jess's limited knowledge—didn't involve wads of cash. And fake passports.

The thought of sleeping in her sister's bed sent ominous chills spiraling through her body as it was—now added on top of her already ill feelings was the fact that there was easily half a million dollars taking up residency in the room. There was no way Jess was going back in there until she had to.

As soon as the sun was high enough in the sky, Jess was up and out of bed. It wasn't as though she was getting any sleep, anyway. She paced back and forth, her thigh scraping against the edge of the nightstand. Outside, seagulls sang their morning tune as they flew overhead toward the water's edge.

Jess needed to run. She needed to get out of this house, clear her head, and go for a jog. Or maybe a doughnut. She tugged on some leggings and a white T-shirt. With one last look at Cass's bedroom door, she shivered, thrusting her hands into her tousled hair and tugging it into a messy ponytail. Her fists immediately balled up, tight . . . tense. She slowly released her grip, forcing the tension to leave her hands and shoulders. It was stupid to jump to conclusions.

Biting her lip, Jess pushed through Cass's bedroom door and snatched the iPad from the closet again. *Think. Think . . . use your damn brain, Jess.* What would Cass use as a password? She punched in the last four digits of her sister's phone number. Disappointment flooded her stomach as the screen buzzed with its annoying *invalid password*.

Jess tossed the iPad onto a chair positioned in front of the bay windows. "Another time," she said to no one.

She grabbed her small digital Leica camera; as strange as it seemed to most people, she loved having it with her on her runs. You never know what you're going to come across and it was through photographs that Jess discovered any town. Locking the door behind her, Jess took off, her tennis-shoe-clad feet slapping the pavement. She found herself along the water, running toward Portland's historic district. It was only a few blocks away and soon she had run the entire length of the water.

God, it really was a beautiful little city. The September air smelled crisp. Like salt and apples. And at seven-thirty a.m., it was virtually deserted, with hardly anyone out yet. She passed her favorite diner, right along the water, and inhaled the smell of fresh baked goods, smiling. Tugging the Leica from her waist belt, pausing to photograph the BECKY'S DINER sign. Wrapping the camera strap around her wrist, she clutched it tightly, adjusted her earphones and the phone that was bound around her bicep, and took off running toward the park ahead.

"Jessica?" A voice called from behind her. "Jessica Walters?"

Jess stopped running, placing two hands at her ribs to control her breathing.

She squinted as the sun backlit a man walking toward her. Dark, unruly hair curled around his ears and neckline and she could just barely make out the muscled physique. He wore a suit and as his arms swung, a gun flashed from beneath the jacket.

Jess nearly choked on nothing at all and her hand around the camera tightened considerably. The image of the basement blur flashed in her mind. Oh God. How did he know her name? She spun, wondering if it was too late to pretend she hadn't heard him. She picked up her pace again, looking down at her camera in hand as if that was what had distracted her. Anxiety crawled across her skin as though she had stepped into an ant farm.

"Jessica!" he called again. Only this time she didn't look back. She broke out into another jog. Footsteps pounded behind her and she ran faster. Nobody who knew Jess well ever called her Jessica. Not unless she was in trouble. The footsteps were growing louder behind her. Shit, he was still gaining on her. Her lungs burned as she pushed herself harder, taking off at a full sprint toward the park. There were bound to be other joggers in there this early, right? Someone would see her and help.

A hand clamped onto her bicep, jerking her back into a muscled chest that was heaving with labored breaths. Jess screamed as the man spun her around to face him.

"Jessica! Jessie, it's me—Sam!" He put both hands in the air, palms up.

"Sam?" She gasped for air, heart pounding against her ribs. "Sam! Jesus, what are you doing? You scared the shit out of me!" Her face fell into her hands and she rubbed the fear from her eyes.

"Me? What are *you* doing? Running like a maniac to get away from me."

Jess's face heated. Years of resentment and anger slammed into her, though she had thought she'd let go of that long ago. She repeated her mantra she had learned the day her parents died: *I am a product of my past; not a prisoner of it.* She pushed the feeling away and somehow managed a tight smile. "And here I thought you were used to chasing the ladies, Sam."

Sam's face dropped even more and for all of a second, Jess's throat fell to the pit of her empty stomach. A flash of tongue caught her gaze as he wet his lips. "Me? Chase?" he said. "Never."

It was a flat-out lie. Jess had known Sam for almost his entire life. And beginning in kindergarten on the playground, he was always chasing girls. Granted, they usually let themselves get caught, but that was beside the point. "It's been a while," Jess added quietly, remembering the last time she'd seen Sam. Their high school graduation party. Heat rushed to her cheeks at the recollection of that embarrassing night. Hell, he didn't need to chase her *that* night.

Sam's brows puckered. "Yeah, it has," he said, chewing the corner of his mouth. "If I recall, you walked out on me after an amazing graduation celebration."

Yeah, she had. She had left him naked in his bedroom as she slunk away from that awful night. Goose bumps pricked along her arms and she darted her gaze away, avoiding those mischievous eyes of his. "Yeah. But that was senior year. After three years of you ignoring *me* all through high school." She crossed her arms, sending him another glare.

She could see his hard swallow and the way his neck tensed with the movement. But then, his full lips quirked in that same endearing way they had when she was a teenager. Sam McCloskey. The boy who taught her how to smoke a cigarette. The boy she lost her virginity to. The boy who ceased being her best friend as soon as her parents died. And the boy she ran from after she graduated. Damn, he could charm the bloomers off an Amish farm girl with that grin. Even after he had abandoned her for three years, she still wanted him so bad that night after graduation. A little charm and a lot of Zima helped make that happen.

"That was a long time ago, Jessie. Can't we just say sorry and move on?" Though his suggestion was light, a storm brewed behind those deep blue eyes of his.

Jess snorted her opinion of that.

"Sam," she said, dropping her voice low, looking around without moving her head. "Why do you have a gun?"

His grin widened as he reached into his back pocket. Flipping open a leather wallet, he flashed a gold badge. "Sorry—didn't mean to scare you. I made detective a few years back."

Jess's eyes squeezed shut. God, she was such an idiot. A detective! Of course. She'd heard something about that from Cass earlier this year.

"Hey." His palm rested on her arm with a reassuring squeeze. "I was so sorry to hear about Cass."

Jess dropped her gaze, becoming suddenly interested in the sidewalk cracks. "Thanks," she rasped.

"It was a beautiful service," he added. "She would have loved the display of roses."

Cass hated roses. She would have wanted gerbera daisies. Pink ones. But Jess didn't expect anyone to know that. It was sweet of Cass's colleagues to send the flowers, even if they were all wrong. "I didn't know you came."

Sam sighed. "Well, you seemed . . . busy. I didn't know if I should say hi."

The irony was that Cass's funeral had been filled with people Jess barely knew and didn't want to talk to. "Still would've been nice to have seen a familiar face that day."

"Yeah," he whispered. Sam shifted back on his heels, running a finger across his top lip. God, those lips. Jess's eyes fell on his soft pout remembering how they dragged across her heated flesh all those years ago. Her chest heaved and she quickly averted her gaze. "Well," he continued, "I should probably get back." He jerked his head toward a black unmarked sedan with tinted windows.

"Yeah, of course." Jess nodded.

As he turned to leave, something different passed along his features. Awareness—realization, perhaps. Jess narrowed her eyes, assessing the new Sam in front of her.

After another moment, he faced her once more, clearing his throat. "Jessie—would you like to grab dinner tonight? Nothing formal—a bite to catch up?"

She hesitated. "I dunno, Sam . . ."

"C'mon." He tilted his head to the side. "Just old friends. Catching up."

Jess swallowed. Just old friends. What a joke. She wanted to believe that was true, but with her and Sam, was it ever "just" anything? That sentiment right there was exactly why she should turn, run home, and not look back. Only instead, she found herself nodding. "Okay, sure. Why not?"

His grin was tight, but it was the most she'd seen him smile during the whole conversation. Tension melted off her back and shoulders. As much as she didn't want to admit it, she was damn lonely. And having someone take her out—someone who truly knew her—might be just what she needed. And Sam was right. High school was a long time ago. . . . Maybe it was time to forgive and move on.

"Is that little Jessie Walters?" Another guy jogged toward them, holding two cups of coffee. He handed one to Sam as he approached. He was shorter than Sam and a little rounder around the belt, but in decent shape. A goatee surrounded thin lips and he smiled at Jess, picking her up in a hug and spinning her. "Wild Walters is back in Portland, huh?"

He set her back on her feet and Jess laughed. "Matt?" She slapped him on the shoulder. "How the hell are you?"

"I'm awesome. Kelly and I just had a baby—a little girl." He dove a hand into his back pocket, pulling out his phone and flipping through some pictures. "We named her Grace after Kelly's mom."

Jess raised an eyebrow. "So you have Grace and Kelly in your home? You poor bastard."

"I know, right? I'm surrounded by princesses!"

Jess smiled and nudged him with an elbow. "She's beautiful, Matt. Congratulations." Jess flicked a glance back to Sam, whose eyes were glued to her as he sipped his coffee. The steam billowed out of the small hole on the lid, covering his face with the fog. There was a tug to one side of his mouth—a smirk forming as he stared.

"Look at you, kid," Matt continued. "You look great. Brooklyn agrees with you, huh?"

"Better than great," Sam added quietly, his eyes slowly raking her body.

The moisture in Jess's mouth dried. So much for "just friends," huh? She shrugged the compliment off. "It's probably more of the fact that with my rent, I can't afford more than one meal a day." Jess looked again to Sam and added, "You guys don't look so bad yourselves."

Sam's mouth twitched higher as he ran a hand over his dark hair and clean-shaven jaw.

"Thanks, Jessie." Matt patted his belly. "Kelly's banned doughnuts from our house, unfortunately."

"Not that that stops you from eating them in my car," Sam interjected. "And getting powder all over my damn leather interior."

"So, you two work together?" Jess looked between the two guys from high school. Where Sam was the bad boy—the one who smoked behind the school and could convince any girl to join him in ditching class—Matt was the goof. The guy who went for the laughs and succeeded each time.

"Partners. For two years now," Matt said, clasping a hand to Sam's shoulder.

"Man, you go away for a bit and come back to find everyone's a detective!" Jess laughed.

"You're kinda in the business yourself, right?" Matt asked. "Forensic photography?"

Jess nodded. It was a morbid job, but she liked it. There was something about looking at the world through a scope. You could drown out the rest of the nonsense and focus in on one thing at a time. No one seemed to understand her motivation though—hell, she wasn't sure *she* understood her motivations. "Yep."

"How long you in town for?" Matt asked.

Jess shrugged. "I have to get Cass's affairs in order. At least a few weeks."

"Our forensic photographer left recently—moved up to Belfast. We could probably talk to the captain. Get you some freelance work while you're here. If you need the money—"

"Matt, I dunno if that's a good idea," Sam interrupted.

Tension knotted in Jess's stomach. "Why not?" She narrowed her eyes at Sam. It was the exact douse of icy water she needed. The reminder of how quickly Samuel McCloskey could turn on people.

His gaze slid to Matt's with a barely visible sigh.

"Don't look to Mattie," Jess snapped. "Look at me."

Sam's gaze slipped back to her, eyes blazing. He stood taller and stiffer and Jess could feel the intensity radiating off his body. "It's not a good idea, Jess. You have to get your sister's affairs in order. You need to focus on that while you're here and not worry yourself with a second job."

His tone sent a shiver down her spine. It was more than just stubborn—it was commanding. An order, not a request. He had a way of doing that . . . even in high school. His suggestions were demands. There were some areas of her life Jess loved to be bossed around—but not when it came to her career. "If I spend all day every day only dealing with Cass's stuff—I'll lose my shit," she said, glaring at Sam before turning to Matt. "I could really use the distraction."

"Then go work at the Portrait Persons kiosk in the mall," Sam grunted.

Jess felt her face go hot. "Sure. As soon as you quit your job and become a rent-a-cop." Sam's teeth gnashed together at the suggestion and Jess shot him an angry smirk. "Yeah . . . not so easy to give up doing something you love, for something else that's only partially related, huh?" She folded her arms.

"Fine, do whatever the hell you want. You always do, anyway." Sam threw his hands up and stalked back to the car.

"Me?" Jess trilled.

Sam called to Matt from over his shoulder. "C'mon, Matt. We gotta get back."

"I'll talk to the captain," Matt said quietly with a wave good-bye.

"Thanks," Jess mouthed as he ran off in the opposite direction.

# 5

Sam McCloskey gripped the steering wheel with such force, he swore his fingers would have blisters when he finally released his hold. He had caught glimpses of Jessie at Cass's funeral, but he had barely noticed how much she'd matured in the last ten years. All he saw the day of the service were the silent tears streaming down her face. The way her long, black eyelashes spiked around her amber eyes. Eyes that now bore experience, passion, and seduction rather than immaturity and childlike rebellion. And those tears—the way her chest quivered with silent sobs—it splintered a crack right into his stone heart. There were only two other times in their lives he had seen those tears spill down her face. Once was the first time she fell off her bike when they were kids. The second was her parents' funeral.

His stomach lurched at the memory of her parents and he quickly pushed them away. Back into the recesses of his mind. There was no time or place in his life right now for regrets. Could he have handled shit better back when they were fifteen and her parents died? Of course. But, come on, he was *fifteen.* And cutting her off as a friend was better than her finding out the truth.

Why, oh why he thought that chasing her down the sidewalk today was a good idea was beyond him. Maybe it was a flash of momentary insanity. Or maybe he was lulled in by the sight of her graceful body running down the docks. Her svelte, lean muscles clenched from under that tight, white T-shirt. A shirt that he suspected looked completely conservative on a hanger in her closet—but on Jessie? Christ, it was practically X-rated; sheer and barely reaching above her navel. The strip of skin revealed there was taut, leading his eyes down to long, muscled legs. Runner's legs.

"Dude! What's the big deal?" Matt's voice spiraled him back into the present. "It's her job back home—and we need a new photographer. At least until we find someone more permanent." Matt reached into the Tim Hortons bag, pulling out a crème-filled something or other and biting in. His eyes rolled back, and he let his head fall onto the headrest. With a mouth full of half-chewed food, he smacked his lips and gave a contented sigh. "Besides—if she has a job, there's the chance she might decide to stick around for a while. Maybe even stay for good. Ever think about that?"

Sam raked a hand down his face, the skin smooth from his morning shave. He *had* thought of that. And that was exactly why he couldn't let her get settled here. Not with a job. Not with a home. Nothing. And he certainly couldn't tell Matt his reasons for not wanting to work beside Jessica "Wild" Walters. It was the one and only request Cass had of him before she died. Get Jessie out of Portland as quickly as possible.

"Jessie doesn't want this coastal life. She made that perfectly clear years ago. She'd be miserable. New York was always her goal."

"Don't be so sure," Matt said, wiping powder from his goatee. "Women hit a certain age and BAM! The only booties they want are the kinds that go on a baby's feet. Less bars, more children."

Sam snorted. That might be true of most women—but Jess

was anything *but* typical. "Somehow, I doubt that's Jessie's intentions. She just needs to keep her head down and stay out of trouble." *Yeah fucking right.*

"Wild Walters staying out of trouble? We're talking about the same girl here, right?" Matt chuckled.

"Yeah," Sam groaned. He'd barely spent ten minutes with the woman and already he was so hard he was piercing the base of the steering wheel. What the fuck was he thinking, inviting her to dinner? He shook his head back into reality. It was a tactic—that was it. He needed to get into Cass's house. And a dinner with Jessie and maybe an invitation for coffee at her place after was a surefire way to get in the door.

He gulped. She looked so lost. So hollow. Those brown eyes of hers were once filled with electricity. But today, she looked vacant. And maybe—just maybe, he truly wanted to catch up with her. Make sure she was okay. A long breath pushed past his lips as he remembered how she made her way toward him at the graduation party years ago. Her stride had been slow, confident. Hella sexy. She was wearing some little halter dress that barely covered anything and she paused before him, a nearly empty bottle of something sweet and alcoholic in hand. Despite the fact that he was nearly a whole head taller than her, she dropped a shoulder confidently, fisted his shirt, and pulled his face down to hers. Pausing just before their mouths touched, she whispered, "I don't want to hear any objections. This is happening. Tonight."

Why the hell she would come on to him after what he did to her was far beyond his understanding. And as he was about to stop her—push her to arm's length—she kissed him. She kissed him in a way that he never knew a kiss could be. Firm, but soft. Wet, but not sloppy. Her tongue thrust into his mouth and he groaned, lifting her onto his hips.

"Jessie," he said. "Maybe we shouldn't—"

"Shut up," she moaned into his mouth. "And take me upstairs."

And despite the warning signals that fired off in his brain, he did just that. Their one and only time together.

"Whatchya smilin' about over there?" Matt asked with his own knowing grin.

"Your mom," Sam shot back.

"Hooohooo!" Matt clapped his hands, laughing. "You've still got it bad for Jessie, huh? I knew it. I told Kelly and she told me there was no way, but I *knew*—"

"I do not have it bad for Jess. Hell, I barely know her anymore!"

"Uh-huh. Look at yourself, man. You're beet red. I've never seen you blush at *anything!* Whatever happened to you two, anyway? You were best friends for years. Every girl wanted to be Jessie and every guy would have killed to have been in your shoes. It always seemed logical that you woulda ended up together."

Sam sighed, pulling into the gas station. What happened to them? It was far too fucking complicated. And if he couldn't explain to Jessie why he walked away, he sure as hell couldn't tell Matt. Sam had a dark side, that's what happened. A side to him that he couldn't fucking forgive himself for, let alone ask another woman to forgive as well. But that night, that one night after graduation, hope sparked inside of him like a piece of flint catching a flame. But before the fire could set, Jess had tamped it out, leaving him alone and never looking back.

But now, here she was, back in Portland; in her hometown where everything probably reminded her of her parents' deaths and all that she had lost. Now with Cass's death? Sam knew when Jessie left this time—it was for good. Nothing tied her to this town anymore. Sam's chest tightened at the thought and yet—maybe that was exactly how it should be.

Jess opened the door to her sister's home, stripping her layers as she walked to the upstairs bathroom. Fucking Sam. Did he think she couldn't handle the job? The job she'd been doing for *six years* now in New York. Or was he afraid what would happen if they worked with each other? As if she was some horny teen who couldn't keep her wits about her with him at her side.

Jess grunted, stomping around the guest room. Sam McCloskey, you are hot, but not *that* hot.

She passed Cass's bedroom, the door still open from that morning. Jess swallowed and ducked into the bathroom, shutting the door behind her. She turned the water on and stepped into the steaming hot shower.

Maybe she should tell Sam about her sister's stash. As a detective, he might be able to help. Jess snorted, sudsing up her hair. Sam's idea of helping was playing protector. No—not protector—*controller.* Besides, whatever was going on in Cass's life before she died couldn't have been good. If there was one thing Jess had learned at the NYPD, it was that no one has a fake passport and stacks of cash for any legit reason. Whatever Cass had been into was bad news. Jess swallowed the lump in her throat. She'd be damned if she was gonna let anyone tarnish her sister's legacy. Nope. She couldn't tell Sam a damn thing. Not yet, at least.

An image of all that money in stacks below the floor flashed in her mind and she shifted under the steady stream of water. That was a shitload of money. Simply having it under this same roof with her was enough to cause Jess sleepless nights. What the hell are you supposed to do when you find stacks of cash in a dead family member's home? The sudden burn for answers flared within her and Jess scrubbed the bar of soap over her body. As though this action would wash clean all that had happened in the last two weeks.

The water pattered across her heated flesh and she closed her eyes as the rivers of water streamed down her breasts and stomach. She fell against the tiled wall, letting her head rest there.

The last night she ever saw Sam was their graduation party.

They were eighteen years old and she was still a virgin. Begrudgingly so. And of all the people in the world, she didn't want to lose it drunkenly to some douchebag in college. No, she wanted someone she cared about. And despite the crazy three years she and Sam had had, she knew he still cared about her.

She had worn a blue pleather miniskirt and a halter top—instead of the sweet summer dress Cass had bought for her. Her sister had been furious; embarrassed. All the other families had lovely photos of their kids posing demurely. Cass had a picture of Jessie giving the middle finger to everyone as she received her diploma. Cass screamed at her after the ceremony, telling her to get the hell out of the house that night and not come back until morning, something Jess had already planned on doing, regardless.

Jess closed her eyes, remembering the feel of his hands on her soft skin. The way he tugged her skirt down and untied her top. He had always been a guy who knew what he wanted; he was her first kiss where she felt as though it was actually a *man* kissing her and not some teenage boy fumbling up her shirt. He was direct, but not pushy. Confident, not arrogant. And Jess had wanted every bit of him. She'd wanted him for four years and every time he ignored her passing glances in the hallway—every time he left a party she had arrived to—it chipped away at her already broken heart. Until finally it was unfixable. But that night—it was his party. He couldn't leave his own damn party. And Jess was determined to convince him. To look him in the eyes and do exactly what she had wanted to do for four years. And with a little bit of liquid courage, she was able to do just that graduation night. Jess kept her eyes closed, trailing her hand down her body as her mind wandered back to that night. . . .

*"That's quite the outfit choice," he groaned, his lips trailing the line of her throat as he carried her into his bedroom, dropping her onto his bed. It was a bed she knew well; the same bed*

*they had played Teenage Mutant Ninja Turtles on together as kids. The same bed where they had giggled over his stepdad's girlie magazines. The same bed they had sat on and smoked their first-ever cigarettes on—and then consequently threw up on moments later.*

*"I was rebelling against Cass." Jess shrugged through a grin, narrowing her eyes in a playful manner. Sam's mouth quirked and he hooked a finger into her black thong, snapping the strap against her skin. She gasped as the sting of pain resonated.*

*His eyes lit up with the momentary acknowledgment of pain. "Did you like that?" he asked.*

*Jess tilted her head, not exactly sure how to respond to the question. "Pissing Cass off?"*

*His smile twitched. "No. This." He tugged the strap once more, pulling it back farther and letting it snap to her skin harder than before.*

*Through clenched teeth, Jess inhaled. The sting lasted only a moment, but the excitement in Sam's tight face lingered.*

*Jess panted and a sudden flood of dampness seeped between her legs. "You're teasing me, Sam," she said with a smile.*

*"And you didn't answer my question, Jessica." He hooked a finger into the thong once more, this time brushing his knuckle against her swollen folds. "Do you like a little pain with your pleasure?"*

*Jess's eyes widened. Holy shit. She had never thought of that before. "You mean like . . . like spanking and stuff?"*

*Sam's pupils dilated and as a car drove by outside, a bright highlight illuminated one side of his face, casting the other in a deep shadow. "To start, yeah."*

*"I-I don't know. Do you like that?"*

*He didn't answer and instead studied her face carefully, his mouth sloping into a soft frown. "Are you sure you want to do this tonight, Jessie?" Sam asked, swallowing. "Because goddamn, do I want you. Have wanted you for years." His voice was raspy, and he dropped his forehead to hers, cupping his hands around her jaw. His touch was tender, and he traced the outline to her chin in a light trail that left a heated path behind.*

*"It sure didn't seem like you wanted me for years," she whispered, fisting his shirt. With a tug, she pulled him against her, his arousal pushed against her own and her body clenched.*

*He growled, claiming her lips with his. It was wild, primal, and the animal nature resonated deep within her as he curled his fingers into her panties. He dragged them down her thighs, and they fell to the floor. "That outfit," he panted, "didn't only drive Cass crazy. Did you see how every other guy in school was looking at you?"*

*Jess nodded. "I saw. But all I cared about was how you were looking at me."*

*"God, you're so hot," he murmured, sliding his lips down her throat. "You know the way you nibble the edge of your pencil in Spanish? I used to stare at you from the back of class, wishing it was me you were nibbling on."*

*Jess swallowed. "It could have been. Anytime. You just needed to say the word."*

*He stilled, muscles at his lower back bunching beneath her palms. Static buzzed between them as drunken partygoers hollered from the other side of the door. Finally, Sam sighed. "Look, Jessie, I—"*

*"I don't want to hear it," Jess snapped. And it was true. She didn't come tonight because she wanted some sort of bullshit apology. She didn't come to reconcile. She came because they were eighteen. Adults. And she was leaving soon. But before she did, she had to get Sam out of her system. Otherwise, she'd never be able to truly move on. Softening her tone, lifted onto her elbows. "Tell me more. About how much you wanted me," she said.*

*"At Halloween. Jake's party—you came in a devil costume," he hissed, closing his eyes. "Jesus, that was hot. You had that red*

*corset and a black miniskirt with fishnets. It looked like you stepped right out of a calendar. It felt wrong staring at you in that outfit. You were so . . . naughty."*

Jess *giggled and shifted onto her hip. "Ohhh, I'm a naughty girl, am I?"*

Sam's *gaze shot to hers. "Are you making fun of me?"*

*She stilled, swallowing, and holding his gaze. He looked so serious; so angry. She shook her head. "No . . . I-I just thought we were playing around. Being silly."*

*"I'm not." The air crackled with electricity and for a moment, all breath stalled in Jess's throat. Was this the same guy? Sam's gaze burned a line down her body and the moment of having the giggles evaporated. His touch splayed along her hip and Jess found herself gasping at the sudden contact. It was more erotic and intimate than the kiss they had just shared and his eyes seared into hers. Dropping her hand to his chest, she felt his heart thunder against her palm. Why? Because of her? All this time, all these years, she thought he hated her for some unknown reason. In reality, could it have been that he was actually as in love with her as she was with him? As her gaze lifted, his face was tight, smoldering. It was all the confirmation that she needed. They locked into each other's stare and Sam brushed his fingers down her cheek before bringing them to the bottom hem of her short skirt. Shadows shimmied along his features and before Jess had too long to study him, his mouth was on her again. With one finger, he entered her. She expected him to be rough; taking what he wanted and not thinking more of it. But his movements were slow, controlled, easing her body into a melting pile of whimpers. Jess cried out, falling back on the pillow, closing her eyes.*

*"Jessica." Sam's voice was demanding, but quiet. "Jessie, look at me." She leaned back up on her elbows, once again meeting his gaze. He gave her a smile that hinted of experience well beyond his years. "Good girl." He pushed two fingers inside,*

*stretching her, and lowered his mouth between her legs. His eyes burned into hers, never breaking focus. Who was this man? He wasn't the Sam that she had grown up with. The new quiet control had Jess trembling all over.*

*It wasn't long until she was clenching around his fingers and light exploded behind her eyes. She fell back onto the bed again, clamping her eyes shut as the spasms took hold of her body. She bit back a cry and fisted Sam's comforter between her fingers.*

*After she finished, Sam put both fingers in his mouth, sucking her flavor from them. "You have a real problem with listening, you know that?" he said quietly, his lips curving. "Turn over."*

*"I want to suck you, first," Jess said.*

*His head moved back and forth slowly. "Flip." He gave a little gesture with his hand and Jess swallowed. Was this some sort of game? A new fantasy? Something he'd seen in his latest stepdad's porn collection? Jess wasn't sure, but whatever it was, she liked it. And the fact that she liked it scared the crap out of her.*

*She did as he said, flipping onto her stomach. "Like this?"*

*"On your knees." His voice was different. Tight. Controlled, but on the edge of falling into something different. Like a car about to spin off the edge of a cliff.*

*Jess did as she was told, pulling her body onto her hands and knees.*

*"You like driving me crazy, Jessie?" he asked.*

*Jess opened her mouth to speak, but didn't know what to say. What was the right answer here? Wasn't it good that she drove him crazy?*

*His hand twisted around her hair, grasping the ponytail in his hand. He gave a tug and her head jerked back. "Answer me, Jessie."*

*"Y-yes!" she cried out. "Yes, I want you to be crazy about me."*

*"I told you to look at me and yet while you came, you looked away. You wore your little outfit to drive me insane." He chuckled and dropped his mouth to her ear, flicking his tongue*

*across the sensitive flesh there. Nibbling the edge, he lowered his voice. "You're a bad girl."*

His flattened palm connected with her ass in a spank that took her completely off guard. She cried out—not out of pain necessarily; but more out of shock. She tightened down there and could feel her desire pooling once more.

Had he really hit her? She clenched her teeth . . . no, no, it was a spank. Not a hit. Lots of couples spank. She turned her head to try to look back at him, but he spanked her again. The third time, she braced herself; this one was harder; a biting sting that resonated across her skin. Between each slap, Sam ran his fingers between her legs, gathering the juices there on the tip of his finger and playing with her swollen sex. He spanked again, this time, landing his palm in the center of her ass so that part of his hand connected with her sex. She cried out loud, something clenching deep within her. Deeper inside than any excitement she'd ever felt before.

Was she actually enjoying this? How twisted was she for wanting it even harder? And how messed up was he for enjoying her pain? But she couldn't deny her body's response to the sudden demand and ownership Sam had over her.

"I want to see this hot ass red with my handprint." He spanked her again, this time positioning himself directly behind Jess and lowering his mouth to her once more. He ran his tongue up her thighs, catching the dripping fluids there. "Fuck, Jessie. You're so wet. You like this, don't you? Please tell me you do. Tell me I'm not alone in this." He sounded broken, and his voice caught at the end as Jess looked over her shoulder, their gaze connecting once more. His eyes glistened with an intensity—a plea—that Jess had never before seen in her friend.

One side of her mouth lifted. "I can't believe I'm about to say this," she whispered. "But holy hell is this hot."

Though barely visible, Sam's muscles relaxed into a sigh and his eyes glimmered with the admission. Licking his lips, he *closed his eyes, trailing his hands over her ass slowly, as though taking in every detail.*

*Long fingers curled around her shoulders and up the back of her neck. Snaking the other arm around her hip, he tenderly flipped her onto her back, resting her against the pillows before lowering his lips to her ear. "I need you, Jessie. I've wanted you—wanted this for so long."*

*The bold sentence rocked through her and Jess was instantly aroused with his admission. She lifted her chin, her eyes seeking his and her chest heaving with the trembling breath. She wanted him inside her more than anything. It wouldn't be Sam's first time, but it would be hers. Did he even know that? She pulsed for him. Wanted it; needed it. But, she didn't trust her voice not to shake in answering him, so she only nodded instead.*

*His fingers traced little S shapes down her arm until they laced with hers and, gently, he pulled both arms over her head, peppering tiny kisses over her jaw and lips.*

*He reached for his nightstand, grabbed a condom, and ripped the package with his teeth. "I need to take this in," he said quietly. "Every fucking second of it." His gaze shifted, studying her face, and he untied her halter top, slipping it down over her heavy breasts. They pebbled, reaching for his touch, his attention, his mouth, his . . . anything.*

*He positioned himself between her legs, brushed a hand over her hair, and kissed her. His tongue moved expertly around hers, molding her mouth; guiding her into being a woman. "You okay?" he asked.*

*Jess nodded. "Yeah."*

*"Good." He smiled and kissed her again. "I don't ever want you to not be okay."*

Jess switched the shower off, sick of constantly thinking about those haunting memories of Sam. Neither of them had lasted long while having sex. Even though Sam was the most experienced guy she'd ever been with at that age, he was still young. A few thrusts later and he was trembling over her body, only he made sure she had one more orgasm before falling asleep with his arm draped over her stomach. Jess had lain there beside him for about an hour.

Her body had betrayed her that night. She never wanted to be the kind of woman who wanted to be hit. She was stronger than that. Playful or not. Sexual or not. She had slipped out from his hold that night, put her skimpy outfit back on, grabbed a final bottle of Zima, and slipped out the back door while Sam slept upstairs. She wanted to drink the thoughts away; the haunting memories and the sadness and loss of her parents not seeing her graduation day.

Jess dried off, wrapping the silky robe around her. She had never stopped thinking about that night. No man had ever been able to make her come like Sam had. And with the limited amount of lovers she'd had since, she always found herself wanting a good spanking.

"Shit," Jess muttered to herself as she found a pair of black dress pants and a button-down shirt. "Damn you, Sam." She was going to walk herself into that precinct today and get herself a job. And if Sam had a problem with it? Well, he could just go to hell.

# 6

Jess stood outside the brick building, looking up. An American flag billowed in the breeze, beckoning her inside. "Here goes nothing." As she entered, pressing into the glass door, Officer Rodriguez looked up from behind the bulletproof reception area. Her eyes widened and she pushed her hair behind one ear. "Hi . . . I'm so sorry, I can't remember your name from yesterday. The pink house, right?"

Jess nodded. "Walters. Jessica Walters."

Rodriguez pressed her lips together before looking down at her desk and shuffling some papers. "Is everything okay? Any other scares?"

Jess shook her head. "Everything's fine, thanks. I'm actually here to see Captain Straimer. I spoke with Detective Matt Johnson earlier. He said you were seeking a freelance forensic photographer."

She nodded, holding up a finger, and picked up the phone. "Sorry, this might take a minute," she said. "I'm not usually out here. Just filling in for someone while they did a coffee run." She hit a few buttons and quietly murmured into the receiver.

Setting it back into its cradle, Rodriguez gestured to a row of seats across from the front desk. "Have a seat. Someone will be with you in a moment."

Jess sat down, shifting her iPad in her lap. She had examples of her work loaded and ready to show off. There was a time Jess's dream had been to hang work in a gallery setting but nobody wanted to see an image of a fingerprint blown up as a thirty-by-thirty print. Not to mention getting around the red tape of privacy issues was more than a little difficult.

In college, she had taken a photography appreciation course for one of her electives. She could give two shits about landscape imagery or portraits of models like Man Ray took. But when Weegee's work of crime scenes flashed on the projector, Jess was automatically drawn in to the morose nature of his images.

"Well, well, well. Here's a surprise."

Jess jumped at the sound of Sam right beside her. She rolled her eyes and crossed her legs. "Shouldn't you be out solving some 7-Eleven robbery or something?"

Sam lowered into the seat next to hers, then sighed. "I knew you would come here first chance you got. It's why I told Laura to call me when you arrived."

Jess darted a glance to Rodriguez behind the glass. She was staring at Sam, hearts dripping out of her eyes. As soon as Jess caught her gaze, she dropped her head, suddenly engaged in whatever paperwork was on the desk. Air pushed through Jess's pursed lips in an exasperated sigh. "Of course. I should have guessed you have every lady in here wrapped around your little finger."

His eyes glittered with Jess's observation and she swore she saw the corner of his mouth raise a fraction of an inch. He tilted his head with mock innocence. "Not *every* lady," he said leaning in closer. "Only the pretty ones."

"Lucky for me, Captain Straimer was good friends with my mom." She leaned in to Sam's ear, her lips dangerously close to his skin, and whispered, "*And* I'm pretty skilled with my little finger, too."

"Don't I remember," Sam whispered back. Tension buzzed in the thick air between them as they locked eyes. Jess's breath sputtered like a stalling engine, only she didn't dare show her hand. She couldn't reveal the effect he had on her. His shoulders locked visibly and Jess smiled at the sight. Apparently, her poker face was better than his.

*Take that, you control freak.* She stood, walked back over to Rodriguez, and gave her a tight smile. "Could you call Captain Straimer this time, please. I would hate to have to report you as not attending to the needs of one of Portland's citizens. Besides, Detective McCloskey and I are done here."

Her jaw tightened as she nodded, olive skin paling to a sickly shade of white, and grabbed the phone, dialing. Jess leaned a hip against the counter, arms folded across her chest. The chair screeched across the floor as Sam pushed off it, stalking toward her. Though it went against every instinct she had, Jess ignored the desire to shrink away from his approach.

He gripped her elbow, dragging Jess into a corner of the room and not letting go once they were there. His touch burned through the cotton fabric and Jess's skin flared beneath her clothes. Jesus, she wanted those hands all over her body. And she hated herself for that. "Jess, you don't know what you're getting yourself into here. Please. Just go home." She thought she could get him out of her system. She thought that being the one to walk away after high school would ease the pain of him ending their friendship for years when she needed him the most. God, she was an idiot.

"Then *tell* me what I'm getting myself into." Jess gave a noncommittal shrug. "Seriously. If I don't understand something, instead of trying to control the situation with me in the dark . . . tell me *what* it is I don't understand." She waited a few seconds in a pregnant pause. Sam held her eye contact, the hard lines of his face dropping even more. Jess nodded, pressing her lips together. "That's what I thought. You expect control. Blind trust when you give nothing in return . . ."

"Oh, for fuck's sake—"

"It's true," she cut in. "This is my job, Sam. It's what I do. And I'm damn good at it. If I can handle the crimes coming through Brooklyn, I think I'll be just fine here in Portland."

Sam shoved his hand into his dark hair, hissing a curse. Finally, he dropped his hand to his leg. "I give up. Do what you want, Jess."

"I always do."

Sam huffed passed her, slamming his shoulder into the door. "Don't I know it," he muttered as the door slammed behind him.

"Jessica Walters?"

Jess took one second to regain her composure before turning to find Captain Straimer standing behind her with a wide grin.

"Well, well, well!" he exclaimed, his smile growing larger. "It's good to see ya, kid. How you doin'?"

"I'm hanging in there. How've you been, Captain?"

"No complaints. What can I do for you?"

"I was wondering if we could talk? In your office?"

Thirty minutes later, Captain Straimer set the iPad down, leaned back in his seat, and stared at Jess. His fingers were steepled under his chin and he exhaled on a sigh. "Well, we *are* looking for a freelance photographer. But you, of course, knew that already." He looked at the images on her device once more, swiping through them. "And your stuff is some of the best I've ever seen. Your flash fill is great, your painting with light is stellar. Your focus is razor sharp. . . ." He faded off, dropping the iPad back onto the table and pinching the bridge of his nose with two fingers.

"So, what's the problem?" Jess asked when he simply stopped speaking.

He cleared his throat, his mouth set into a straight line. "I knew your parents quite well. And with everything that's happened—with Cass—I have to consider the possibility of a conflict of interest."

"Captain—"

He held up a hand to silence her. "Hear me out. What if there's a mugging with a similar situation as your sister's? How do I know you won't have an emotional break because of it? Are you sure you're ready to do this sort of work again? And so soon after . . ."

Jess's fists clenched in her lap and she forced them to relax. "If I was a man whose sister just died, would you be going through the same inner turmoil about hiring me?" When he didn't say anything, Jess had her answer, and nodded. "That's what I thought. Captain, I'm good at this job. I love that my photographs help piece together the puzzle, giving voices to the dead. Call any of my superiors in Kings County—they'll tell you. I'm the best. And I know my limits. If I think I can't handle a case, I'll step away." Jess put her hands up in a Juliette Gordon Low type of way. "I promise. Girl Scout's honor." Little did he know, she had never actually *been* a Girl Scout. And technically her sister's murder wasn't her case, so if she happened to stumble upon those files, she wouldn't be breaking the promise either. Even still, her body flushed with the lies.

Straimer finally nodded. "Very well. But I'm putting you in weekly meetings with our force psychologist. If he clears you with the first meeting, then you're all set."

"Sir—"

"I don't want to hear it. I would make a man do the same

exact thing," he snapped. Jess swallowed and nodded, choosing her battles.

"I assume NYPD has your background check and other paperwork they can send me?" Straimer slipped his glasses onto his nose and handed Jess her iPad back.

"Yes, sir. Thank you, Captain. You're not going to be disappointed."

# 7

"You have got to be fucking kidding me!"

"Detective, you might want to consider lowering your voice." Straimer's eyes narrowed, but he held that controlled manner that Sam always admired.

Sam took a deep breath. "I'm sorry, sir. This seems crazy. She's a recent victim's sister. On a case we haven't even solved yet, for Christ's sake . . ."

"McCloskey, she's not going to be on her sister's case at all. She's seeing the staff psychologist as part of the stipulations. She's down there right now talking with Tong. And if I think for even a moment she's not capable of handling the job, then she's out."

What could Straimer possibly be thinking? Never mind her sister's recent death—what about her parents' cold case hit and run? And the sheer amount of men on this force who would eye-fuck her daily. Sam's teeth gnashed together. Jesus, how the fuck was he supposed to function with that girl around every curve.

"Captain, I know it sounds like I'm questioning you here,

but please. I know Jess better than you. Cass was in deep with this drug ring. The latest drug compound wasn't FDA approved yet and they had people smuggling it in from Canada. I'm telling you, Cass's job had her back and forth from Maine to Canada monthly. We're so close, I can feel it. And Jess is incapable of staying out of trouble. If Cass—"

Straimer seemed to have been considering what Sam was saying until the door barged open with Matt knocking as he entered. "Johnson," the captain said, cutting Sam off, "knocking is meant to be done from the *other* side."

Matt eyed the two men chatting before dropping into the chair in front of Straimer's desk. "Sorry, boss. What's the word in here?"

Sam swallowed, gulping the sentence down. He liked Matt—he was a good detective and a great partner. But what they had on Cass was top-secret information. He couldn't leak it, not even to a buddy. Not even to his partner.

"We were just discussing Ms. Walters," Straimer said, staring at Sam. "She'll be starting with us as soon as possible."

"Hey!" Matt laughed and clapped once. "All right. Jessie's joining the team."

"Hopefully, there'll be time for her to dip her toes in with some petty crime," Straimer added, looking at a stack of papers on his desk.

"And if not?" Sam chewed his top lip, fingers tight around his hips.

Straimer shrugged. "She'll have to sink or swim."

"And what? Contaminate our crime scene in the process?"

Straimer crossed from behind his desk, shoving the stack of papers into Sam's chest. "You think so little of her? Check out this history, sent from the NYPD. In her six years on the job, she's never once contaminated a scene. In fact, she's helped solve a few cases alongside the arriving cops and first responders, by seeing things they missed. They call her Macro over there because she's able to see things through the lens that most people can't catch on the scene." Straimer shoved Sam's chest— not hard enough to be aggressive, but enough for Sam to know he'd been pushed enough for one day. "You find me a photographer with that strong of a history and I'll replace Walters. Until then, she's staying."

The muscle in Sam's jaw twitched as he skimmed the first couple pages. Damn, he hated being wrong. She was *better* than good at her job. There were notes from her superiors about her attention to detail, stellar work ethic, and solid case duties. "But her sister wasn't just murdered at any of these crime scenes." Sam shook the papers.

"No. But her parents had died. And she still kept it together."

"Fine," Sam snapped, tossing the papers onto Straimer's desk. "Anything else?"

"Not for now."

Sam stalked out of the office, Matt's footsteps echoing just behind him. "Well, you were awfully quiet in there," Sam growled.

"Yeah," Matt said. "Probably because I agree with Straimer. C'mon, man. Give the girl a chance." He lowered his voice, checking down the hall to ensure no one was coming. "She needs this. Be a friend."

Of course Matt agreed with Straimer. He didn't know the half of it. Only a select few knew of the crazy, tangled web Cass had gotten caught in this year. And for what? Some extra cash? Sam still didn't understand why or how a girl who was on every honor roll, a girl who wore cardigans and shopped at Michaels and made fucking Christmas wreaths as presents every year became involved in such an insane lifestyle. There had to be more about Cass's involvement with this ring. No,

Sam didn't expect Matt to understand why Jess should stay as far away from the Portland PD as possible, but Straimer sure as hell should have known better.

Sam grunted, grabbing the emergency cigarette he always carried in his billfold. He pulled it out, twirling it in his fingers. The white paper was dingy, tobacco falling out of one end, and it had been bent more than once. He rolled it in his hands, lifting it under his nose and inhaling that fading smoky scent. He exhaled slowly. Eight years without a smoke. Eight goddamn years of twitching and eating and being irritable so that he didn't land the same fate as his stepdad—his mom's third husband. He was amazed that the cigarette he carried around hadn't disintegrated after all these years.

"Hello? Earth to Sam!"

He snapped out of his daze, tucking the cigarette back into his wallet. "Sorry. What'd you say?"

"I said, if I didn't know you better, I'd think you were keeping secrets from me."

Sam swallowed. "Secrets? What the hell makes you think that?" Sam was a damn good liar and he knew it. But that didn't mean it was a quality he liked about himself.

"Oh, come on." Matt's voice lowered as he stepped in closer. "It's so obvious." He paused, head dropping to the side.

Sam's pulse jumped as Matt studied his face. He kept himself relaxed, forcing his breath to remain steady.

Finally, Matt playfully slapped his shoulder. "It's obvious you're still in love with her! Just ask Jessie out, already."

Sam wanted to breathe a sigh of relief, but refrained. They were partners; they weren't supposed to have secrets from each other. But Sam had his orders when he had stumbled onto Cass's picture in border control paperwork. Only, she wasn't Cassandra—in the pictures and the paperwork, she was Cynthia. If he hadn't already known her, he never would have noticed. The fake passport was that damn good. But soon after this discovery, it became pretty clear that there was a leak within the department and Straimer made sure that only Sam and a select couple of people on the force knew of her involvement. Especially with Straimer's attachment to the Walters family—he didn't want this information leaked any more than Sam did.

Sam cracked a smile, winking at his friend. "As a matter of fact, we're going to dinner. Tonight." Whether or not she was still interested in going out with him . . . well, that was a whole other story.

Jess gripped the evaluation form handed to her by the staff quack. "Rash and quick to act with more regard for others' lives than her own." Jess snorted, crumpling the piece of paper and shoving it deep into her purse.

Thank God Straimer didn't see that as enough of a reason to cancel her position. Jesus, what a laugh Sam would've had at that, huh? Wild Walters and her little death wish. Is it a death wish simply to put someone's safety above your own? Especially when that someone is a civilian.

"As if that's a bad thing," she mumbled, and then clomped up the stairs to the front door. As she hovered the key in front of the lock, she heard a quiet scraping sound coming from the other side of the door. Inside the house. Every muscle in her body stiffened and the tiniest beads of sweat gathered at the nape of her neck, dripping down her spine like a roller-coaster ride.

Another noise. Like footsteps. And through the beveled glass door, she saw a sliver of a shadow move briefly.

Panic rose in her body from her stomach up to her throat like high tide and she slipped to the side, out of sight. Pressing her back into the pink vinyl siding, she forced herself to inhale deeply. Breathe. Stay calm. With one hand, she punched in the numbers 9-1 and kept her finger hovering over the final 1. Having worked for the police, she didn't want to call unnecessarily. But damn if she wasn't going down without a fight. Whoever this asshole was who kept sneaking into her house was going down. Now.

Quietly, she moved back to the door and slipped the key into the lock, listening for any signs of stirring. Whoever was there had gone silent. Still. Waiting for her entrance. Only they weren't expecting her to be ready for the fight. Slipping the pepper spray off her key ring, she left the house key dangling from the lock and swiftly threw open the door, spraying the offensive, burning stream into the foyer.

"Ah!! Son of a bitch!" A ladder wobbled and Dane alternated between covering his tearing eyes and grasping on to the ladder for balance. "Jess! It's me! What the hell?!"

"Dane?" Jess squealed, her own eyes burning. She threw the pepper spray down and ran to steady the ladder for him. "Oh my God. What are you doing here?" The spray caught in the back of her throat, launching her into a coughing fit. "Come down from there; let's get out of the foyer while it airs out."

"Jesus Christ," Dane muttered while climbing down the steps. His eyes were rimmed bright scarlet, matching the dark hue of his lips. Using his knuckles, he kneaded his eyes.

"Stop," Jess said quietly, taking his hand and guiding him into the kitchen. "Stop rubbing them, it'll make it worse." She ran water over a paper towel, handing it to Dane. "I'm sorry. I heard noises from inside the house and assumed it was an intruder."

Dane lowered his hands, his eyes still watery and red. "Sorry. I noticed yesterday that this light was out in the foyer. Figured since you were staying here, you might wanna be able to see at night. I still had Cass's key; I used to always let myself in if she wasn't home."

Jess sighed, pressing her fingers into her temples. Was it the pepper spray or just life that was giving her this awful headache?

"I appreciate your help, I really do . . . but you can't keep coming in here. Not anymore."

Dane met her eyes and they flashed a brilliant, wet blue. He sniffed, running the back of his hand under his nose. "I know. I'm sorry. It's habit, I guess."

Jess sighed. If Dane and her sister were as close as they seemed, and if he helped renovate this house himself, he probably saw it as a second home. That's not an easy thing to give up. "What if—if you knock and I'm not here . . . leave me a little sign outside. Something that lets me know you're inside and there's nothing for me to worry about."

Dane nodded, holding Jess's gaze. His tongue peeked out from the seam of his lips, wetting them in a swift movement that left Jessie staring at his pout. Without thinking, she tore her eyes from his mouth. This was a man her sister had some sort of connection to—he was *not* up for grabs.

"Absolutely. Cass has those ceramic frogs on her front steps. I'll turn them so their back is facing out if I'm here. Again—I'm really sorry. I wasn't thinking."

Jess nodded and her heart squeezed for Dane. "It's okay," she said, offering him a slight smile. "Now we have a plan. I'm sorry for spraying you."

His lopsided grin rose on one side, crinkling his kind eyes. "Can't say it's the first time a woman sprayed in my face."

Jess snorted a laugh, stunned by the brazen joke. She tossed a dish towel on the counter next to her at him, which he caught with a wink. "Gross!" she laughed and pointed toward the bathroom. "Go rinse your eyes out. It'll help."

That wicked smile grew wider before he slipped inside the bathroom. The faucet turned on, and the door was slightly ajar.

"You shoulda been a spy, you know that?" Jess called out from the kitchen as she leaned over the sink and flushed her own eyes out. Even though Dane received the brunt of the spray, residual traces burned her eyes, too. Grabbing two glasses from above, she filled them with water.

Moments later Dane was back in the kitchen standing before her and shaking droplets of water from his hands. Jess tossed him a hand towel from the oven. "And *you* should definitely not be a spy," Dane laughed. "If I was really in there waiting to attack, I don't think pepper spray would have deterred me."

Jess handed him the glass of water, shoulders sagging with her sigh. "You got me there."

His calloused fingers scraped against her soft skin and he offered her a warm smile. "So, how you holding up?"

Crunching her shoulders to her ears, Jess shrugged and hugged her arms against her body. "I dunno. I'm managing, I guess." Dane nodded, dropping his gaze into the water as though suddenly fascinated by it. "What about you? How are you doing?" Jess asked quietly.

Dane swallowed, his jaw clenching with the question.

After a moment, Jess shook her head. "I'm sorry. I shouldn't have asked."

"No, no. I asked first." He cleared his throat and continued. "I'm not great—but, hanging in there. I forgot to tell you that Cass throws this big party here every other weekend. People usually know just to show up on the first and third Friday of every month." He ran a hand across his forehead. "I'll find the guest list and try to spread the word it's been cancelled."

"What?" Jess shook the cobwebs from her ears. "You're kidding, right? My sister throws a monthly party? That doesn't sound like Cass."

Dane nodded. "Yeah. It's always a masquerade. And usually she makes partygoers bring something crazy—last time they had to bring a whole fish."

Ew. And also, holy shit. Why hadn't Cass been that fun when Jess was around? Because Cass had to be the guardian when Jess was younger, that's why. She didn't get to be a kid again until after Jess moved out. It made sense but didn't lessen the sting. She never experienced Cass's fun side.

Jess slid a glance to the kitchen table where she had tossed the black-and-pearl mask she had found yesterday. Well, that was one mystery solved.

"The guest list can be hard to track sometimes because it sort of spreads by word of mouth, but I'll try. In the meantime, you might want to stay somewhere else on Friday. Lock the doors, turn off the lights. You know, just to be safe."

The stash of money and goods in Cass's baseboards flooded Jess's mind. A party with Cass's friends would be the perfect way for Jess to find out more. "Don't worry about it, Dane. It would be nice to meet some of Cass's friends." *Friends, ha.* To Jess's knowledge, they hadn't even come to the funeral. Then again, Dane didn't either.

Dane shifted, unease flickering in his eyes. "I don't know if that's a good idea . . ."

Jess glared. "Why?"

"Well, for starters, it's an anonymous party. With the masquerade, people keep their identities under lock and key. And—" Dane gulped. Actually gulped, cutting his words off mid-sentence. "Look—I just don't think it's a good idea. Your sister wouldn't have wanted you attending one of her parties."

Dane finished the rest of the water and set it down in the sink. "I need to get going. Thanks for the drink." He rushed for the door, but Jess cut him off before he made it there.

"What aren't you telling me?" Her voice had venom in it— but something more, too. Desperation.

Dane looked to the ceiling, his lips moving, mumbling silently to himself.

"Dane! Please?" Jess grasped his elbow, shaking him until he looked back down at her. "Please," she said once more. "I've been finding . . . stuff. About Cass. And I need to know the truth. This party could be good for that."

"Oh, you'll find stuff out about her at one of these parties," he murmured, rolling his eyes. Dane inhaled slowly, letting the air pass through barely parted lips. "Your sister . . ." he started, and Jess hung on to his every word, leaning in. "These parties weren't your average . . . they were fetish parties."

# 8

---

"Fetish parties?" Jess repeated, tension winding inside of her. Her fingers curled around something and she didn't realize it was Dane's shirt until she broke her gaze from his and glanced down. A numbness took hold of her and even though she and Dane were a little less than an arm's length away, Jess felt his proximity in the very depths of her bones. The soft hum of the radiator lulled her into deep thoughts and flashes of Cass in situations that she never wanted to imagine.

"Whoa," Dane said, but Jess could barely register his voice. "Easy." Strong hands gripped her shoulders, holding her body steady, and Jess blinked as Dane's piercing blue eyes came back into focus.

"A fetish party," Jess said again. "What kind of—" she cut her own words off with a hard swallow. "You know what? Never mind, I don't want to know."

"Yeah." He shook his head and sniffed. "She never would have wanted you to know that about her."

Something here wasn't adding up. Sure, Jess and Cass didn't necessarily share all the details of their sex lives with each other . . . but Jess surely would have known if Cass was into something *so* extreme. Right?

Jess lifted a tentative hand and swept a stray piece of hair from her cheek. Then again—she never would have expected to find stacks of money in her closet, either. Or a passport in someone else's name.

Dane's eyes narrowed, and he leaned so close that Jess could smell the cinnamon on his breath; see the flecks of gold in his otherwise crystal blue eyes. "I didn't think it would upset you this much—I'm sorry. I shouldn't have said anything."

Panic swelled in Jess's chest. This world—Cass's world— was one she knew nothing about. She didn't know who to trust or who to talk to. Hell, how could she even know that what Dane said about his and Cass's relationship was true? Cass never mentioned him to Jess. None of her friends at the funeral seemed to wonder where he was. And other than one photo on a shelf, there was no evidence of their friendship.

The tiniest bit of sweat broke out along Jess's hairline and she resisted wiping it away. It would only draw more attention to her nervousness. "Nothing. I-I'm just realizing how little I actually knew about my own sister."

Dane's face softened. "Look, if you really want to have the party, you can. Hell, it's your house now. I feel guilty—it's not what Cass would have wanted. Let me know what you decide. I'll come and help."

Jess opened her mouth to protest, but Dane cut her off with a look. "Seriously, Jess. I won't take no for an answer. How many dominatrix parties have you thrown? You *need* my help with this."

Her mouth clicked shut and his stern look never wavered. Maybe it was naïve, but Jess wanted to believe Dane—she wanted to believe that her sister had someone in her life looking out for her and taking care of her. It was an area where Jess had dropped the ball more than once. Cass was the caretaker; Jess was just the taker. Nervous energy took hold of her body and she forced her hands to relax onto her hips, finally nodding after what felt like a year of silence. "Okay."

"Good," he said. "There's a closet at the back of the kitchen . . . a small one that's below the cupboards in the pantry. She has a keypad lock on it. I think her code is zero-eight-one-five."

All the hairs on Jess's neck lifted and her spine straightened. "Code?" Her heart skipped. "Zero-eight-one-five . . . what significance is that?"

He folded his arms in a way that was deceptively casual, watching Jess closely. His expression was reticent, his voice tight as he answered. "Who knows? Might just be a random compiling of numbers."

*0815.* Jess ingrained the numbers into her mind, forcing clear any bit of fogginess. Something in her belly flopped and suddenly her number-one goal was to get Dane the hell out of this house so that she could run upstairs and unlock her sister's iPad.

Dane's stern mouth was set but showed the tiniest hint of a curve as several seconds ticked by. His gaze was a show of strength; a test. Jess knew there was something more to this, but as she was held captive by those silvery blue eyes of his, something deeper resonated within. A fevered sweat lashed along her hairline and Jess tensed, willing her body to cool itself. There was a desire within her to please this man; to do whatever it was he wanted. To feel the surge of excitement that went hand in hand with earning his approval.

An unconscious shiver rolled down her spine as Jess blinked, her eyes flicking to her feet. Fuck. Why was it so damn hard for her to hold his stare? As challenges went, it should have been an easy one. Heat spilled across her cheeks and his voice above her was dark, commanding. And she refused to be lured in like a fish caught on a line. Instead, she followed her eyes slowly up his powerful legs, taking her time to soak in the sight of him. Red fabric poking out from Dane's zipper caught her eye, pausing the inspection momentarily. Jess's flush quickly faded and with a stretch of her neck, she stood a little taller, the curve of her lips confident.

Those sharp, silvery blue eyes were suddenly much less intimidating and her grin widened in response to their oddly long silence.

"What?" He mimicked her smile with a lighthearted tone that she liked about him.

"Dane," she said, inhaling his spicy male scent, leaning forward. "Your fly is down."

His gaze dipped, following Jess's. And instead of being embarrassed, and quickly zipping it up, he sauntered toward his toolbox, collecting the items. Once packed, he stood tall, with that same subtle quirk to his lips, and winked. "So it is," he said, leaving the fly wide open, red underwear peeking through.

That confidence—that damn easiness that he can manage. Most men who have his sense of dominance are terrifying and alpha. They hate defiance . . . but Dane, he was different. Dominant, sure, but there was a playfulness there; an amusement. And in some ways, Jess found that quality even more unnerving.

Dane smiled and squeezed her arm reassuringly. He glanced at his watch before his eyes widened. "Damn, is it six already? I need to go. I'll come by tomorrow if you want—to check on you."

"That's not necessary—"

Again, he gave her a look that would have silenced a roaring lion, studying her for a moment that lasted an eternity. "I'll see you tomorrow." He yanked the door open, dropping a hand to his fly and zipping it up with a wink.

Standing there on the other side of the door, with his fist raised and mouth agape, was Sam.

# 9

Sam's eyes narrowed, momentarily stunned, before his gaze dropped to Dane's fly, then back and forth between them. "Hello," he said coolly, sucking the inside of his cheek. His sharp nose and angled cheekbones stood out against the tight line of his lips. He extended a hand to Dane. "I don't think we've met."

"Dane," he answered quickly, grasping Sam's hand in a tight hold. "I'm a friend of Cass's." Only they didn't look like strangers. Dane's eyes flashed that intense silver that Jess was becoming so well acquainted with and the cords in his neck roped with tension. "Well, thanks again, Jess, for the water. I'll see you tomorrow."

Sam held his ground like a marbled column as Dane moved beyond and out the front door. He turned slowly to Jess. "Tomorrow?" Jealousy cracked at the edge of the question and it made her clench with excitement and fury at the same time.

She didn't answer and instead raised an eyebrow. "What are you doing here, Sam?"

For the moment, he seemed genuinely surprised. "We had a date."

Jess snorted, placing a finger in the air. "This is not a date," she said. "You never said the word *date*. In fact, I believe your exact words were *two friends catching up.*"

Sam took one step toward her, his gait commanding. His entire movement dominated any room he entered. Without thinking, Jess took a step back, her butt knocking into a small table. His lips quirked. "Nervous?"

She tugged her shirt down—an old, anxious habit. "No," she lied. He flicked another glance at the hemline of her shirt. Damn, he still knew all of her ticks.

His smile twitched higher. "So . . . dinner?" He shifted his weight so that all of it was resting on one leg. The outline of Adonis-like muscles dipped and curved from beneath his soft-looking V-neck shirt. And his jeans clung to his ass and thighs—just tight enough to show the brief stirrings of an erection. "If you want to change, I can wait." He lowered himself onto the couch in the adjoining living room. "Of course, if you prefer the buttoned-up look, that's fine, too," he added with a grin. "It's fun to cut loose a tightly wound skein."

Jess forced herself to look away. "After your little stunt at the precinct, I thought it would be clear that tonight was cancelled."

"Well, that's the problem with assumptions, isn't it?" He leaned back into the leather couch, kicking one leg up over the other. "I'm here now. We might as well spend some time 'catching up.' Especially since we will apparently be working together now." The last sentence was said with a biting sarcasm that made Jess's skin crawl. There was an implication of disapproval that she utterly despised. As if she needed his consent or blessing for any life choice. He lost that fucking privilege when he abandoned her at her mother and father's funeral.

She folded her arms. "Maybe I made other plans tonight."

Sam's eyebrows arched over two blue eyes. A different blue than Dane's. Deeper, darker. Like an ocean just before a storm.

"Oh, yeah? With that guy?" His head jerked to the direction of the door where Dane exited.

"Maybe."

Sam rolled his eyes. "Oh, please. Dane Murray would never date you. Not after . . ." Sam let the sentence drop, rubbing his lips together. "Shit," he muttered.

Jess swallowed. "Not after what? Knowing Cass? Dating Cass?" She finished for him, quietly. "I *knew* you had met him before. You might be a damn good liar, Sam McCloskey, but I know you. Don't forget that." She cleared her throat and turned to straighten the vase near the front door. When he didn't answer, she spoke from over her shoulder. "Anyway, you're right. I don't have plans with Dane. He's just nice and helping out around here."

Sam pushed off the couch, strolling over to Jess. "Dane's not good people, Jessica. Stay away from him."

Jess twirled, dropping a hand to her hip. "How so?" What did Sam know? Dane didn't seem like a bad person, but he did seem like he had secrets. Then again, so did everyone in this damn town. It was toxic. It bred secrets that festered inside you until your lies became too large to contain anymore. They quickly replaced your heart; your blood. Until you were nothing without them.

Sam didn't answer right away. "You just have to trust me on this."

*Trust.* The word caught in the back of her throat. "Trust?" The bitter laugh cracked across her tongue like a whip. "You? You've got to be kidding me, Sam." Jess heaved a sigh and shook her head. "Dane said he and Cass never dated."

Sam snorted. "And you believed him?" His breath was heavy and his presence behind her even heavier.

"Based on track records, I have more reason to trust Dane than you."

Cupping her jaw, he tilted her chin up until their eyes connected. "Hey—I'm sorry. For bringing up Cass like that. It was fucking insensitive of me."

Jess ground her teeth into the corner of her lip. "Wow. An apology from Sam McCloskey? Call the *Portland Press Herald.*" *Too bad it was an apology for the wrong infraction,* she thought.

The light danced in his eyes, but he didn't crack a smile at her quip. He studied her face, circling his thumb around the edges of her mouth. "I mean it, Jessie. I'm sorry." A flutter warmed her belly, as she could feel his gaze in every inch of her body. His dark hair was messed up and looked like he had spent the day running his hands through it. Jess lifted a hand, and though the movement went against every thought she had, she couldn't resist feeling that silky hair between her fingers once more. Did it feel the same still? She smoothed it with a palm, scooping the strands between her fingers. Yep—same thick, luxurious, inky hair he had in high school. She resisted the schoolgirl sigh that was caught in her chest and instead cleared her throat.

His brow furrowed and Jess nodded, that familiar tightness settling in her chest again. "Your hair. It, um, needed a little help," she said, offering a shrug.

She moved away, a spray of scarlet spanning her cheeks, but he pinched her chin, not allowing her the chance to cop out. "Let me take you to dinner."

"Is there a question hidden in there somewhere?"

His jaw jumped as that little half smile twitched to life. "Please, may I take you to dinner?"

They were locked in a staring contest so intense that Jess could feel the electricity throughout her whole body.

She curled her hands around his, lowering them to her sides. "Let me go change."

\* \* \*

Sam finished the last bite of his steak, watching as Jessie nibbled on a french fry. The silky green dress she wore dipped low across her cleavage as a breeze drifted through the open window. Her nipples hardened, peaking the soft material of her dress. Sam didn't bother adjusting his pants as an erection stirred.

Her dark hair rested straight and silky down her back with one section that fell over the front of her shoulder and ended just above the swell of her breast.

Sam leaned back in his seat, studying the woman across from him. A woman. No longer the girl he knew. It was hard to believe she was the same person.

Jess tugged on the silky strands and shifted in her chair. "What?" she finally asked, eyes widening.

Sam smiled. "Nothing," he said. "Can't a guy look at his date without being subject to scrutiny?"

"This is not a date," Jess muttered again. Only this time, it didn't hold quite the resolve it had earlier. A ghost of a smile appeared at the edges of her sweet little pout.

"I like the straight hair," Sam observed. "I mean, I liked the curly hair, too, back in the day. It suited you then—wild, uninhibited. Straight is sophisticated, though." Honestly, the girl could be bald and he would still have steel between his legs.

"Thanks," she said. "I can't believe we never ran into each other in the ten years I've been gone."

"Well . . ."

She blinked, surprised. "Well?"

Sam shrugged. "I've seen you a few times. When you've been back in town visiting or whatever."

"Why didn't you say hi?"

Sam shook his head, air hissing from his lips. Jesus, why did he say anything at all? He leaned onto his elbows. "Never mind. Forget it."

"Tell me." Jess's hand darted across the table, her nails dragging across his flesh as she held his hand. Her touch sizzled across his skin and heat swelled low in his stomach. Raw, primal heat. "At the very least, I deserve an explanation from you, wouldn't you say?"

He lifted his eyes to hers. Hell, what could he say to that? He did it for her own good; there was no way he could tell her the truth—not now, and certainly not back then. And she deserved to be with someone who wasn't lying to her every fucking moment of every day. He slid his hand out from under hers. And pulling away from her touch might be the damned hardest thing he'd done all day. Swiping a napkin over his mouth, he sighed, placing it on the table next to his plate. "Jessie, I was young. And stupid. And I thought you deserved better than me."

Her voice broke and he couldn't be sure if it was the warm lighting or tears dancing in her eyes, but gold flecks shimmered as moisture clung to the edges of her lashes. "*That's* your answer?" she whispered. "You felt I deserved better than you?" She snorted and shook her head. "My parents had just *died*, Sam. I would have befriended Charles Manson back then if he had let me cry on his shoulder."

This was a bad idea. The whole night. What the hell was he thinking? That they could hang out and be buddies for the time she was back in town? Every second she spent here put her life in more and more danger. And the more time he spent with her, the less likely he was to let her go. Even if it was exactly what she needed. He was a selfish bastard. She sure as hell shouldn't trust him. He pulled his wallet from inside his jacket pocket, yanking out a credit card and tossing it onto the table.

"Sam," Jess began quietly. "I-I missed you." Her gaze fell to her lap. "Still do, actually."

There it was. Those words, that tone. It was exactly what he was afraid of. It shattered him. And what could he say in response? That he missed her, too? Because he did. There wasn't a day that went by that he didn't think of her. And God, he wanted her. He wanted Jessie in his arms, in his bed, in his mouth—everywhere. "I know you won't believe me, Jessie. But I miss you, too."

She leaned across, draping her hand gently on his. The touch spiraled through him, seizing his body. Maybe this could work? Maybe he could keep her safe—protect her if they managed to be friends once more. She lifted his hand into hers, turning his palm face up as a smile curved on her full lips. God, that smile. It could nearly thaw out his icy heart. *Nearly*. She exhaled, the air blowing a stray strand of hair from her eyes. "Remember when we had our palms read?" Her eyes shimmered, nearly gold, but far more valuable than any metal. She chuckled quietly to herself. "She said we were destined to be together forever." Jess snorted and the moment of tenderness dissolved into quiet sarcasm. "Stupid hack."

"Maybe not," he answered quietly, not even sure why he answered.

Jess swallowed, her face flushing a shade of pink that reminded him of her nipples. The waitress handed Sam back his card and he scribbled a signature with a tip. It hurt when Jess left him in the middle of the night after they made love at his graduation party. He replayed that night over and over in his mind. How soft her skin was. The way the miniskirt would inch up around her thighs as she moved about the party. The feel of her ponytail wrapped into his fist. And it hurt like a motherfucker when he woke up, realizing she had left without a good-bye. But he deserved it. He deserved every bit of it when it came to Jessie.

Shit. Sam swiped a hand down his face. This was not the conversation he wanted or planned to have tonight. "Let's get you home, huh?"

"Yeah. I have a big day tomorrow." Her brows wiggled and though there was still a spot of sadness in her gaze, she twitched a grin in his direction. "First day on the job and all."

He locked eyes with Jessie. His Jessie. Anger and frustration and passion swelled in him and he hated that she could stir up all these emotions he wished he didn't have. Her being in his precinct was the absolute worst thing right now. Somewhere, there was a mole. And even though right now, Jessie didn't seem to suspect anything, if that person discovered that she was suspicious of Cass's secret life—there wasn't a doubt in his mind that she'd be the next target. "Don't remind me," he grumbled, pushing out of his chair.

She stood as well, scooting her chair with the backs of her legs. "Thanks for dinner." She strolled past him in a whiff of cherry blossom scented perfume.

"Anytime," he muttered, rushing to get the door for her. Through the slinky silk of her dress, the outline of her ass moved like water and he could see the faint trace of a thong underneath. He shifted himself from within his pocket. He wasn't normally one to shy away from an erection. Hell, maybe he was going about this all wrong. Maybe it was high school all over again and they just needed to fuck. Get it out of their systems, so that the tension would dissolve and they could work together without getting too hot to focus.

Sam bit his lip to abstain from groaning. Christ, this girl would be the death of him. As they walked the couple of blocks back to Cass's house, a cool autumn breeze rushed by them and Jess shivered, running her hands over goose-pebbled flesh.

Sam shuffled out of his jacket and draped it over her shoulders. "Here," he said, his hands lingering at the lapels.

Cass's house—now Jess's house—was only a couple of blocks off the water. Not exactly oceanfront property, but pretty damn close. But the house wasn't close enough for Cass to be operating a smuggling ring right out of her home. They had had a watch on her house for weeks and when she went in for the night—she was just that. In. The light in her bedroom would turn off and there would be no activity until the following morning. And yet, the following day, a new batch of oxy and this new mystery drug would be on the street. Though Cass had confided in him somewhat, it was damn obvious she had been hiding something. The way she'd swallowed nervously, her eyes shifting around the interview room—she hadn't trusted anyone.

Though he doubted her fear came from being in his presence, he had begun looking at his fellow officers and detectives differently. It was as if she had known something about his squad. Or maybe it was just a hunch.

As they approached Jess's door, she pulled out a set of keys. "Thanks again for tonight. It was nice . . . 'catching up,'" she added with air quotes. Flinging the jacket from her shoulders, she handed it back to him.

"You know," Sam said, "it actually was." And he meant it. His eyes traveled the lines of goose bumps racing over the revealed flesh at her sternum. "Jessie—I know this question sounds stupid in light of why you're in Portland, but . . . are you okay?"

She paused and those coffee-bean eyes lifted to his. In the inky night, they looked darker than usual and they twinkled as she nodded.

"I am."

"You don't seem it," he said quietly, stepping in closer and cupping her jaw. His finger trailed the line up to her ear where he pinched her lobe between his thumb and forefinger.

"I'm as okay as can be expected," she said, and lowered her gaze in a lazy way that also managed to be sexy as hell. "I guess that's a night, then, isn't it?" Jess's eyes fluttered in a series of blinks and she ran a tongue across her perfectly plump lips. Not in an inviting way—no, that wasn't Jessie's style. It was a natural act of her simply wetting her lips.

Sam stiffened at the sight of her moist mouth. Jesus, he wanted that tongue on him—every fucking sweltering inch of himself. He stepped in closer, unable to stop himself. He was like a wolf with the finest cut of steak being dangled just in front of him.

With his other hand, he brushed into her smooth, glossy hair. The strands were like silk between his fingers and his mind flashed back to their night together ten years earlier. How he had wrapped his hand around her ponytail, struck her ass hard, and tugged her into submission. And her body's response to it was utter perfection. She had melted around him, loving every second. Or so he thought.

Sam traced her jaw with his fingers, running his hand down the tender skin at her neck, so delicate, he feared he would tear her like tissue paper. He held her still and made the mistake of stroking his thumb over her slick bottom lip. It was warm and wet, just as he had remembered it all those years before.

The edges of her teeth peeked out, grazing his thumb, and he hissed at the feel of her nibbling on his skin. Finishing the gentle bite with a soft kiss, she let her lips linger on the pad of his thumb.

And with that one little movement, Sam was done for. He tugged her into his arms, his hands tangled in her hair to pull her head back. His lips slanted over hers, covering them with a searing kiss. He wanted her hot. He wanted her branded—his, even if for just one more night.

Sam groaned in her mouth. She was pure; her innocence effervesced on his tongue and her muscles became rigid as he kissed her the way a man should kiss a woman. He gave her the kiss he'd always wanted to when he was a teenage boy. And after all these years, she was so different—a woman. And yet, still the same ol' Jessie.

He parted her lips with his tongue, licking over them as he thrust inside with the firm kiss. Rapture tore through his senses like a series of fireworks exploding as she whimpered on his lips.

He released his hold on her and Jess stumbled back against the door. He glared down at her, a flush reddening the apples of her cheeks. Her amber eyes darkened as she pressed her fingertips to her swollen lips.

Sam panted, catching his breath, as equally unnerved inside as Jess looked on the outside. He knew he should stay away. Knew she was a hell of a lot safer that way. But when it came to Jessie Walters—damn, he was already a goner.

# 10

Jess cleared her throat. Holy crap, did that really just happen? She had thought Sam was a good kisser back in high school; it was nothing compared to the kiss they just shared. What else had he managed to perfect in their years apart?

His erection, still impressive in size (not that she had expected that to change at all) was nestled at the apex between her thighs as they kissed. It tore right through her to the fire in her belly as she moved her hips over his rigid cock with her lips on his.

"Would you like to come in for . . . for some coffee?"

"Fuck the coffee," Sam growled, and then kissed her again. "I'll take the cream, though," he whispered against her lips, pressing her back against the front door. Jess lifted one leg around his hip, squeezing him with her thigh muscles. Who gave a shit about what the neighbors thought? Once she sold the house, she'd never see them again.

Jess fumbled for the knob behind her, dropping the keys in the process. "Shit."

"Let me." Sam dropped to his knees, his nose lingering at her sex for a moment with a slow inhale. "Jesus, you smell delicious." He grabbed the keys and opened the door, scooping Jess into his arms and kicking the door shut behind him. His lips barely missed a beat and landed quickly back onto Jess's.

With closed eyes, Jess reeled into an alternate universe. One where she and Sam were together again. Tangled in each other's arms with no other problems; no dead sister with mysterious items buried deep in her closet; no job conflicts or power struggles between her and a man who so clearly wanted to dominate her.

Sam reached the top of the stairs and turned for the master bedroom.

"No," Jess whispered. "I'm on the left." Sam paused, peering into Cass's open door for all of a half second. He turned and shouldered Jess's door open, lowering her to her feet.

"Put your hands above your head, Jessica." His voice was darker, suggestive, and it ripped through Jess right to the center of her simmering core.

Sam clenched his jaw, his eyes sliding over her body. "Hands. Up," he said again, as he stared at her with a heated look in his eyes. The command was rough and something in her chest lurched. His eyes on hers were so sexually charged that Jess flushed as she gathered the courage to meet his demands.

"Why?" Jess whispered. She knew the answer to this. He wanted her helpless. Immobile. The thought spiraled fear through her body down to her toes. *Fear and—excitement? No. Not excitement . . . just fear,* she lied to herself.

"Because," he said with a predatory step toward her, "I'm going to tear that dress from your body, press your breasts against that wall, and show you what you've been missing all these years by paddling that tight ass of yours."

The breath left Jess all too quickly and she felt light-headed. Yes, his answer had shocked her, but damn if her body's reaction to it didn't shock her more.

Sam's steps toward her were slow, controlled. Was he ever

not in control? Jess rolled her shoulders back, which hitched her breasts with the movement. He paused momentarily, eyes flicking to her tight nipples as a smile encompassed his mouth. As though he saw right through her charade.

"Is this how you want me?" She slowly raised her arms high above her head, leaning onto the wall behind her. She felt sensual in the position. Womanly. And her sex pulsed between her legs.

"Almost," he growled. And in an instant, he had both of her hands locked in his, her back pressed against the cool wall. Burying his nose into the curve of her neck, he nipped the soft skin there. "Did it take everything within you to do as I asked?" He unzipped the side of her dress and with a quick flick of his fingers, it fell in a pool of silk at her feet. "If I recall, you have a hard time listening to me—or anyone else, for that matter."

"Oh, I listen." Jess stretched her neck to give him more access. "I just don't always obey."

He chuckled as his teeth grazed her throat. "That's the understatement of the year, babe. Try never."

"Maybe it's just *you* I don't like listening to. Ever thought of that, Sam? Or should I call you *sir?*" Jess mocked with a lifted brow.

Sam's hand came down on Jess's hip, squeezing with a force that made her whimper and she was suddenly drenched. He grabbed a fistful of her hair, tugging her head back. Nudging her panties to the side, he slid two fingers inside of her. They pumped in and out in surprisingly gentle motions and Jess's legs wobbled beneath her. "*Sir* works. So does *master,*" he answered.

*No fucking way. Not even if Sam was on his deathbed and that was his dying wish.* "Would you settle for King of My Orgasmic Domain?"

"Absolutely," he answered, nodding slowly. "Though, you

might find it hard to say all that while you're writhing in absolute bliss."

"Someone thinks awfully highly of himself."

He glanced down to her peaked nipples and ran his hand down her outstretched arm to circle them tenderly. "You should know, I don't approve of your making fun of me, Jessica," he growled. "I think that hot little mouth of yours could benefit from a ball gag."

His denim-clad steel pressed against the side of her hip—but his restraint was far more impressive than her own. He didn't rub against her. Didn't even attempt to undress.

For ten years, Jess had not only avoided this sort of bedroom behavior, but had avoided Sam. And for what? Because she had some sort of convoluted definition of what was sexually acceptable? With Sam, nothing was off limits, it seemed. And damn, she liked it.

He caught her lips in his and he tasted like peppermint. Parting the seam of her lips with his tongue, he delved in with a hunger—a hunger for Jess. And with his fingers still pulsing inside her, he whispered against her mouth. "Turn."

Panting, she did as she was told this time with no arguments. He still held her hands firmly in place above her head and pressed her palms to the wall. "Do not move these hands. Got it?" From behind her, she heard the fumbling of a belt buckle and the distinct drop of pants to the floor. "Answer me, Jessica. Do you understand—don't move your hands."

"Yes," she rasped, her voice low with a huskiness she barely recognized in herself.

"Yes what?"

Jess tightened, peering at Sam from over her shoulder. Her gaze narrowed. *No fucking way.* "Yes, *Sam,*" she answered pointedly.

His hand came down on her ass with a hard spank and she cried out.

"Wanna try that again?" he growled, his palm smoothing the tingling skin on her backside.

"Yes, Mr. McCloskey," she said again with an inward smirk. Pushing his buttons was so damn easy.

His grin twitched. "Closer," he said. His hand connected with her other cheek, the slap ringing through the quiet room. "But not quite." He dove his fingers into her pussy once more, sliding in with ease. "One more try, babe."

"Yes, Detective," Jess answered. The paddle that followed was the hardest yet and he tweaked her nipple with the other hand. Sensual pain spiraled through her body and her vagina clenched, pulsing with the same excitement she felt at the core.

There was a tightening deep inside her and the delicious feeling of a shudder. Fuck—she was close to coming. And from what? Being slapped around? She swallowed and dropped her cheek to the cool wall.

From behind her, there was a sound of clothes rustling. She peeked over her shoulder to find Sam completely naked now. Gloriously nude and looking like he stepped out of one of those sexy cop calendars.

His hard cock brushed against her thigh, a bit of pre-cum glistening at the tip as she looked over her shoulder. The sight of him did things to her—her body became more aware in his presence, responding in ways that were entirely out of her control. Broad shoulders led to a defined chest that was sprinkled with dark, coarse hair. A narrow waist arched into six ripped sections of ab muscles and a deep V where his cock jutted forward. Veiny. Large and flanked by a trimmed mass of curls. Jess's mouth watered.

Clenching her eyes shut, she dropped her forehead to the wall in front of her. Sam lowered to his knees, nudging her ankles and spreading her wide. "Open up for me, baby."

She spread her legs, crying out as the first contact of his warm tongue lapped across her swollen clit. Her knees buckled and Sam caught her at the hips, steadying her above him. "Fuck," Jess cried, "give a girl a little warning."

Sam didn't remove his mouth from between her legs and his chuckle was low and vibrated against her. "Those hands better still be on the wall," he finally said.

Jess looked to her palms, still flattened in front of her. "You think *I* would disobey *you?*" Then she gasped as his teeth nipped her swollen bud.

"I so badly want to make you come." He nipped her clit again, this time holding on and dragging his teeth over the sensitive skin there. "But if you keep acting out, punishment will be necessary."

Jess's body squeezed—everywhere.

"I felt that," he whispered. "You want to come, Jessie? Then obey me." He moved his tongue faster and faster over her, alternating the staccato movement with luxurious long licks. She was close—so damn close. One hand fisted and she slammed it into the wall before her with a shattering cry. Sam pulled his mouth from her and she was left cold, alone as the building orgasm faded.

"No," she whimpered.

"I could so easily make you cream for me." His touch was barely a flutter against her swollen lips, but she ached for that touch so damn bad. "You know what to do, Jess. Give me what I want and you'll get what you want."

Jess swallowed, her entire body warmed, flushing a bright red, and she was suddenly thankful that neither of them had bothered to turn the light on. Her lips parted and a voice that didn't sound like her answered. "Yes, sir." It was barely above a whisper; Jess wasn't even sure why she had uttered the words when everything inside her was screaming not to.

Sam's gasp was barely audible, but Jess heard it nonetheless. His excitement reverberated in the room, his grip on her hip tightening. He didn't think she'd give in, Jess realized. And the fact that she did excited him. "Good girl." The words were tight. Intense.

He dove his tongue inside of Jess, thrusting in short, sharp movements. Her body bucked against him, and she bit down on her lip to keep from crying out.

One finger danced around her pucker, stroking the seam from her pussy to her ass. The feel of his finger lingering in that area made her tighten everywhere, pulling her away from the near ecstasy of the moment. His hands slid from her waist, spreading her wide. "I want you to come for me. Come, Jessica." He entered her with two fingers, pulsing them in slow, controlled movements as his tongue lapped at her clit.

He added pressure and another finger slid inside her, circling her aching, throbbing sex. Light exploded behind her eyes, and she convulsed, clamping around his finger with spasms so strong, they echoed everywhere in her body. She was splintered; simply fragments of what was standing there moments ago. And then she was in the air, Sam's arms surrounding her as he carried her to the bed, setting her gently on her back.

Digging around in his pant pockets, he pulled out a foil square and crawled over her.

The bedspread was soft against her burning ass as Sam positioned himself on top of her. Jess swallowed, looking up at him. His arms were columns on either side of her head and she ran her fingers up his corded muscles. A chunk of hair fell into his eyes as they searched her face. "You okay?"

Jess swallowed and nodded. "I want to taste you," she whispered.

The concern etched onto his brow softened, morphing into something darker. Desire. Lust. "There'll be lots of time for that later," he answered. "For now, I need to be inside of you." Tearing the condom open with his teeth, he had it out and onto his cock in seconds.

He grasped Jess behind her knees, tugging her down to him.

Licking his palm, he stroked himself and Jess slid her hand over her tender breast down her flat stomach until she reached her clit. Circling the area, she couldn't take her eyes off Sam's cock. The tip pressed against her and as he entered her, Jess's body stretched to accommodate his size.

She gasped, unable to help the exclamation and Sam stilled above her.

Before he could ask if she was okay, Jess reached behind, clawing at him with her fingernails and driving him deeper inside of her.

"Fuck," he hissed. She squeezed his muscled ass harder—it was firm beneath her palm and she curled her legs around the backs of his thighs, pulling him deeper toward her body. With a roll of her hips, she pumped against his thick cock. "Baby," he said, "if you want it rough, you just say the word."

Jess's eyes sparkled and Sam chewed the inside of his cheek, staring at her. "But *you* gotta say so."

Jess whimpered. "Please, Sam. Fuck me hard."

Sam shuddered, his eyes closing as a ghost of a smile turned his lips up. He leaned down, running his nose from her collarbone up to her jaw. Flicking his tongue at the base of her ear, he whispered, "What's your safe word, babe?" His dick was absolute steel inside of her and Jess squirmed, loving every moment of stretching pain his girth brought.

Safe word? She gulped. Holy hell, she'd heard about safe words before—but they were needed for the serious stuff, right? Like bondage and whips and chains . . . a thought silenced the voices in her head. If Sam needed her to have a safe word, then it's likely he's actively involved in all that. "How about *shitthathurtsyoumotherfucker?*"

Sam chuckled, its sound a low vibration in his throat. "Baby," he said gently. "I want to fuck you hard. I want to feel my balls slapping against your pussy. But if I don't know your safe word, I can't proceed how I know you want me to." He moved his hips, the thick underside of his shaft dragging a path backward and Jess cried out. The fear that he'd pull out entirely and stop was terrifying. Rationality was not something that was prevalent in this situation—for as much as her brain was saying she would be perfectly fine if he were to stop right now, her heart and body were screaming otherwise. He paused, leaving his head just barely inside of her.

Jess arched forward, desperation consuming her, and her plea was answered with a fluid thrust that sent shockwaves trembling down her body.

His warm breath on her ear was distracting and she couldn't think—could barely breathe with him fogging her head. She didn't have a set safe word. Up until tonight, she never knew she would need one. But she did want to be fucked. Hard. Hard enough to make her forget—replace the bad memories of Sam with something new. Something good. "How about . . ." She looked around the room for inspiration. Her eyes landed on Sam's, the blue twinkling in the moonlight like a precious gemstone. ". . . *sapphire*," she answered. "*Sapphire* is my safe word."

He nodded. "Sapphire," he repeated. "You ready?"

Jess nodded. Her eyes dropping, she leaned her head toward the ceiling. "God, yes."

Sam threw both her legs over one shoulder so that she was partially at an angle. Where most men would have simply jackhammered into her, Sam was more controlled than that. He began slower with deep sensual thrusts that slammed directly into the knot deep inside Jess. A tension built there like a rubber band being twisted over and over again. Each thrust ended with a flick of his hips so that he wasn't just hammering the spot with his head, he was stroking it.

"Yes," Jess cried, diving both hands into her hair. "Fuck me, Sam. Harder."

He listened, slamming his cock into her faster now with a

rhythmic pace. One hand slapped her ass as his finger glided against the seam, landing at her asshole once more. He slid one finger inside and she moaned with the unusual feeling. It hurt—but in the best possible way. The same sort of tenderness she felt when she lost her virginity to Sam. That line where pleasure and pain intersect and you can't tell the difference in what you're feeling.

He lowered his lips to her nipple, his teeth locking down against the pebbled nubs. They were far too sensitive and conflicting sensations spiraled through Jess until she was a writhing, wriggling mess beneath him.

"Don't move," Sam growled, and then laced his hand in hers. His face softened and he leaned in, lips parting Jess's. His kiss was deep, and full of demands that Jess feared she'd never be able to meet.

"I've thought of no one but you for years," he whispered in a moment of vulnerability, and then pressed his thumb against her clit while maintaining the impressive pace of fucking her. Sam trembled from above Jess, the shaking growing more and more with each thrust. Sweat covered their bodies. Jess slid her hand down the length of her body, until she reached his tight balls slapping against her. She squeezed and tugged as Sam groaned, throwing his head back.

He was fighting it, too. The tension in his face built as he bit his bottom lip. "Come for me, baby." His voice was different. Undone. Neither of them would last much longer—pleasure this great was never sustainable.

Jess didn't answer—no, couldn't answer. No words could escape her lips. She felt unraveled and so, so close to coming that she was afraid Sam would stop if she did anything to disturb his flow.

"Jessica," he snapped, his hand connecting with her ass once more. She yelped at the contact. "Answer me, goddamn it."

"Yes," she managed.

He spanked her again, tweaking her clit between his thumb and forefinger.

She gulped. "Sir . . ." she added. "Yes, sir."

As soon as she submitted to his demand, she could feel his cock harden from within her. His thrusts grew deeper and longer and he dropped his mouth to hers again, his already roped muscles tensing as he shivered from above her body. He pulled out of Jess, snapping the condom off just in time for him to come on her breasts.

He was captivating, beautiful; and the moonlight sliced across one side of his face and dark hair, casting a blue light over his entire body.

As he finished, he gathered his cum onto the tip of his finger, tossing Jessie's legs open, and ran the fluid into her ass. Dropping down between her legs, he tongued her clit once more. The final searing tremors ripped through her and Jess dove her hands into Sam's dark curls, grasping his hair as her sex spasmed against his lips. Her release was hot, wet, and even after she finished, Sam continued licking her in long, soft motions.

She fell back, panting. Sam was exactly what she not only wanted, but needed. And holy hell, was that terrifying. The man she had been running from all these years was the exact person who could help her get over past trauma that he helped create. But maybe that's exactly how it was supposed to be; maybe the creator of the pain is sometimes the only one who can eradicate it?

Jess swallowed. No, that can't be right. She had run away for a reason. She had avoided Sam and all that he represented for a *reason.* You can't be with someone if you don't trust them to stay by your side when things get rough.

Jess hopped up from the bed, curling into her robe.

"Where you going?" Sam asked, rubbing the tension from his face.

"Shower," Jess said.

A wolfish grin caught the moonlight streaming in through the slats in the blinds. "Want some company?"

Jess swallowed. "If you want." She hugged the robe tighter around herself. "I just need a quick shower, that's all." She inwardly begged that he could read her body language. She needed a minute to herself. A moment to evaluate what the fuck she had just let happen.

At that, Sam sat up, leaning his elbows on his knees. "Everything okay?" His brow pinched with concern.

"Fine." Jess could feel her lips tightening with the response. Sam was smarter than that—he would know something was up. "It's been a long day, Sam . . ."

He nodded, slipping his boxer briefs back on. "I understand. I'll be right here when you get out."

She wanted to protest. Tell him that he didn't need to stay the night, but somehow the words choked in her throat. The house was quiet—eerily so, especially at night. Jess was used to the hustle and bustle of New York and her tiny two-room apartment. Part of her wanted to be alone and the other part wanted someone else in this house. And she just couldn't bring herself to kick Sam McCloskey out.

# 11

When the sound of water hissed from the bathroom, Sam dropped back down onto the bed. Had he pushed her too far? She'd been through a lot in the last couple of weeks. Sam knew deep down that there was nothing wrong with his lifestyle choices. But whenever Jessie looked at him that way—shit, she might as well have shattered his innards to pieces.

This wasn't a lifestyle for everyone—it was something that he had to keep reminding himself of. The problem was, Jess seemed to enjoy it . . . until she didn't. And unfortunately, those lines she kept drawing were invisible to everyone but her. The BDSM life was all about trust. The sub had to trust her master and vice versa. And it was clear that Jess was far from trusting anyone, most of all Sam. Not that he could blame her one bit. How do you trust a master who doesn't even trust himself?

Awareness prickled over his body. Shit. Here he was in Cass's house; he knew what he needed to do for the job, but it felt like a betrayal of Jess. It wasn't the reason he kissed her. But the question was: Would Jess believe that if she ever found out? Well, hell . . . add this to the dozens of secrets he needed to keep from her and the reasons why he and Jess could never be a proper couple.

Sam stood, peeking out of the guest room. This was for Jess's safety, he reminded himself, but the excuse felt weak even in his own head. The shower was still running, a bit of steam seeping out of the partially cracked bathroom door. He would just slip into Cass's bedroom, find what he needed, then be out of there.

He stepped into the hall, freezing as the floorboards moaned under him like an alarm announcing his presence. He paused, waiting for any indication that Jess was onto him, but the water kept running. He moved on into the bedroom. It was cleaner than clean—hell, he always thought *he* was a tidy person, but Cass put his habits to shame.

A quick look around was all he needed. He slipped into her walk-in closet, flipping through the clothes on the hangers. It appeared that they were first arranged by season. Then by type of clothing, then by color. "Jesus," he whispered. "OCD much, Cass?" The girl liked her control, that was for sure. Then again, who was he to judge?

At the bedroom bay windows were two club chairs and a little table with a small bookshelf to the right.

He rushed to the books. Shit . . . which one did she put those pictures in? He dragged a finger across the top line of books, organized yet again to perfection. Only one stuck out the tiniest fraction. As though she had put it away quickly, not stopping to make sure it was perfectly in line with the others.

Sam yanked the book from the shelf with a quick glance at the title. *Molecular Biology and Eastern Medicine.* Yep, that was Cass for ya. Smarter than her own good sometimes.

He opened the book and flipped through the pages, then turned it upside down, shaking it for any loose items. *Dammit, nothing.* One specific page was dog-eared. Something about how pharmaceuticals were studying alternatives for various

chronic and terminal diseases. Herbs versus prescription medicines and a whole paragraph containing medical jargon.

*Yeah, yeah, blah, blah, blah,* he thought as he shoved the
book back into the shelf and grabbed another, flipping it open.
Where the hell had she put them? He went through several
more before pulling out *Heart Disease and Western Medicine
Hurdles.* His lungs tightened as he flipped open the cover.
Bingo.

The light flicked on above Sam and he jumped, slamming
the book shut. For all of a moment, his throat dropped to the
pit of his stomach as he turned to find Jess standing in the doorway, light spilling in from the hall around her shadowed figure.
Her hair was wet, curly, wild. Just how he liked her and his
cock jumped at the sight. Her silky lavender robe was tied
loose around her waist and the swell of her breasts curved from
underneath. It only fell to midthigh, leaving her muscled legs
revealed, Sam noted, as his gaze traveled the length of her body,
taking in every minute detail.

"What are you doing in here?" she demanded.

Sam dropped the book onto the side table, strolling over to
Jessie. He didn't like that his job required him to snoop. And
he hated that he had to lie. "I was just having a look around."

"For what?"

Sam's ears prickled and for a moment, he considered telling
Jess the truth. He opened his mouth to speak, only his tongue
wouldn't move, like he was suddenly paralyzed.

No, he couldn't tell her the truth. Not right now. It would
just put her at more risk. The hardened detective took over and
Sam shrugged. "Just looking around."

"Why?" she snapped, and Sam's senses tingled. She seemed
awfully defensive.

"Cass was a part of my life, too, Jess. I was just . . . remembering."

"Well, maybe instead of looking through her shelves, you should be out there looking for her killer." Jess swallowed and her jaw set to a hard line. Despite the firm exterior, her voice cracked. Her dark eyes danced, moisture brimming around their depths as her expression dipped, paler than usual. His heart raced at the sight of her so broken; completely shattered before him. He wanted nothing more than to wrap his arms around her and blanket her from the sorrow. "B-besides," she continued, "it's not like you'll find anything relating to her death in here." She blinked rapidly as she spoke and her eyes flitted around the room and she gave a quick tug to the hem of her robe. Sam pressed his lips together in thought.

That rapid fire of blinks and the absence of eye contact—his mind wandered back to middle school, when she would lie to her parents about where she and Sam had been. That same quick-blinking frenzy would give her away with every lie. The way she would tug on the bottom of her shirt or sleeves when she was nervous. Jess knew something about Cass's situation—something in this room. He flicked a quick glance around, but nothing was overtly out of place that he could tell. Unless she had already seen—his gaze dropped to the book he had left on the table.

"Babe," he whispered with a step toward Jess. "I give you my word, I will find your sister's killer. I'll search for him till the day I die. But you have to know that with these robbery-gone-bad killings, it's like searching for a needle in a haystack. There were no prints, no DNA at the scene . . . we don't even have a murder weapon."

"Don't give me that," Jess snapped. "I don't buy the whole robbery-gone-bad scenario . . . and if *I* don't, then I know *you* don't."

Sam groaned, rubbing his eyes. He should have known she'd shove her nose into official police business. Exactly the reason Straimer should have never let her on their force. "What makes you think that it's more than a robbery? Did you find something?" He lowered his voice and took another step, closing the gap between them.

"N-no. It's just a feeling." There it was again. Blink-blink-blink. And a quick tug on her hem.

"Jessie, without knowing what it is you know, I have to assume this is a plea to make sense of a terrible tragedy." With an outstretched hand, he rubbed her arm. "I see it all the time in victims' families—"

Jess wrenched her arm from his touch and damn if that didn't feel worse than a sock in the gut. "This isn't 'some victim' we're talking about here, Sam. It's my sister. It's Cass. And you know I'm right. This wasn't a random killing. She was—" Her voice cracked, and Jess dropped her head, shaking it while looking at the floor. "She was involved in something."

Sam's body stiffened. She knew. The question was, how much did she know? Did she have new information? "What was she involved in?"

Jess shrugged. "I don't know." She rubbed a hand over her arm, soothing herself.

Sam's expression softened and he cupped Jess's neck, pulling her into his chest. "So, tell me what you *do* know, then." He paused, stroking his fingers through her wet tangles. "I wanna find this bastard, Jessie. And if you know something . . . you have to tell me."

She stilled beneath his hands. This secret she was keeping— it was dangerous. And could end up getting her killed. The thought chilled him until his blood froze into icicles within his veins. He'd already failed once in keeping Cass safe. He'd be damned if he'd fail again. No matter what it took, Jess would survive this. And Sam would see to it that she did.

Jess tilted her chin to him, her eyes darkened by the low-lit room. Her mouth parted, voice cracking with the beginning of a sentence. "I found—"

A deafening ring sounded from the bedroom. Jess's head snapped in the direction of the ringtone. "That's my cell," she said, clearing her throat.

"Leave it." Sam's hold on her shoulders tightened and he turned her attention back to him.

"But—"

Another ring tone blared through the house. Shit. This time it was Sam's work cell interrupting the quiet night. He muttered a curse and moved past Jess to the guest room. Rummaging through his pant pockets, he found his phone.

"McCloskey," he said in a voice that was all business. "This better be good, Matt."

There was a sigh from the other end. "It's anything but good, man. A body was found in Deering Oaks Park."

"I'll be there in ten minutes."

"Sam, give Jess a call if you can. I left her a message but she didn't answer."

Sam raised his gaze to catch Jess leaning against the doorframe. "Don't worry. I'll tell her."

## 12

A chill crept into Portland's evening without the warmth of September's sun to thwart the coolness. Deering Oaks Park was only a few blocks away and the change in Sam's body language was notable. Gone was the guy who offered her his jacket and placed a gentle hand at the small of her back. Gone was the man who claimed her lips and body as his own. In his place was a brittle and hardened detective, whose determination was almost as palpable as the tension between them.

From across the street, red and blue lights swirled about like the dance floor of a club. First responders bustled around tirelessly, taking breaks only to step outside of the yellow tape and guzzle some coffee.

Rodriguez ran by them, her glare shifting between Jess and Sam as they arrived together. Her shoulder brushed Jess's and she quickly cast her eyes down as she rushed beyond them to her squad car. Jess couldn't help the flare of triumph over her, as stupid as that was. The girl really didn't *do* anything to her other than follow Sam's orders earlier. Jess made a mental note to bring her a coffee and patch things up. Especially if they were going to be on cases together.

As Sam and Jess approached the body, a mixture of dread and excitement deep in her belly stirred like disturbed sediment at the bottom of the ocean floor. This was what she lived for. She thrived on it. The crime scenes, the adrenaline. It was almost as though the world was clearer through the lens of a camera than through her own eyes.

"The body was found like this—" A woman interrupted Jess's thoughts, not even waiting for them to fully arrive at the scene before getting them up to speed on the situation. On the surface, the man looked peaceful, lying face up on a park bench with a blanket covering him almost to the neck. To a passerby whose only goal was to avoid eye contact and get home, he simply looked like a drunk, sleeping off a nasty hangover.

"It looks as though rigor recently set in, so without getting him on the table, I'm gonna estimate his time of death to be around eight o'clock or so." The medical examiner froze, her eyes locked onto Jess's briefly. "Who's the new girl?"

Jess held out a hand, quickly retracting it. Stupid. You can't touch a person's gloves at a crime scene. After a mental face palm, Jess offered her a warm smile in its place. "Jessica Walters—Jess. I'll be filling in as the CS photographer."

"On an interim basis," Sam added quietly, circling the body.

"Nice to meet you. I'm Christine, the ME." Using the back of her forearm, she brushed silky, jet-black hair out of her eyes and smiled in return. "Welcome to the team." Then, leaning in, she flicked a quick glance at Sam before adding quietly, "Even an interim team member still gets to play the game, ya know?"

"Can we get back to the dead body here?" Sam snapped, hands clamped to his hips. He slid a final glance to Jess before circling the body. "Cause of death?"

From the other end of the crime scene, Matt caught their attention, jogging over for the debriefing.

"Based on the contusions on the back of his head, I would say some form of blunt force trauma is most likely, but there's no murder weapon yet." She dropped to a crouch at the top of the man's head, pointing at the base of his neck with a gloved hand. "See this? From the shape of the contusion here, it looks accidental. As though he fell in a struggle and hit his head."

"Rock?" Sam asked, crouching along with her.

Jess stepped closer to see the unusually shaped bruise.

Christine shook her head. "No, definitely not a rock. Something thinner. Longer. The blood is lower on his skull as if whatever struck him spanned the entire base of his neck. If the killer moved the body after, it could have been the impact that killed him. It may have even broken his neck. I'll have to open him up to know more."

Jess tightened her hold on the camera, clenching the macro lens in her other hand. A chilly breeze caught her curly hair, lifting it in the wind.

"And nobody saw anything? At eight o'clock?" Matt asked, his gaze circling the area. He ran a hand through his hair and muttered a curse. "This is Deering Oaks Park. Tons of people are out at that time . . . walking their dogs, jogging. Someone must have seen *something.*"

Jess stared vacantly at the man. "It's a big park. Back in high school, I'd hear homeless people fighting here all the time and barely give them a glance. I've seen couples break up, car accidents, drug deals. People have blinders on."

Sam nodded and Jess was surprised he even heard her. "Yep," he said in response. "And after the fact, no one thought to check if he was more than a sleeping bum in the park." He raised his gaze to meet Jess's, mouth drawn into a tight line. "Or a dead bum and no one cared."

But if you looked a little closer, he was so clearly not a bum, despite the fact that he was covered with a gray wool blanket. Beneath that ratty blanket, the tiniest knot of a tie peeked out. John Doe's jawline was smooth; clean shaven. His hair gelled.

This was no bum; he was a man with a paycheck. A home. Jess gulped. Maybe even a wife and children.

Jess lifted the camera to her eyes and scanned the bench. Her lens magnified the scene: the grain of the wood; the rusty texture of the metal; the dry, cracking blood at the base of his neck. It was easier to focus on what was only within that circle; easier to block out the rest of the world and see one thing at a time. She zoomed in on the armrest, noting the dried blood. It matched the color of the painted bench almost exactly and if you weren't zoomed in, it would have simply looked like a splatter of paint on the iron armrest. Lowering the camera back around her neck, she leaned in to Sam. "There's blood on the armrest of the bench," Jess pointed out. She had only meant it to be a quiet observation, but everyone turned to look at her.

"Of course there is," Christine said. Though she didn't roll her eyes at Jess, her tone indicated that she wanted to. "He's been bleeding out onto this bench for hours now."

"Yeah, I know that," Jess said, managing to keep her voice calm. "But here." She walked over, pointing at the base of the bench. She knelt and as her hand hovered near the bench, Sam grasped her elbow, a heavy look in his brows as he slapped a pair of gloves in her hand. Jess quickly slipped them on. "Here," she continued. "His head is propped on the back of the bench and this crevice here. But look on this side of the armrest. Blood." Jess knelt, pulling in closer. "And a hair follicle, I believe."

Sam knelt beside her and Jess could feel his heavy breaths at her shoulder. "I think you're right."

"Can I get a tag?" Matt called out as Christine knelt on the other side of Jess.

"We would have found that with our sweep when the body was moved," she said quietly. "But I agree. I think the armrest is our murder weapon."

Pride swelled within her and she smiled at Sam, who still

barely glanced her way. She quickly dropped the smile. He was a different man on the job; determined, grim. He regarded her as though she had run up to the body and rubbed her DNA all over the corpse.

Sam stood, closing his eyes and holding both hands out in front of him, as though he was imagining the confrontation that took place. "If he was pushed in the struggle, fell back, and hit his head on the armrest here, the impact could easily have been enough to be our cause of death. Our perp probably got skittish, laid him out on the bench, and took off." Sam opened his eyes again and let his hands rest on his hips. "Let's get someone here to measure where he would have been standing to fall and hit his head in that exact spot." Unlike Matt, Sam didn't need to yell the command. He held a presence that made people listen no matter how quietly he spoke. A fact Jess knew all too well.

"All right," Matt said on a sigh. "We got a John Doe. A murder weapon. No wallet, no cell. Nothing at all in his pockets except a bit of lint."

"Let's sweep the area, boys," Sam said, turning to the officers behind him. "Find me something." Then, he added more to himself, "Find me anything."

"Okay, Jessie." Matt squeezed her shoulder with a smile. "Work your magic."

Rolling her shoulders back, Jess moved toward the body, but was quickly blocked by Sam's broad chest. "Just a minute," he said, and then glared at Matt. "We need to do our survey. Go take some surroundings first. We'll call you in a bit."

Jess bit down on her tongue. Was he being disagreeable simply to exert his status over her? Or was this the procedure in Portland? She pasted a smile on her face and tilted her head. "Yes, *sir*," she answered pointedly.

His blue eyes twinkled, a heated look warming his hardened expression. One side of Jess's mouth tilted and she turned in a swift pivot, making her way to the other side of the pond. Most of the officers were canvassing the area and while it wasn't a big deal for them to be in the surrounding images, she preferred hers cleared of people if she could help it. Hitching her tripod under one arm and holding the flashlight in the other, she followed the path, curving around the still body of water. It would make less of a difference if random bodies were in her wide shot. They'd be barely noticeable.

She walked to the edge of Deering Oaks Lake and plopped her tripod into the soft dirt. Biting down on the flashlight to free her hands, she screwed her camera into the tripod.

As she took a light reading, a duck waddled her way, quacking. Jess looked down at it. "Shoo!" She waved her hands in the air, only another duck came waddling over, too. "Shoo! Get outta here!" She sighed. Park wildlife . . . probably so used to random people feeding them, they trusted everyone. At the edge of the pond was a small sandbar that sloped into the water.

Jess turned the camera and, with a quick light reading, snapped a couple of images. Looking through the lens, she found the center of the image focused on several ducks gathered together, pecking around a few objects in the dirt.

Jess walked over, and the ducks went wild with her approach. The amount of quacking must have been heard from across the lake. There, one corner of a wallet was buried in the dirt with ducks trying to peck it out of the sand.

A few feet away was a lanyard, a corner picture of John Doe sticking out of the sand. Another duck had what looked like a cell phone in its beak and Jess leaned in to grab it. The scene was already contaminated with duck shit as it was. If that duck flew away with the phone, they'd never get it back. She lunged for the duck, just barely getting hold of the plastic casing. Ducks quacked and the whole crowd of them flew away at the immediate threat. Her elbows sank into the muddy sand with her less-than-graceful landing and as she pushed herself to her feet, she accidentally hit a button, illuminating the screen. The contacts page was a white beacon in the dark, quiet night of the park.

Jess pushed off the ground, moving to stand once more when a name in the phone caught her eye. Cassandra Walters: 207-555-0198.

This had to be John Doe's phone, right? Her gaze shot up across the lake to where he lay lifeless. This man . . . he was somehow connected to her sister. Panic surged in her throat, catching like a too big gulp of water on a hot day. It was too coincidental that he was murdered only a couple weeks after her sister's death.

Swinging her head around the area, she saw that no other cops were near and she lunged for the lanyard, careful not to touch it or move it in any way. "Dr. Richard Brown," she whispered and her voice quivered. "Who the fuck are you and how do you know Cass?" She squeezed her eyes to get a better look in the darkness. The man in the picture was definitely their victim.

Jess hit the button, making Dr. Brown's phone go dark once more before snatching her own phone from her back pocket. Sam could not know that she saw her sister's name in here. He was certain to find it on his own eventually—and as soon as he did, Jess would without a doubt be taken off the case. But maybe—just *maybe,* if he thought he could keep her in the dark, she wouldn't be removed from this investigation. Jess inhaled the crisp night air and it burned against her lungs like a refreshing slap. Cool. Alarming. Finally, she punched in Sam's number.

"You're gonna want to meet me over here," she said. "Now."

What had Jessie found now? Sam gathered a couple of uniforms to join him on the other side of the lake. Partially because if she had in fact found something important, he wanted to jump right on it. And partially because he and Jess being alone together in a dark area right after he had—he sighed, forcing his thoughts to stop raging.

Their night together was clearly a mistake. She knew it, based on how she had run trembling into the shower, and he knew it. Even if he was more reluctant to admit it. Where Jessica Walters was concerned, he couldn't keep it *just* about sex. And now they had to work together, for fuck's sake.

She was down by the water, bent over something in the dirt, face buried in her camera. Her tight ass was tilted high in the air, her jeans riding up the center of her crack revealing the curve of her luscious ass. Sam forced his gaze to what she was staring at. He couldn't be so fixated on her body. Not when he had a job to do.

"Walters," he said, "what've you got for me?"

As she spun to face him, Sam stepped back as a potent and hideous smell hit his nose. "What the—" His eyes scanned her body, clothes covered in some foul-smelling tar-like gunk. "Jesus, Jess. Did you fall in the lake?" He covered his nose with the back of his hand. A few officers behind him snickered.

She tipped her head, not at all amused with his observations. "No," she said, walking over to them. "I had to fight a duck to retrieve this." She dropped something into his hand—a phone.

"Did it shit all over you in the process?"

She glanced down at her shirt, brushing off some of the gunk. "Basically," she mumbled.

Sam bit back the chuckle in his throat and one of the officers behind him coughed. Right—the phone. "How do you know this belongs to the vic?"

She shrugged. "I don't. Not for certain, at least. But, a few feet away, I saw these." She pointed to an ID tag sticking out of the dirt.

Sam sauntered over, pulling his pants up at the knee slightly before lowering to a crouch. "Dr. Richard Brown," he read aloud. "Straimer said you've never before contaminated a crime scene." He held the victim's phone up. "Guess tonight changes that, huh?" He turned to the officer. "Bag this," he commanded.

"Yes, sir."

Jess's brown eyes sparked with passion. "Does *everyone* call you *sir?*"

"Around here they do." A grin twitched at the corners of his mouth. "What else did you find?"

Jess nodded her head and Sam followed closer to the water's edge. "You and I both know that the phone contamination isn't my fault." He should've known she wouldn't let that comment pass quietly. "If that duck had gotten away, you never would have seen it again. My record's still pure as the damn first snowfall of the year."

Humor danced in Sam's eyes and he could feel them crinkle with his smile. "What do we have here?" He sank to the ground once more and Jess followed, her knees brushing his as she lowered.

Sam wasn't accustomed to people not answering him and when he was met with silence, he slid her a look.

She was staring at him with narrowed eyes. Her mouth was tight, though the corners turned up ever so slightly. "I want to hear you say it. That contamination was not my fault. Say it, Sam. I'm fucking good at my job and you know it."

Sam smiled and his fingers itched to comb through those silky dark curls of hers. "I can honestly say you're good at your fucking . . . *job*," he added after a pause, dropping his voice with a quick flick of his eyes back at the officers.

Jess swallowed. "I never believed you doubted my abilities in the bedroom," she said, raising an eyebrow at him. "But you do doubt my work. And I want to hear you admit you were wrong."

Sam sighed. "Fine, the phone's contamination was not your

fault." He leaned in and he could smell her shampoo lingering on her damp hair. Cherry blossoms. He turned his attention back to the dirt. "So, what do we have here?"

"A wallet, it appears. I can't guarantee that it's his, but I didn't want to *touch it* until you did."

"You snap some pictures of it already?"

Jess nodded, and Sam lifted the wallet from the ground, shaking some loose dirt from it. He flipped the billfold open, and there was Dr. Brown's beaming face on a Maine driver's license. "Yep," he grumbled. "It's him, all right."

"So, it wasn't a robbery gone bad, was it? Otherwise, they would have taken his wallet. But instead, they threw it into the pond, hoping we'd spin our wheels figuring out the John Doe."

Sam opened the billfold, where a couple of twenties were stacked inside and shook his head. Jesus. *Another* staged robbery gone awry. But this one was sloppy—not like Cass's scene. Anyone who knew what they were doing would have dumped the wallet and phone far from the scene. "It appears that way, huh?" He scratched at the stubble on his chin and looked out at the glittering lake. A faint light cast shimmering highlights across the top. "This case just got a whole lot trickier," he said. Looking behind him, he jerked his head at Donelly. "Get me a bag, kid!"

"Sam—" Jess hesitated, her voice cracking. That simple crack tore Sam's insides. He couldn't bear hearing her like that. Vulnerable.

He pushed to his feet and held out a hand for her to take. She looked to his hand, then to his face, her eyelids lowering, narrowing in defiance. She rose to her feet without another glance at his palm.

"Can I photograph the victim now?"

Sam shoved his hand deep into his pocket. "Yeah. Christine should be finished for a while, at least."

She nodded and, gathering her equipment once more, headed back the way she came. "Hey, Jessie?" he called after her and she turned, her hair fanning out around her. "Do you have a change of clothes with you? You smell like shit."

She shook her head and smiled before calling back, "Maybe because I've been rubbing elbows with an asshole all night."

# 13

Jess wasn't even sure what time she fell into bed last night. Two maybe? She came back to the house nearly a zombie. Somehow she managed to stay awake long enough to strip herself of the shit-covered clothes and upload the images to her laptop before landing face first into her bed. It wasn't until she heard the doorbell buzzing that she was pulled from her REM sleep.

Shaking the cobwebs from her brain, she padded down the stairs to the front door, stealing a quick glance in the hallway mirror. It was a wonder she didn't scream at the horrifying reflection looking back at her. *That's exactly what happens when you shower, then fall asleep on damp, unstyled hair,* she thought. She threw her wild curls into a quick ponytail, then, licking the pads of her fingers, swiped the dark spots under her eyes.

The doorbell rang again.

"Coming! Jeez, impatient much?"

Cass's front door had a beveled glass window cut out with no curtain adorning it. Jess had no peephole and no way of hiding her presence if she didn't want to open the door. She stilled at the shadow of a man from the other side of the door. It didn't look like Sam—he was thinner. The hair was too dark to be Dane's. Unlocking the door, she cracked it open wide enough to speak through. "Yes?"

"Good morning, Ms. Walters. We met the other day at Cassandra's service." He held out a hand, which Jess took tentatively through the slim opening. "I'm Gilles." His voice had the tiniest accent—Canadian? Beneath an expensive-looking suit, he had broad shoulders and a slim waist. A taupe shirt was left casually unbuttoned around his neckline and accented his grayish brown eyes.

"Hi, Gilles." Jess wracked her brain. He didn't look familiar in the least, but she had met a lot of people in the last couple of weeks. It was possible she had simply forgotten him. His jaw was freshly shaven and held the faint aroma of a cool spice. "You'll forgive me—there were a lot of new faces at the service."

His head dipped in acknowledgment. "Of course."

Deep lines were etched around his eyes and mouth and his eyes traveled the curve of Jess's body as she held firm her place in the doorway, wedging her foot on the other side. "What can I do for you?"

He paused before answering, a leering grin sliding along his thin lips. Jess shivered as he leaned casually on the doorframe. "I wasn't sure what your plans were for this home—but I find it simply stunning. I come to town rather frequently from Montreal on business and I was looking into purchasing an investment property. Should you be interested in selling your sister's home, I would be quite interested."

"Um . . . okay." Jess knew her wariness hadn't come from nowhere. Nothing about Gilles screamed dangerous and yet fear knotted in Jess's chest. He did everything right—wore the right clothing, was well groomed and friendly. And yet—he was off. As though he was an actor reading from a script.

"I'd compensate you rather generously," he stated, and then reached into his jacket pocket, pulling out a folded paper. "Have your lawyers look it over."

"I haven't decided what to do with the place yet. . . ."

"I understand. I'm in no rush. I simply wanted to express my interest and show you how serious a buyer I am."

Jess stifled a yawn. "Okay. I'll look over it."

"Very well," he answered with a tip of an invisible hat. "I'll be in town for the next week. Feel free to call me with any questions."

He turned and gracefully loped down the steps. As Jess moved to shut the door, she thought twice, poking her head out. "Mr.—uh, Gilles?" He turned, looking up. "How did you know my sister?"

His face softened. "I was the international pharmaceutical representative with her company. I worked with her quite often."

Jess nodded, though it still felt as though she was missing a piece of the puzzle. She didn't think Cass knew her colleagues well enough for them to come from another country to her funeral. Then again, she was quickly learning there was a lot she didn't know about her sister.

Jess shut the door, locking it behind her, and padded into the kitchen to make some coffee. As she unfolded the offer Gilles had given her, air caught in her throat, spiraling her into a fit of coughs. There were way too many zeroes behind that offer! One million? *Dollars?* She had to be reading this wrong—there was no way this house was worth *that* much. Even in downtown Portland. It wasn't even fucking waterfront property.

She dropped the letter, backing away from it slowly as though it was a loaded gun pointed directly at her. With a quick glance at the clock, she swallowed. She had spent the better part of two hours uploading images when she got home last night so that she wouldn't have to wake up early.

After a quick shower, Jess spent a little more time on her eyeliner than usual and after a thorough blow-drying of her hair, it smoothed down past her shoulders, blossoming from wild tangles to smooth and sophisticated. She couldn't help the sweet relief she felt at seeing the transition. Damn, she hated those curls. They were unpredictable; untamable. *Much like me,* she thought while staring into the mirror. Then, quickly shaking the thought away, she threw her now-sleek hair into a low bun and tossed her hairbrush into the sink. Grabbing her purse and keys, she eyed the folded offer from Gilles resting on the front foyer table. She hesitated for all of a second before grabbing the offer and stuffing it into her purse. She needed to see Cass's estate lawyer anyway. She might as well let him know about the offer, right? What was the harm in that? She'd be out of her mind to turn down such a high sum of money. Hell, for that price, she could buy a brownstone in Brooklyn of her own!

She gulped, her mind switching to Sam at the thought of going back to Brooklyn. Would he miss her if she left? Jess shook her head. "No. Not if. *When.* When I leave." She rolled her eyes in spite of herself and closed the front door behind her, locking up. "Jesus, there I go, talking to myself again."

Loneliness ripped through her core and she paused, looking up at the gabled home. If she closed her eyes and thought hard enough, she could almost hear Cass's voice in the whispering breeze. Almost smell the fresh scent of the cucumber-lime soap she used. Jess's throat tightened and one lone tear escaped from the corner of her eye. "Damn," she whispered, swiping it away. There was a sadness—no, an emptiness inside her that she rarely let herself embrace. Because allowing the tears, allowing that sadness, was admitting defeat. It was losing the battle.

She pressed her palm to the door; the textured wood was grainy beneath her fingers. "I'll get him, Cass. I'll nail the bastard." She tapped the door twice and turned to head down the stoop. A black sedan parked on the street sped away in front of her as she walked at a brisk pace to the precinct. She needed to run down to CSU—or whatever they called the department here in Portland—and check on the data of that phone. Even if they sent the printout information to Sam today, he still needed to sift through it. It was probable that he wouldn't discover Cass's name in that contact list until late today. Maybe even tomorrow, if Jess was lucky.

Unfortunately, it was all too probable that Cass's name on his phone could ping within the CSU search. The computers tended to find links before humans did, and her name was already in the system. Jess swallowed, the moisture going down hard like a fistful of marbles.

The walk to the station was quick, but with each step closer the more nervous she became. She'd never done anything like this before—hell, she'd never had reason to steal evidence until recently. The hardest part would be slipping in without Straimer, Sam, or Matt seeing her.

The glass doors were ice cold beneath her palm as Jess pushed through with a quick look around. Flashing her badge, she raced for the elevators, keeping her chin down and eyes cast low. The less eye contact she made, the more likely she'd get out of there without getting caught.

The elevator doors pinged open and she stepped on, hitting the button for the annex.

"Jessica, right?"

*Shit.* Jess looked up to find Christine offering her a warm smile as she took a sip from a steaming mug.

"Yeah. Christine, hey. Well—Jess, actually. Get any rest last night?"

She sighed and even though she had a lovely face, her almond eyes were framed by bluish circles. "Not enough. Never enough," she added with a quirked eyebrow. "Going to the annex?"

Jess nodded, patting her purse. "Yep, just dropping off the memory card."

"Oh, great. I'll walk that way with you. I have to check on some evidence later."

Every muscle in Jess's throat clenched. Taking a breath slowly in through her nose, she released it, forcing her muscles to relax with the exhale. "Great." Though it was wobbly, she still managed to force a smile.

Luckily, the annex was a pretty big space with a lot of different departments. Christine split off at a fork in the hallway, offering Jess a small wave before turning. Relief rushed over her body, powerful and strong, and as she walked up to a caged window, she handed over her temporary ID badge, the memory card, and the prettiest smile she could muster up.

"Hey there," Jess said, grinning. "Just dropping off the photos from CS1452."

The man behind the counter grunted some form of a hello as he grabbed her memory card, flipping it over in his meaty fingers. He wasn't young, but also not exactly old. Nor did he seem all that thrilled to be down there logging evidence and crime scene information.

From below the counter, he produced a plastic bag and a sticky tag and jotted down Jess's information from her ID. Standard procedure almost anywhere you go. "You gonna need this card back today?"

"Nope, I've got other blank ones at home if they need some time. Hey—how are the victim's phone logs coming along?"

The man's eyes narrowed and the dull color seemed to spark the slightest interest at her question. "Why?"

Jess shrugged, forcing nonchalance into her voice. "Just curious." When he continued to stare through her, she added, "Christine was actually asking."

The tightness around his lips and eyes finally relaxed with a nod. "I'll check for you." Tossing the labeled bag with her images into a TO BE FILED bin, he smacked his fingers along the keyboard before looking back to Jess. "Yep, finished this morning actually."

Relief hissed through Jess's body and her hands involuntarily clenched around her purse's shoulder straps. "Oh, cool. Could I see them? Christine wanted to have a quick look. She's down here somewhere and said she'd be by soon."

This time, he didn't seem to be so suspicious and with a jaw-popping yawn and a click of a button, he stapled the printed sheets together. "You know the drill, right? These can't leave this area here without a detective signing them out. I need you to hand me your cell phone while you have evidence in hand. No pictures, etc."

Jess froze, feet cemented in place momentarily. He was supposed to put her information into the computer as having checked out the evidence . . . only he didn't. Hell, maybe she had a shot at getting away with this.

With another swallow, Jess realized how dry her throat was. But she had totally been ready for this. And reaching into her purse, she pulled out the dummy cell she'd kept on her since losing her phone a couple of weeks ago. If someone was going to try to steal her shit, at least they'd only get a crappy free Android. She handed him the burner smartphone and waited. An elephant might as well had been sitting directly on her chest because damn if she could barely breathe.

He turned it over in his hands, looking at it momentarily before tossing it into the drawer below him. "Cool. You can have a seat over there." He slid her badge back over the counter to her and the sigh of relief spiraled down to Jess's toes as she took a seat.

From under the table, she pulled out her real phone. Okay,

yes, she knew what she was doing was wrong. And technically illegal. But Dr. Brown's death was related to her sister's. She could feel it. She just needed to find the damn link. It was far too coincidental that he had Cass's number in his phone and somewhere in these records was an answer. Just maybe not the answer she hoped for.

Placing the stack of papers on her lap, she scooted her chair under the table. Then, placing one sheet on the table as though she was reading, she kept the rest out of sight of cameras and other people. She leaned far over the sheet she was "reading" as though deep in thought. And thank God for the ScanApp; one by one she scanned the pages onto her phone. Every few minutes, she would take a page she already scanned and bring it up to the table, to look like she was still reading.

It took longer than she hoped and a clicking from the hallway caught her attention. She looked up to find Christine walking her way. Jess hadn't scanned all of the pages, but what she had was enough. For now. Dropping her phone quietly back into her bag, she prayed the damn thing didn't start ringing.

Jess smiled and waved at Christine as she filled another cup of coffee. Damn, she was such a nerd. Smiling and waving? Seriously . . . could she look any more guilty? Gathering the papers and stacking them quickly, Jess rushed back to the evidence counter, handing them over. Her fingers trembled as he took the stack from her and carelessly shoved the papers into a manila envelope. Then, labeling them, he tossed them into another bin.

Again—no logging of her name. Nothing typed into the computer about her checking the papers out. It was almost too easy, which made panic rear its ugly head once more. Nothing was this easy. Was it simply the difference between a major city's police department and a smaller city?

Best not to ask questions, she thought, turning with a slight wave good-bye. Always best to keep your head down and slink away into the shadows. . . .

"Jessica!" The guy called out and Jess cringed at the sound of his voice. A sharp breath nearly sliced her esophagus as she slowly turned to see the guy slapping a palm to his forehead. "Your phone!"

Jess's pulse raced in every pressure point of her body. She was pretty sure if she continued at this rate, she'd have a heart attack before the end of the week. "Oh, right," she said, and rushed to grab the burner phone from him. "Stupid me, huh?"

He offered her a half smile before going back to reading the newspaper and she nearly ran the whole way to the elevators and out of the precinct.

Portland was a lovely city. Especially in September. With tourist season over, you were left with mostly locals, which was perfectly fine with Jess. The downside was that certain areas became absolutely barren with very few people walking around.

Jess walked for several blocks, taking a moment to inhale the fresh, salty air that blew off the ocean. Every few minutes a breeze would catch her hair, whipping it around her face and neck. The tension melted from her body as she walked farther and farther away from the police station. This sort of dry, beautifully cool weather only existed in New York for all of two weeks a year. But if you could handle the winters, most of Portland's summer and fall was beautiful, like this.

Jess waited at a stoplight for the little white walking man to blink. There was only one car coming and she moved to cross the four-lane road, figuring she had plenty of time to make it across. Only, the black sedan coming at her didn't slow down—it sped up. A screeching sound echoed down the street as the tires peeled, careening closer and closer.

The black car skidded directly at her. She bolted out of the way, to the other side of the street, but the car followed her, swerving into the right lane, closest to her. Jess lost her footing, stumbling on the edge of the sidewalk and falling headfirst into a lamppost. The last thing she heard was the screech of tires before everything went black.

# 14

"Fuck, that's hot!" Sam almost dropped his coffee cup when the steaming liquid nearly blistered his lip. He quickly set it on his desk, reaching now for a cool glass of water.

Matt's desk sat facing his and his buddy raised an eyebrow, tossing his keys to the side and taking a seat. Sam lowered his brows to a scowl in response. "What?" he growled.

"You're in quite the mood today." Matt's gaze leveled to his as though he could read what was wrong, then he turned his attention to the computer screen. "It appears our good doctor was a trauma specialist. Worked mostly in the ER at Mercy Hospital."

"Well," Sam said, and pushed his seat back. It screeched along the floor like an owl diving for a capture. "Should we go have a chat with some of his friends? See what sort of mischief the ol' doctor was into?" Sam grabbed his jacket off the back of his seat, throwing it around his shoulders. He caught the eye of Laura, the newest officer to join the force, just in time to find her warm smile and a small waggle of her fingers in his direction. She was sweet. Always aiming to please; happy to oblige. She was pretty enough, too. But she didn't do it for him.

His mind swept to Jessie for the millionth time that morning. The taste of her resonated on his tongue and lingered like a fine wine. Yep, Laura was nice. But Jess was what he craved. Having Laura would have been like having a can of tuna to compensate for craving lobster. The two just didn't compare. And in the end, he might no longer be hungry after the tuna, but he certainly wouldn't be satiated.

What was it about Jess that drove him so damn wild? Was it their history together? Or was it the same challenge a rancher saw when a wild horse was brought to the stable? The game of dominance; of breaking. Either way, he was neck deep in shark-infested waters and surrounded by blood.

"Hey man, let's go." Matt jerked his head in the direction of the door and Sam followed.

"If you plan on getting doughnuts today, then we're taking your car, asshole."

Matt grinned, jingling his keys. "Not a problem."

The drive to the hospital was a joke—they might as well have walked. Only then, Matt wouldn't have been able to justify the stop at Holy Donut. And Sam had to admit as he licked the cinnamon from his fingers that that was one *damn* fine doughnut.

The hospital was large, brick, and held a gothic presence about it that Sam always found a bit creepy. Maybe it was just hospitals in general. His mom never gave a crap about him most of his life; she spent her time with her face in vodka bottles, moving from husband to husband, most of whom were complete losers. If they weren't beating the shit out of Sam's mom, then they were beating the shit out of Sam. And usually, he would put himself in the way of their fists just to give his mom a break. Only, she never seemed to care; never seemed worried about Sam's well-being. It wasn't until she married Bill that either of them learned what love could be.

Bill was good to both Sam and his mom. He was tender with

her and showed Sam how to fix up bikes. They shared cigarettes and Bill would tell him stories of when he fought in Vietnam and the "damn hippies" who opposed him. Sam smirked at the memory, looking back up at the hospital. Only Bill hadn't lasted long—lung cancer took him away far too early in life while Sam was only a junior in college, only four years after joining their little family. Those were the only four years of his life that he could remember his mother being sober more often than not. Any other time in his childhood and she was falling down, wasted.

His mother was never equipped to handle that sort of trauma; she avoided the hospital, only coming to visit her husband a handful of times. But Sam didn't leave his side. His professors understood and Sam took three months off school to care for the only father figure he had ever had in this exact hospital. After Bill died, his mom soon shacked up with another loser who beat her too hard one night, snapping her neck.

An "accident," he claimed. Never mind the fact that she had a fucking year's worth of scars and bruises covering her body. But her wounds were inadmissible in court—those scars, those bruises, could have come from anywhere, the prosecutor said. And since she was no longer alive to testify that he was abusive, he served one year for involuntary manslaughter and was out in six months on good behavior. It was that moment Sam knew he wanted to go into law enforcement. He wanted to put the bastards behind bars who didn't deserve the freedoms of everyday life. He wanted to make a difference.

"Dude," Matt said, holding the door open. "You're off in lala land today, huh? C'mon."

Sam nodded, cursed his trembling hand, and entered those doors again. As long as he didn't have to go up to the fifth floor, he'd be fine.

As soon as they entered the ER waiting room, the two men were assaulted with announcements over the intercom, beeping, rolling gurneys, crying patients. That smell—that god-awful hospital smell flooded Sam's nose and a wave of nausea overtook his body. He gritted his teeth and flashed his badge to the woman seated at the reception area. "Good morning," he said. "We need to talk with any of the trauma doctors on staff today."

The woman arched an eyebrow and cocked her head with sass that would put even Jessie to shame. "I think they might be a little busy," she said with a hand gesture to the various patients waiting to be seen.

"I realize that," Sam continued. "But this is about one of your own. A Dr. Richard Brown."

"Dr. Brown?" Concern flickered in her dark eyes. "Is he okay?"

"I'm afraid not. He died last night."

The woman gasped and fell back into her seat. "Oh my God. Oh my God!"

"You knew Dr. Brown well?" Matt asked, flipping open a notepad.

"Not *that* well," she admitted. "We worked together a bit, of course. He was a good man. A nice guy and a great doctor," she said, her voice drifting off at the end.

"Is there anyone we could talk to who might know him well? A friend? Nurse or fellow doctor?"

The woman nodded. "Yes. Y-Yes, of course. Please have a seat and I'll page Dr. Moore. They were good friends."

Sam had turned to grab one of the few available chairs away from the bleeding, oozing, and coughing patients, when he caught movement from the automatic doors. A stretcher was being rushed in by two medics. Sam's heart damn near stopped. There on the gurney with a bloody rag pressed to her head was Jess.

# 15

There was a low thrum pulsing at Jess's temple, but other than that, she felt fine.

"Please," she said, trying to sit up. "Is the stretcher necessary? I could have walked here."

"Ma'am, please lie back. It's policy if we are called to a scene where the patient was unconscious to not allow them to walk."

*Ma'am? Hmph.* "It seems a bit like overkill," Jess said, looking once more to the fluorescent lights above her. "I was out for, like, a second."

"You were out long enough for a passerby to see the whole thing and call nine-one-one," a prickly man beside her snapped.

"What the fuck?" a voice from her left shouted.

*Typical of an emergency room,* Jess thought. *Angry people annoyed that they have to wait so long to be seen.*

"What the hell happened?"

"Sir, you're going to have to step back, please," the female paramedic stated with an outstretched palm.

The voice was closer this time. Louder. And sounded an awful lot like—

"Sam McCloskey. I'm a detective with the Portland Police Department." Jess groaned, her headache suddenly pulsing harder behind her eyes. "And I need to know what happened. *Now.*" His hand was around hers and Jess attempted to sit up once more. "Jessie." His voice was softer now, and worry lines etched around tired eyes. "Are you okay?"

"I'm fine, this is just procedure." A hand clamped down on her shoulder, tugging her back down onto the gurney. "All right, already!" Jess shouted with a side eye at the paramedic.

"Jesus, you're bleeding." Sam's voice cracked as he brushed the hair back from her temple and Jess caught a glimpse of his fingers shaking.

She turned to pudding inside and warmth spread through her belly. She knew deep down that he cared—but he wasn't exactly the most vocal guy when it came to his feelings.

"It's just a little cut. I don't think it'll even need stitches."

Sam spun away from her, his hands tugging through his dark hair. "Stitches," he repeated, then muttered a curse.

"How did this happen?" Matt was at her side and Jess hadn't even seen him there.

"I was crossing the street and some lunatic didn't stop at the light. . . ."

"According to our witness, the unmarked car sped up upon seeing you crossing the street. Almost hit you and as you were running to get away, you tripped, hitting your head on the lamppost." Jess shot the paramedic a glare and he shrugged. "What? They're cops."

"Detectives," Sam and Jess answered in unison.

Sam's jaw jumped. "Someone tried to run you over? Were you even going to tell me? File a report? Anything?"

"McCloskey," Matt shushed him, looking around the waiting room.

"Follow us," the paramedic said, rolling Jess into a private room. "You all can talk in here while you wait for Dr. Moore. He'll be treating you today."

Sam shot his partner a look, and Matt nodded, heading over to reception.

"What's going on?"

"Nothing you need to worry about," Sam said.

"Is it about our case?" Jess pressed on. "It's about the case, isn't it? This was Brown's hospital."

Sam waited until the paramedics moved Jess to her bed, then closed his eyes, clenching them shut so tightly that she could count the wrinkles on either side. Jess could have sworn she saw him silently counting to ten. When he opened them, his tongue darted out, wetting his full lips, and Jess felt a clench of desire from below. That tongue. Hell, he was good with that thing.

"Yes, it is about our case. No, you may not be there for the questioning."

"But—"

"No."

"It makes sense, though—"

"Jessie. *No.*"

She sighed. There was a light knock at the door and Matt entered with a man in a doctor's coat following behind him. He was a little older than Jess, with the tiniest bit of white peppering his dark hair and trendy black rectangle glasses.

"Hi, Jessica." Dr. Moore looked at the chart, then back at her with a smile. "Your friend here tells me you had a little run-in with a pole?"

"Lamppost," Sam corrected, glaring at the doctor.

"Yes." Jess continued to tell her story for what felt like the billionth time that day.

"Well, let's have a look, shall we?" Dr. Moore rolled a seat over to Jess's side and Sam stood on her other side, running his thumb over the back of her hand in circles.

Dr. Moore did all the typical medical things—checked her heart rate, blood pressure, eyes, and ears.

"Dr. Moore," Jess said while he shined a tiny light into her ear. "Do you know Dr. Brown, by chance?"

Sam squeezed her hand until her fingers crushed together.

Dr. Moore paused, clicking the light off and shifting to face her. "He's a good friend of mine, actually."

Jess turned to Sam, eyebrows raised. He had three seconds to tell the doctor about his friend or she would.

His lips pursed and though Jess's hand in his hurt from the force, she refused to show pain. Not to Sam. Not in this moment.

"Why don't we let him fix you up first, Jessie. Then we can talk."

Dr. Moore continued his examination, but a new crinkle tightened at his brow. Worry lines deepened at the corners of his eyes and his lips turned down into a frown. "Is Rich all right? We had a couple of drinks last night but he promised me he was walking home. I even took his keys." Dr. Moore swallowed, meeting Sam's eyes. "Was going to give them back today." He rolled the chair back, looking to the ground. "Please, whatever it is, just tell me. Is he in jail?" The doctor swiped a hand down his face. "He's going to lose his medical license someday."

"He's not in jail," Sam answered.

"Does he get drunk often?" Jess prodded further.

"No!" Dr. Moore answered quickly. Too quickly. And he knew it. "He doesn't get drunk often. . . ."

Jess raised her eyebrows, encouraging him to go on. "But . . . ?"

Dr. Moore spoke on his exhalation. "But, when he does drink, he tends to go a little nuts. He's an all-or-nothing kind of guy." His gaze dropped to Matt's badge, which hung on his belt loop. "Can you tell me what this is about?"

"In a minute." Sam flicked a glance to Jess. "How is she, Doc? Does she need any stitches?"

Dr. Moore gave a shaky smile to Jess. "No, you're lucky—it appears as though you just cut your head. No stitches needed. I'm going to send you home with some antibiotic ointment and painkillers in case your body starts to hurt once the adrenaline wears off. You should avoid sleeping for at least four hours in case you have a concussion. Do you have someone who can stay with you to ensure you'll remain awake? If not, we can set you up with a bed here where we can monitor you."

"Um—"

"Yes," Sam snapped. "She has someone."

Matt snickered from the corner but coughed to cover it up when Sam glared in his direction.

The doctor ripped a prescription from his pad and handed it to Jess. He lifted his hands in question, then dropped them to his knees with a slap. "So?"

Sam looked pointedly at Jess before opening the door with a gesture for the doctor to follow. "Let's talk out here," Sam stated.

Dr. Moore's eyes lowered. "In public? Where any of my or Rich's patients could hear? Absolutely not. I've been more than cooperative."

There was a look in Sam's eye that suggested he was about to go super alpha all over this doctor's exam room, just as Matt stepped in. "Dr. Moore, we have some terrible news about your friend. We're sad to tell you he died last night."

Dr. Moore sank to his chair once more, his face draining of any color that was there. "What?"

"Was there anyone you can think of that he had any disturbances with last night? At the bar or in his personal life?"

"You—you suspect he was murdered?" Dr. Moore swallowed, looking between Sam and Matt.

Sam finally stepped in, lifting his clenched fist from the

doorknob. "Yes. We have reason to believe it was accidental, but that his death was the result of an altercation."

"What time did you two part ways last night?" Jess asked.

Dr. Moore's face fell into his hands and he rubbed at his eyes. "It was early . . . I mean, for the drinking crowd, it was. We finished our shift here around four and hit happy hour at the Little Tap House. I think we left around seven-thirty."

Jess slid a glance at Sam, who met her eyes. That sounded about right—if Rich had left the bar around seven-thirty, that would have put him in the park at just before eight, his approximated time of death.

"He had no altercations at the bar? No one giving him a hard time?" Matt peered from above his notebook to catch Dr. Moore shaking his head.

"Then what did you mean when you said 'he's going to lose his license someday'?"

Dr. Moore opened his mouth to speak, but his voice caught, breaking with emotion. He took a moment to compose himself before starting again. "Rich was not the best at holding his alcohol. He didn't have a girlfriend, but he had a lot of companions." Dr. Moore met Sam's eyes as if Sam could read his thoughts.

"Companions?" Sam questioned. "Any names you can give us there?"

Dr. Moore shrugged. "I doubt they're real names. Candy, Cookie, Mystique . . . etc."

"So he would go to prostitutes?" Matt asked.

"That's what I assumed they were. Though he never confirmed it one way or another."

A shiver descended down Jess's spine. How the hell was she supposed to get any questions in around these two?

"He had no other family? Ex-wife? Anything?"

"No, his parents are both gone. No siblings, no wife, no kids."

"And where did you go after you left the bar?"

"I had much less to drink than he did. My wife ordered take-out at Boda, which I stopped to pick up on my way home."

"What time was that?"

"As soon as I left. Seven-thirty, seven-fortyish. I was home by eight-fifteen."

Sam nodded to Matt, who walked over and handed Dr. Moore his notepad. "Could you write down your address and your wife's name so that we can verify that?"

Dr. Moore looked terrified and his already red eyes bulged even more. "You think I'm lying?"

"We've got to confirm everything. Protocol," Sam said, though his voice was hardened. Edgy.

Jess cleared her throat. "It's just standard procedure, Dr.—what's your first name?"

"Marc," he said, swallowing.

"Marc," she said, sending him a small smile. "We just have to verify everything. In the same way you need to run tests even when you don't suspect the symptoms will lead to a positive diagnosis. As long as your story is as you say, you have nothing to worry about."

He nodded, but his eyebrows were still tight in the center.

"That is the whole story, right?" asked Sam.

He sent them a shaky nod before standing. "Yes." His voice was clipped as he scribbled the information into the notebook. "If there's anything else I can answer for you, please let me know."

Sam snapped his own Moleskine notepad closed, tucking it into his back pocket. "Thank you for your help, Dr. Moore. We'll be in touch."

Marc turned for the door, looking to Jess. "Rest up tonight. You should be fine to go back to your routine tomorrow, but I'd like to see you in a few days for a follow-up. And if any new symptoms develop, call me." He handed her a card.

*Bingo,* Jess thought, a triumphant inner smile warming her chest. A follow-up appointment was the perfect way to get some questions answered. "Thanks, Dr. Moore."

When he left, shutting the door behind him, Sam looked to Matt. "Can you handle the bar and wife questioning?"

Matt's gaze shifted between Jess and Sam and he nodded. "Of course. Won't be the same without you, though, puddin'," he mocked, batting his eyes.

"Really, Sam, I'll be fine for a few hours if you want to go—"

"You'll be fine? *Fine?* You were on your own for a few hours this morning and were nearly killed."

Jess rolled her eyes. "That's a bit melodramatic. Some guy behind the wheel just lost control—"

"That's not what it sounded like," Sam snapped. The muscle at his jaw twitched and his dark blue eyes creased in concern.

Jess's eyebrows shot up. "What? You think someone intentionally tried to run me over? Who the hell would do that?"

His gaze dipped below her eye line, avoiding her stare. Instinct kicked in, surging like a jolt of electricity through her body. He had a theory. . . .

Sam cleared his throat on a cough, fiddling with some Band-Aids on the counter. "The next eight hours are the most important after a head injury. If you grow tired with a concussion, you won't be able to keep yourself awake. I'm coming with you and that's that."

Jess pressed her lips together. Eight hours alone with Sam. She knew of a few things that could help pass the time.

# 16

Sam went for his car and was back in front of the hospital in such a short time that Jess was certain he must have broken quite a few laws. All in a detective's day's work, huh? She slid into the passenger seat where he was double-parked. The sedan was understated, but inside it had all the high-end upgrades. Leather seats with warmers. Serious speakers. Polished in a way that the most OCD person would have been content to sit in it. Cass would have friggin' loved it.

"Wow," Jess said, looking around. "It's like the Batmobile."

"That makes you, what? Catwoman?"

Jess shook her head. "No way. I'm a good guy—Batgirl."

He laughed. "Okay then, Batgirl. You hungry?"

"Not really," she said.

His lips tightened. "Did you eat anything for breakfast?"

"No . . ."

Sam didn't say anything further, but he chewed the side of his mouth for the remainder of the drive. Within minutes, he was pulling the car into Jess's driveway. "We should have walked." Jess rolled her eyes and climbed out of the car.

Sam slipped out and was at her side in seconds, offering a helping hand. "Walk?" he said, an incredulous look on his face. "Batgirl doesn't *walk*," he said, grinning.

With a chuckle, they approached the door, nearly stumbling over a large black box with a scarlet bow. A note was taped to the front.

"What's that?" Sam's demeanor shifted.

Jess's bones ached as she stared at the mysteriously wrapped package. "I don't know," she said, opening her door. Entering Cass's house, she set the large box onto the foyer bench.

Sam's gaze traveled from hers to the box and back. "Well? Aren't you going to open it?" he grunted.

"Later." Jess raised one shoulder to her ear, wandering into the kitchen in an effort to look nonchalant. The box called to her from the foyer, but she'd be damned if she was about to let Sam in on it. What if it was something pertaining to Cass? "Need anything? Food? Water?"

"No," Sam said, coming up behind her. His presence there was nearly tangible and tingles of awareness danced down her arms. "I'll get us some lunch while I fill your prescription."

"I said I wasn't hu—"

"I don't care. You need to eat."

Jess turned to face him and his arms wrapped around her waist. His hands fell on her hips with a gentle squeeze. "Or you could just stay here." Jess tilted her chin toward him. Everything clenched inside of her as those deep eyes of his locked onto her.

His lips tipped up on one side. "You need to rest," he told her, but even as he said it, his grin spread.

Jess pushed onto her toes before he could object and slanted her lips across his. He inhaled a sharp, shocked breath through his nose, his muscles stiffening beneath her touch. Excitement throbbed between her legs as she ran her tongue along the seam of his lips, nibbling the corner. He groaned and as one hand scooped urgently into her hair, the other dipped under her top, kneading her tender, heavy breast and rolling her nipple between his thumb and forefinger. The lace of her bra scraped against the ultrasensitive skin. Jess bit back a sigh and stroked Sam's erection through his dress pants.

"What am I going to do with you?" he groaned against her lips.

"Fuck me until I forget all about today?" Jess offered, batting her lashes.

Sam chuckled. "Perhaps," he said. "But first, you need to rest for a bit and I need to fill these." He waved the prescriptions in the air.

Jess pushed her bottom lip out in a pout. "You're not much fun."

Sam leaned in, drawing a line down her ear until he nipped her lobe. A growl rumbled from his throat as he flicked his tongue out. He whispered, his hot breath sending shivers through Jess. "I'm not fun, huh? You sure about that?"

Excitement rolled through Jess's body and despite her attempts to keep him from seeing it, her body trembled. His eyes flashed with triumph before he grabbed his keys.

He slipped through the door with a final glance at the box. Jess forced her eyes not to follow his and instead wiggled her fingers. He pointed at her. "Rest, but don't fall asleep. I'll be back soon."

Jess waited until she heard his car drive away and even then, she leaned out the window to ensure he was gone. She ran to the box, tearing the note from the front. She was never great at unwrapping gifts patiently. It read:

*For tomorrow night—to help you blend.*

That's it. That's all the card said. Jess flipped it over in her hands. Nothing was on the back either. Was it even meant for her? If it was, then it must have been from Dane—he was the only person Jess knew who was aware of the party. Or was it a gift for Cass? From someone who didn't know she died—

Jess gulped, shaking the thought away. No, she was letting her imagination run away with her. After tearing the bow away, she lifted the lid. Inside was the most stunning dress Jess had ever seen. She gasped as she lifted the black sheath gown and held it up to herself. The main dress was strapless, but over the top was a sheer black lace with crystals placed strategically over the material, creating a shimmer effect.

"Whoa," Jess exhaled. It was exquisite. Expensive, no doubt. Also inside was a classic pair of black Jimmy Choos and a mask. Not the sort of cheap mask with an elastic string that clips around your hair—no, this one was even more beautiful than the pearled mask she had found under Cass's couch. It had an adhesive on the back to stick to your face and wire inside to mold to your features. The shoes alone cost more than Jess spent in a year on clothing and panic took hold of her lungs at the thought of possessing items worth so much.

She shoved everything back into the box and ran upstairs to Cass's bedroom, tossing it into her closet. With a gulp, she fell to her knees, prying the floorboard up and snatching Cass's iPad.

She quickly punched in 0815—the code Dane had given her for the closet downstairs. People always reuse passwords, right? Her lungs expanded with a held breath as she waited. It buzzed to life, illuminating an e-mail account she had never seen before. A momentary rush of relief and excitement took hold of her body before she could realize what exactly she was doing, prying into a section of Cass's life that she wasn't sure she was ready for yet. But there wasn't time to hesitate. Not when other people Cass knew were also dying. "Sorry, Cassie," she whispered, clicking open the first e-mail within the archives. The first date was from almost a year and a half ago.

Dear Master,

Thank you so much for taking me on as your student. Despite what my friend may have led you to believe, you must know I'm doing this for myself. I've spent a lifetime taking care of others and being the woman they all expected and wanted me to be and now, I need to discover who the real me is.

You asked me to regale you with why I find this life so appealing? I've watched from the sidelines for several months—well, years if you include reading books and watching movies. And I finally had to ask myself, do I truly want to spend my life as a spectator?

I look forward to seeing you soon without our masks and learning all that you can offer me.

Warmest regards,
Cece

Jess gulped. Cece? The next e-mail in the thread was this man's—this "Master's" response. His text was bolded; his font choice masculine and blocky.

**Dear Cassandra,**

**There is no need for the pseudonym around me. I, too, look forward to our first meeting, as I have had a close eye on you at the masquerades for quite some time. I'm so glad Monsieur Punir introduced us. Though I'll admit, I was rather surprised. To my knowledge, Punir never shares.**

**Meet me tomorrow at lunch, outside your office building. There's a coffee cart that has the**

**absolute best espresso in all of Portland, hands
down. It's my lifeline, that cart.
Until tomorrow,
Master**

A slamming sound from downstairs caused Jess to jump. A
coffee cart outside of Cass's office. Combined with her questions for Dr. Moore, Jess had quite a few field trips coming up.

"Jess?" Sam called from downstairs. Her heart leapt into her
throat as she froze, sitting on the floor of her sister's closet, iPad
in her lap still. "I got us some Thai—coconut fried rice, right?"

Jess gulped. He remembered her favorite.

"You're not asleep, are you?" he yelled again.

"No!" she answered, tossing the iPad into her guest room
and clambering down the stairs. "No, I'm up." Even though
she knew rationally that she had nothing to be nervous about,
her heart slammed into her chest. She had done nothing wrong,
opening a package that was left at her door. Reading her sister's
e-mail was not immoral or illegal at this point. Though a soft
little voice at the back of her head reminded her of Dr. Brown's
phone records burning a hole in her phone.

Sam narrowed his eyes at her. "What's wrong?"

"Nothing," she lied. *Master.* The term Sam had wished her
to call him last night.

Sam's gaze traveled to the empty table where the box no
longer sat. Jess was certain he noticed its absence, but instead of
making a big deal out of it, he sauntered into the kitchen, grabbing two plates. "Eat," he demanded, setting a plate down in
front of a chair. Jess lowered herself to the seat, grabbing the
takeout container and spooning some out.

"Boda?" Jess asked with a smirk, spooning some rice onto
her plate.

Sam shrugged. "When the doctor mentioned it, it suddenly
sounded awfully good."

"Not to mention, you could ask some questions while waiting on the food to be ready," Jess added matter-of-factly.

Sam caught her eye, mischief glinting like a spark in the middle of a dark night. "Guilty as charged," he said, grinning, and spooned a heaping mass of meat and noodles into his mouth.

They ate in comfortable silence for a few minutes until Jess remembered Gilles from earlier. "Something weird happened this morning," she said.

"Other than your near-death experience?" Sam grumbled.

Jess continued speaking as though he hadn't said a word. "A man came by and made an offer on Cass's house."

Sam's fork slipped through his fingers, landing on the floor with a crash. Jess jumped at the sound. The muscles around Sam's shoulders and neck bunched as he bent to retrieve the fork.

"This is prime real estate around these parts," he said, lifting his gaze to meet hers. His eyes burned through her as he held eye contact. There was something more to that simple look; something needy. Terrified. Possessive.

"It must be. He offered me one million dollars for it. For a *pink* house," she snorted.

Sam's grip on his fork was tight and his knuckles drained of blood, fading to a creamy, pale color. "A verbal offer?" he asked tightly.

"No, he had a formal offer on paper. He's only in town for a bit and he asked me to have the estate lawyer look it over."

"In town? Where is he from?" Sam tilted his head casually, but his voice was on edge; brittle and ready to crack at any moment.

"Canada. He was a drug rep who worked with Cass. Said he has to come here a lot for business and wanted to invest in a place where he could stay."

"Could I see the offer?"

Grabbing her purse, she rooted through the too-full bag. The folded sheet of paper was now more crumpled than something worth a million dollars *should* be, but whatever.

Sam's eyes flitted over the paper. He swallowed, folded it, and handed it back to Jess. "Well, that's a hard offer to refuse. What are you going to do?"

"It's a lot of money. Even if I were to stay in Portland, with one million, I could buy something smaller—something more suited to me and still have a nest egg."

"Stay?" His eyes rose to hers and Jess's breath caught with the absolute masculine beauty this man exuded. Vulnerability flashed momentarily in his eyes and he quickly recovered, returning himself to the stony gaze she was used to.

With a swallow, Jess went back to eating her lunch. "I don't know. Maybe. I have a lot to figure out still." When she looked back up, Sam was staring, an animalistic hunger glistening in his eyes. "What?" she said. He didn't answer, but his brows pulled together. "Sam, *what?*"

"Won't you miss Brooklyn? Your friends? Your job?"

Jess froze midbite, her fork halfway to her mouth. "You trying to get rid of me, McCloskey?" She was kidding—mostly. But even as she made the joke, the truth of it resonated across his face. "Oh my God," she whispered, dropping her fork. "You *are*. You are trying to get rid of me." The realization caused a numbness that spread through her body like a cancer; fast, aggressive—deadly. "I'm so stupid," she snorted, shaking her head.

"No." He stood, pushing his chair back. "That's not what I'm—"

"You're chiming in a little too late, Sam," Jess snapped, grabbing her plate and tossing it onto the counter. She'd barely had five bites, but any hint of appetite had evaporated with the realization.

"Jess," he growled and though his tone was low, it was all business. "Jessie, *stop.*"

But she didn't. She couldn't. How could she be so stupid? Of course he would push her away. It was what Sam did.

"Jess, listen to me. I've been trying to avoid these feelings for years, but I can't. I just *can't.*" His hands gripped her shoulders, halting her nervous pacing, and he hooked a finger under her chin, dragging her gaze up to his.

His eyes were hungry as he towered over her, his touch firm, but tender. "I tried. I tried everything. I've tried for the better part of a decade to ignore you, move on from you, pretend you don't exist. But it's impossible, Jess."

"You—what?"

"I want you," he blurted out. He said the words quickly as though if he didn't speak fast enough, he may never say them.

The gasp caught in her throat. "But you had me. You *always* did." He was standing over her and with a quick flick of his hand, her bun was loose, hair cascading down her back. With that finger still curled around her chin, he gently tilted her head back.

Jess swallowed, the fear tying into a knot low in her belly. "Sam, your, um, lifestyle—I don't . . ." *What? Want it? Like it?* That was a total and utter lie and both Sam and she knew it. ". . . understand it," she finally settled on. "Help me understand it?"

Sam looked taken aback for all of a moment before his eyes searched her face. When he didn't answer her, Jess shifted underneath that heavy gaze of his. "I'm just not sure it's right for me."

"Jessie," he said, and the low rumble of his bass sent vibrations trembling over Jess's body. "Let me see if I can find a way to explain it to you." He laced her fingers into his and tugged her into his body. Then, leaning back on the table, he grasped her ass with a hand pulling her against his erection.

"Remember how we used to shoplift freshman year?"

Jess swallowed, her throat like cotton. She nodded a response.

"That rush we got as we stuck something small in our pockets and walked past the security guard—it's a similar rush. It was thrilling. Scary, even. It's the same reason why you love horror movies. And riding motorcycles. You willingly climb onto a bike with little protective gear, twist the throttle, and revel in the flip-flop that rolls in your stomach as you careen down the street at dangerously high speeds."

"Okay, yes, motorcycles are dangerous. But horror movies, roller coasters, and, and even shoplifting . . . they're not. Not really," Jess offered quietly.

"Aren't they? You put your life in the hands of the operators of a roller coaster; in the hands of the movie producers with horror films. You have no control over where the ride or the story will take you. A safe dominant-submissive relationship should be that way, too. It's not about pain necessarily. It's about the unexpected. You have no control and it's exciting and terrifying. But if your dominant does his or her job right, the ride is fucking amazing, baby." He leaned in close to her ear, nipping at the base before whispering. "Let me take you on a ride, Jessie."

She shivered against him as his thumbs circled her nipples through the thin cotton of her shirt. He kissed her then and Jess was surrounded by tingly, delicious warmth as Sam's massive arms wrapped around her body, encompassing her entirely in the kiss.

"Lie on the table," he rasped as his touch hovered over her bandaged cut. With tender fingers, he brushed her hair away from her forehead. "I'll be gentle this time," he added, tracing those same fingers down her face and jaw.

Jess lifted herself onto the table, scooting his food off to the side. "You won't hurt me." But even as she said the words, she wasn't entirely sure she believed them. Because in reality, Sam *had* hurt her. He hurt her when he abandoned her. And that first night they experimented with this after graduation. But, she had liked it. Too much, in her opinion. "I'm not worried about that."

"Yes you are." Sam's features sagged, darkening. "And you should be," he whispered. "Not all doms know how to control themselves," he added.

The admission caught her off guard and she swallowed hard against a lump forming in her throat. "But you do?"

Sam didn't answer and, instead, his lips fell on her once more, kissing away any possibility of clarification.

His lips trailed down her throat as his fingers played with the hem of her shirt. Lifting it quickly over her head, he dropped it to his side onto the floor. His fingers were nimble as he undid her bra and it popped open, releasing her from its bondage. The straps dragged down her arms, leaving goose bumps racing behind.

Sam dipped his head to her full, aching breasts, circling his tongue over the hardened peaks. A deep moan growled at the base of Jess's throat as Sam's tongue flickered across her sensitive nipples. He pulled away, leaving Jess alone and chilled.

He stood before her, pants tight at the zipper and unable to tear his eyes from her. "Clothes off. Now," he demanded. "And lie back."

Jess did as she was told, momentarily taken aback by how easily she obeyed his orders; how natural it felt. What a difference a day makes, huh? Just yesterday, she was fighting him on each and every command. But now? She was pudding beneath his capable hands. Jess wiggled out of her pants and thong, stealing a glance out the open windows. Any nosy neighbor could peek in and see her in her birthday suit at any moment. The idea opened the floodgates between her legs. The thought of someone watching them; desiring her; envying her for having Sam. She shivered and licked her lips.

Sam's gaze followed hers to the open window and his eyes darkened to the deepest blue she had seen. The sort of blue that reminded her of the darkest part of the ocean where undiscovered creatures resided. "Does that excite you?" he asked. "The thought of someone watching us?" It was as though he could read her thoughts—or maybe she just needed to disguise her facial expressions better.

"What if it does?" Jess arched her back with intent and spread her legs wide for Sam. The ceiling fan breezed down and despite the cool gust of air, she felt hot, sweaty, and achy all over. She needed him in her and on her. The lack of his touch was almost painful and her sex pulsed.

Sam dropped down so that his face was between her legs. She could feel his energy there and she wiggled in front of him, scooting herself closer to his lips. "Please, Sam," she begged. His sexual prowess reverberated and the need for him ripped through her. He puckered his lips and blew a warm breath over her swollen, throbbing sex. Opening his mouth, he hovered above her, still not touching, and Jess whimpered. He dropped a soft kiss, his lips covering her clit before he pulled away, standing once more.

"I don't share." Though it was a whisper, his voice held the dark promise of punishment if she were to ever suggest such an act again. Walking to the windows, he yanked the curtains closed. "You should remember that," he said. And though the sentiment was serious, there was a satisfied gleam in his eyes. As though he liked knowing something that turned her on so voraciously. And he liked withholding that gratification from her. He was turned on by denying her of exactly what she desired—it was a scary revelation to have. And yet, it was exciting to recognize that within him. Denying it simply made her want it all the more.

Sam dropped his pants and with quick flicks of his fingers, his shirt was unbuttoned. Afternoon sunlight streamed in through a crack in the curtain and caught the side of Sam's body, highlighting the contours of his roped muscles. His erection pierced forward, thick, veiny, and ready. Moisture clung to the tip and Jess's lips parted at the sight as though she were in the middle of the desert parched and Sam was her oasis.

"Put your mouth on me." His eyes glanced down at his cock and back to Jess.

She licked her dry lips as Sam approached, opening wide and brushing her tongue along the ridge at the underside of his shaft. She took him entirely in her mouth until he hit the back of her throat, then pulled out, dragging her teeth lightly along his skin. As she circled her tongue along his head, the pre-cum caught there when she pulled away, leaving a strand connecting them. Jess looked into Sam's eyes as his hand found her nipple once more. Jess nibbled the ridge before taking him whole again.

Sam hissed, biting back a curse, and pinched her nipple. The sensation was felt all the way between her legs. "Baby," he growled, "it's taking all my restraint right now to be gentle with you." He pulsed his hips against her mouth, pumping faster. His erection tightened against her tongue. His excitement growing right along with his size.

God, she missed this. She missed him. And not just how sexy he was or how hot he made her. She missed their conversations; his company. She just missed *him*. Her best friend.

Jess moaned as she took him deep into her mouth once more. As he pulled out and away from her, Jess felt empty without him. She wanted more; wanted all he had to offer and then some. She sucked harder to counter the friction of him pulling away. He grunted and grasped her hair as though it was second nature before quickly releasing. "Shit," he mumbled, his hand hovering at the bandage at her temple. "I won't last long enough to fuck you if you continue that."

Dropping to his knees, he ran his tongue along her length, pausing at her engorged opening and thrusting his tongue inside before he moved to her clit with quick, feather-light flicks. "Close your eyes and keep them closed," he said from below.

Jess did as he asked—it was an easy command and she relaxed into the rhythm of his tongue against her hot flesh. She savored the familiar contact. Even if it had been years—well, other than last night—Sam's lips, his tongue, his teeth had changed very little. And for once she relished in the familiar rather than the unknown.

There were few men who had the ability to shoot a ripple through her typically composed and confident attitude. Though not the most organized of all the Walterses, she was easily the most stubborn. And she hated, *hated* the thought of herself being submissive to any man in any way. Even if the actions spurred a waterfall between her legs.

Jess's hands clutched the edges of either side of the table, knuckles white as Sam's pace sped up against her. Two fingers entered her, spreading her wide and circling the knot deep inside. His other hand cradled her hip possessively and a tingling sensation spiraled down Jess's body.

The tightness that built between her legs was too much and Jess wiggled against it for more—more of Sam, more of a release. More everything. Just as she was damn near ready to explode, there was a lack of touch on her. A breeze wafted across her flesh and Jess whimpered, her eyes fluttering open. Where did he go? Why did he leave?

His hands shackled her wrists, pinning them above her head and his body scraped the length of hers, his thick erection pressed into her, nestling between her legs.

His mouth closed over hers, blazing with urgency. His

tongue stroked inside her mouth devilishly and his hands restricted her movements as they pinned her arms above her head. "Don't come yet," he ordered, his voice ripe with challenge.

"I can't guarantee anything," she whispered, her eyes still closed with his command.

His erection pushed slowly inside of her, spreading her opening around his girth. Each pulse inside of her massaged deep, leaving moments of ache that faded quickly into pure bliss. Jess sighed, lifting her hips to meet his thrusts. They were controlled and fluid in each bit of movement.

"Open your eyes, baby." Jess blinked open, her long lashes causing fuzzy webs within her vision. "I want you to come with me," he whispered, dropping a hand down between them. Using the tips of his fingers, he drew small circles over her clit. His touch glided across her smooth skin and Jess moaned as sweat gathered between her breasts.

The world was spinning beneath Jess and despite the fact that she was certain she didn't yet have her footing, she didn't want the ride to stop. If anything, she wanted it to go faster. She wanted to throw caution to the wind and know this man and everything about him that might have changed in the decade they had been apart.

He filled Jess entirely, deliciously stretching her beyond where she ever thought she could go. She rolled her hips over his length, craving something deeper. Longer. More. Pain split her, but she didn't even care. He was firm and throbbing, his body making promises that Jess begged to keep true to.

He met her breath pattern with each inhale and exhale. "Yes, Jessie. Fuck, yeah," he rasped, and then dropped his head back. On either side of her head his hands were clenched in an act of restraint that was most impressive.

"Sam," she groaned. "Put your hands on me." Jess pushed

harder into him. "Please, now. Touch me—I need your hands on me."

His answer was a forward arch and one strong arm wrapped around her waist, lifting her at an angle off the table and pulling her close to him. Jess cried out, lifting her body as his hand slid under her ass and he drove himself even deeper into her. She crushed her lips against his and he met her tongue, stroke for stroke in a wet, searing kiss. His teeth clamped down on her bottom lip and she felt his smile against her mouth. "Did I say you could kiss me?" he said, but a hint of playfulness was within that rasp.

"Shut up," she said, grinning. Clasping a hand behind his neck, she pulled his mouth down to hers, but instead of kissing him again, she waited, a breath away from him. Sam took her mouth this time in a sensual kiss. He claimed her lips with his, meeting her tongue with a sweep of his own, each thrust an erotic stroke.

She was so close. Every part of her body was tight and far too sensitive. Heat flashed over her skin, tingling down to her toes. They flexed as he thrust deeply into her. "I'm going to— Sam, I'm going to . . ."

Sam groaned, arching his back as he gave one final plunge, rolling his hips with the movement. Spasms rocked through Jess's body as she clawed at Sam's back, clutching his skin, pulling him closer to her. Jess felt her body clamping onto him as the final tremors shuddered through her. He grunted against her, burying his face into her shoulder and nipping the tender skin there. His release was hot and wet as he spurted inside of her. His coarse chest hair scraped against her tender nipples and Jess twitched below him as her orgasm faded away.

He collapsed on top of her, careful to put the weight on his elbows. Dropping a light kiss, he brushed his mouth across hers and the touch sent another spark lighting in her chest. Jess trailed her fingers over the tight muscles at his shoulder and followed the curved lines down to his biceps. He brushed the hair off her moist brow and studied her face for an eternal moment. "It's my promise to never leave you like I did before. Never again, Jess," he whispered, pressing a kiss to her forehead.

It was the words she always longed to hear. For years—hell, for more than a decade. But there was something lacking in the confession.

"Jess?" he asked quietly, his hands brushing over the tight lines forming between her brows.

"That wasn't an apology," she whispered, sitting up, forcing him off her. "And it wasn't an explanation," she said louder.

His eyebrows drew in, lines tight at the corners of his mouth. "I'm sorry, Jess. I really am. I—I was young. And stupid. Come on, we were fifteen."

"I know," she said, her voice hoarse. "We were fifteen. And I was newly orphaned. Jesus, Sam . . . I didn't even know if Cass would get custody of me at that point. I thought I was gonna end up in a foster home or something."

"I'm sorry," he repeated quietly.

The dinner table was smooth and polished, contrasting her raw, unhinged grip on it. "Why? Just tell me *why* you did it."

Sam was silent, more concerned with the patterns of the floor than with Jess's needs at the moment.

"I can't forgive you until I understand why!" Jess shoved off of the table, grasping for her clothes and tugging them over her head.

"I can't tell you why, Jessie. Please. Just know that I'm sorry and that I had a good reason." Sam followed her, pushing to his feet. Reaching for her, he ran a palm down the length of her arm, entwining her hand in his.

She wrenched away from his hold. "No!" Air dragged through her tight lungs. God, she hated that he had such an effect on her, but it was what it was. And he probably *always* would have this effect on her. "No," she tried again, calmer. "Try again when you find the courage to explain."

He grabbed his clothes, dressing slowly and making his way to the front door. With a resigned sigh, he turned to face her.

Hope sparked in her belly. She wasn't asking for much—an explanation, that was all.

Only, instead of a reason, sadness washed over his features with a final lick of his lips. "You can't sleep yet, Jessie. You know that, right?"

She nodded and brushed a piece of dark hair that fell onto her forehead. "I know." She folded her arms, leaning against the wall.

His dark blue eyes studied her, never leaving her face but shifting in subtle movements. As though he was reading every aspect of her expression. He studied her thoroughly as though he might lose his vision at any moment and never wanted to forget her.

"I drove to New York once. Freshman year of college. Like a goddamn puppy looking for its owner, I searched for you. And I even found you—a waitress at some booty restaurant where you wore short shorts and tight shirts. Guys ogling you from every angle. And I realized, what the fuck was I going to say to you? You had moved on. I needed to do the same." The muscle at his jaw ticked and his eyes found hers again. Only this time, they weren't the same soft gaze. They flashed with regret. "But I never did move on. I always thought of you. Every little thing would remind me of you. Anytime I used sugar cubes instead of loose sugar." He smiled at the memory, dropping his gaze to the floor and dragging a hand through his messed hair. "Anytime I passed by a coffee shop that offered a tuxedo latte. Whenever there was a girl with curly dark hair and eyes so deep they could read me without my saying a word." He swallowed, clearing his throat and turning for the door, head shaking. "But I can't give you the explanation you want, Jess."

Sorrow gripped her heart. She wanted to forgive him blindly. It's what Cass would have wanted. But she couldn't. She knew herself and she could never let this go. Not knowing the truth would eat away at her like a parasite. "You broke my heart, Sam McCloskey. And you can't even tell me *why* you did it. Get out."

And that was exactly what he did.

# 17

That afternoon, Sam could barely concentrate enough to catch every couple of words. Jess's run-in with the lamppost could not be a coincidence. Was it a message to him? A message to get her away from here?

Sam looked to his notes, tapping the pen against his Moleskine pad. That look on Jessie's face as he left her yesterday was enough to wrench his guts into a sailor's knot. Could he tell her the truth? At least as it stood now, time might win her back. Time might dull the ache of him being a stupid, selfish teen and walking away from her friendship when she most needed him. But if she knew the real reason, he doubted she could ever forgive that.

He gripped his pen so hard that his fingers ached beneath the cheap Bic plastic. No, it was unforgivable. *He* was unforgivable.

And it didn't matter even if she did accept his apology. She needed to get *out* of Portland—not be planning her future here. Cass's death had made that crystal clear. What Sam needed more than anything were the images from inside that damn book.

The tip of the pen tapped rapidly against his notepad as he flicked it between his fingers. Damn, he could use a smoke right about now.

"Detective?"

Dr. Moore's wife looked at Sam, a worried expression marring her delicate features. He darted a glance to Matt, who was glaring at him in response, mouthing the words *what the fuck* to him from behind Mrs. Moore.

Shit. This was exactly why Jessie being in town was terrible. It was bad for him, bad for his job, and dangerous for Jess.

Sam cleared his throat. "I'm sorry, Mrs. Moore. Could you say that last part again?"

She looked back to Matt, twisting her hands in her lap. "I said, I feel awful about Rich. In all honesty, I never liked him much. He was always wanting to go out with Marc—I think it's the difference between single friends and married friends." She scrunched her nose, flipping silky blond hair behind one ear. "Different priorities, you know?"

Sam refrained from rolling his eyes. "Did you feel as though he was a bad influence on your husband? Did you and Rich ever get into any fights?"

"Oh, no, nothing like that," she said, shaking her head. Her pearl necklace clacked with the movement and she fiddled with the top buttons of her cardigan. Jesus, she looked like something out of *The Stepford Wives*.

"We heard that Rich enjoyed company a lot of nights," Matt began, shifting his gaze from Sam to Mrs. Moore.

She shrugged, arranging some items on the coffee table, fluffing a vase full of peonies. "Oh? I wouldn't know. I was never invited to join them on their boys' nights."

"So, Marc never talked about Dr. Brown's paid escorts?"

"What?" Her voice was suddenly shrill and she no longer cared about the bowl of flowers being perfectly arranged. "When? When did they hire escorts?"

"We can't be sure, ma'am." Matt eyed Sam from across the

room and though silent, his communication was blatantly obvious. "We are looking into a recent transaction from last night—" Matt barely had the words out before Mrs. Moore was throwing a coffee-table book across the room.

"Son of a bitch!" she shrilled. "Marc knew that I would not stand for that once we were together!"

Matt's eyes lifted to meet Sam's and he nodded an encouragement. "So, Marc and Rich used to hire escorts . . . together?"

Mrs. Moore pressed her lips together, smoothing berry lip gloss over her top and bottom lip. "I-I don't know." She immediately returned to straightening the flowers.

"Uh-huh." Sam clicked his pen, rising to his feet. He moved to the mantel, looking at various framed wedding pictures. "So, if I were to dig a little deeper into your husband's past, I wouldn't find any arrests for solicitation?"

Mrs. Moore gasped. "No!"

"And you realize," Matt interrupted, "if we discover that you've withheld information, you could be considered an accessory to murder?"

That was a bit of a stretch—they didn't even know who Rich's killer was yet. But the sentiment was true enough. Withholding information could be punishable.

Punishment. Sam's mind wandered once more to Jess's tight, tanned ass as he spanked her the other night.

Mrs. Moore swallowed and her eyes widened to cartoon levels. "Is that true?" She looked to Sam, who nodded.

"Lying to two detectives certainly doesn't look good, ma'am."

Her gaze dropped to the floor and she wrung her hands in her lap once more. "I don't know a lot, but I know that Rich and Marc used to hire paid escorts. Marc swears he never did anything illegal with them—he would just use their company for medical events that he needed dates to. But he did say that Rich always made things a little more . . . personal with his escorts. Bringing them home and stuff." She offered a little shrug with one shoulder. "I never understood why. He always had women falling all over him. And he dated all the time—non-paid dates. It didn't seem like he would need to hire anyone for . . . *that.*"

"Thank you, Mrs. Moore. To your knowledge, your husband has not called the escort service since?"

"No!" She looked damned near close to tears, her cheeks reddening and she fanned herself with the palm of her hand. "I can't speak for Rich, though. He was always with a different bimbo every night," she said through gritted teeth. "And the second you try to set him up with a nice girl he could settle down with, he disappeared on you. I introduced him to the sweetest little brunette from my church . . . oh, sure, he was nice enough to her, but clearly she wasn't his type." She sat taller, rolling her shoulders back. "Last night—my husband—he wasn't found . . . you know . . . with an escort or anything? Was he?"

"No, ma'am," Matt said. "To our knowledge, Dr. Brown may have called an escort service after Dr. Moore left for the night."

She sighed, falling back onto her couch in relief.

"One last question," Sam said. "Do you know the name and number of the escort service they frequented?"

Her jaw slackened and even despite that golden spray tan she sported, her face paled like porcelain china. "No. Of course not."

When they finished their questions, Sam and Matt left the Moores' home. Sam sighed. "Do you think she knows more than she let on?"

"Nah, not after you hit her with that accessory bullshit."

Sam scratched his chin, starting up the car. "So you don't think she has the number to that escort service?"

"Why?" Matt joked. "You lookin' for a date?"

Sam winked, diving his hands into his pockets. "How long have we known each other?"

"Decades," Matt said, smiling.

"And in that time, have I ever needed to pay for sex?"

"Hey," Matt said, putting two hands up in surrender. "A guy like Richard Brown certainly didn't need to pay for it and yet he did. Don't ask me why people do what they do! But I'm certain our good friend Dr. Moore will remember the name of the service. I'll check in on him a little later."

"Yeah," Sam said, "it's just . . . usually when people are telling the truth, they don't turn ghostly shades of white."

They continued walking in silence, and Matt pulled his jacket tighter around himself. "Jesus, it's getting chilly. I know a place up this way—best chowder you've had in your life. Wanna eat?"

Sam nodded and followed as Matt led the way to Mary's. He froze at the entrance. Oh, Sam knew Mary's, all right. He knew the owner all too well.

"Won't Kelly have dinner on the table for you? You sure you want to spoil your appetite?"

"Are you kidding?" Matt held the door open. "Kelly can't make a bowl of chowder to save her damn life. I won't eat much . . . just enough to take the edge off. Besides, she's always ranting about portion control. Leaves me fucking starving by bedtime."

Sam swallowed a curse before entering. Maybe she wouldn't be working today. It was a Thursday afternoon, after all. Most business owners didn't—

"Sam McCloskey," a husky voice said from across the room. "As I live and breathe. What the hell are you doing here?"

Sam gritted his teeth, cringing momentarily before turning to find Mary standing there. "Hey you," he returned, offering her a kiss on the cheek. Mary had short, spiky black hair, striking green eyes, and lips that looked like she had red lipstick permanently on. He didn't know quite how she kept the color so consistent.

"How the hell are you, Sam?" Her green eyes twinkled as she looked him over.

"I'm great, how are you?"

"Better now." She arched an eyebrow in his direction.

"Mary—this is my partner on the force, Matt Johnson. Matt, this is Mary. Owner of the greatest chowder house in all of Portland."

Mary puffed a gust of air from the side of her mouth. "Portland? Try all of Maine." Then, looking back to Matt, she added, "Nice to meet ya. Have a seat." She gestured to a table, putting some paper place mats and silverware in front of them.

Mary's lithe body moved like a cat around her restaurant. Elegant, graceful, and with just enough spunk that you could never be sure if she would turn and purr against your hand or claw your eyes out. He had never been with Mary sexually— but they ran in the same circles. They were both doms. Though he didn't doubt for a second that a roll in the hay with Mary would be hot—having to fight tooth and nail to maintain control when they both so desperately needed it. Yet, it never happened.

There were only a small handful of BDSM clubs in the area and the regulars tended to get to know each other quickly. Luckily, Mary was a seasoned veteran and knew better than to bring up the lifestyle in front of anyone new.

Sam excused himself while Matt played around on his phone and headed to the restroom. He made eye contact with Mary for all of a second before she casually set her things down and followed him inside.

"Well, well, well," she said as Sam checked the stalls for anyone else in the bathroom. "You're the last person I expected to see stroll in this afternoon. Looking for a date tonight?"

She sidled up in front of Sam, clutching his lapels and dragging her knee up his inner thigh. He snatched her hands from his jacket, forcing them to her sides. "No," he snarled. "I'm seeing someone. Sort of."

She arched a black eyebrow in his direction, those scarlet lips curling into a smile. "Oh?" She pouted, exaggerating the expression. "Such a shame. I thought tonight might finally be the night we could play."

"My partner brought me here . . . I didn't realize where he was taking me until it was too late."

"Well, you're always welcome . . . it's your choice that you never show up."

"It seems best to keep the lives separated." He groaned inwardly at the irony of his life now. It was the antithesis of keeping it separate. A high school love whom he now worked with becoming his submissive bedroom partner.

"Well, will I be meeting your new lady tomorrow night?"

*Tomorrow night?* "What's happening then?" He lowered his gaze at Mary, her tight leather skirt and thigh-high laced boots covering slim hips. A tight corset came only just below her belly button, revealing a strip of olive skin.

Humor flashed across her face. "Oh, Sam. Don't tell me no one invited you?"

"To what?" He knew of every goddamn BDSM party in this town. There wasn't a club or privately hosted party he hadn't been invited to.

"The masquerade, of course," she said on a laugh. "I've seen you there before."

"Is it taking place at a different venue?" he asked.

"Not to my knowledge. Did no one tell you? The key to enter this time?"

"No. It's been cancelled," he grunted, narrowing his eyes at her. "Cass passed away—so the party's been cancelled."

Her face slackened, suddenly serious. "The house mom died? What the hell happened?"

Sam swallowed. He hated lying, but damn if he wasn't a pro at it these days. "Robbery gone bad down by the wharf. So, unfortunately, whoever invited you had it wrong."

Mary snorted, shaking her head. "If you say so, bubby." Tossing a rag over her shoulder, she swung her hips toward the bathroom door, throwing a wink over her shoulder. "Except I was sent the info *today* by Monsieur Punir, himself."

Panic swelled within Sam. "Seriously? And it's in the same pink house?" Mary nodded, opening the door with one hand. "Wait—what's the key?" he growled, rushing toward Mary, backing her against the doorframe. She sighed and grabbed his cock, squeezing.

"Do not push me as though I am one of your babes. Got it?" She twisted his balls like they were in a vise before shoving him back against the doorframe.

He gritted his teeth. "Fine." Damn, he quickly remembered why they had never had a full-on fuckfest. He'd be black and blue all over by the end of it. "Just tell me the key."

She smirked, running a palm down his chest and hooking her finger into his slacks. He grabbed her wrist, stopping her from going any further. "Sorry, honey. You'll have to just figure it out like the rest of us." She nudged the door with her shoulder, sauntering out of the bathroom.

Sam gripped the sink, his face nearly as white as the porcelain. "Son of a bitch," he whispered.

# 18

Jess woke the following morning close to eleven, but spent an hour in bed scouring Dr. Brown's phone records. Outside of Cass's contact information in his phone, the only other link between them she found was a call from Cass to the doctor's office. Since he was a doctor, then it was absolutely possible that they knew each other through pharmaceuticals.

Jess circled her knuckles around her red-rimmed eyes. She slept great through the night . . . she had absolutely no reason to be tired. That was the funny thing about sleep though, wasn't it? The more you get, the more your body thinks it needs. She checked her phone, once more. Nothing. No missed calls. No texts. She had kicked Sam out, but still. She expected something by the way of communication. Maybe she was stupid for holding out hope that he would come clean with her. Matt had promised to call her if there was anything job-related, though part of her doubted Sam would have allowed that. Where were Sam and Matt right now? In New York, the detectives would likely be at the victim's home, searching for clues.

Jess slipped into the shower, shivering despite the steaming water that pelted her body. Tears swelled at the back of her throat and she fell against the chilly bathroom tile.

*Thump, thump, thump.* It was quiet, but Jess just barely heard the knocking over the steady stream of water.

She turned the shower off, towel-dried her hair quickly, and threw on her silk, lavender robe as she headed down the stairs.

*Thump, thump, thump.* The knock was steady and firm. She stole another quick glance at the clock. Hell, it was almost lunch already? That's what happened when you slept your day away.

Jess swung the door open, and yelped when she saw Dane standing there, leaning against the doorframe. She pulled the robe tighter, not sure exactly why she was so startled. "S-sorry," she apologized. "I was expecting someone else."

Dane's smile tipped toward his eyes and his gaze fluttered briefly down to her bare legs. The robe barely covered to her midthigh and Jess tugged on the hem. "My apologies for interrupting."

A bit of water from her damp hair trickled down her chest, creeping its way between the robe and her skin. As it dripped over her nipples, she could feel her body's reaction as they became hardened peaks. She opened the door for Dane, quickly hugging her arms to her chest after. "Come on in. Um . . . can you give me a minute to dress?"

Dane nodded. "Take your time," he answered quietly. "I have some things from the truck I can unload while you get ready."

Jess began up the stairs, stopping to turn back to him. "Things?"

"For the party? Tonight? If you recall, I promised I would assist you."

*Shit.* She had completely forgotten about the party tonight. "Right. Oh, yeah. The party."

His eyes flashed as Jess shifted her weight back and forth and placed a hand on the banister. "I can always try to cancel it. . . ."

"No," Jess answered sharply. "No. It's fine. I was hoping to join my colleagues for a questioning today, but I guess I don't have to go—"

"Your colleagues?" Dane interrupted. "You mean Sam, right?"

Jess swallowed as Dane's face darkened. She stretched her neck to each side. She had nothing to be ashamed of with Dane. He had no hold over her. No say in where or who she spent her time with. "Yes. With Sam. And my other colleague Matt, as well."

He regarded her with quiet reserve. The sort of stoic calmness you see in royalty or someone who never once questioned his control of a situation. "You can go," he prodded. "I'll stay here and set up, if you like."

Jess didn't know how she quite felt about that yet. Dane? Alone in Cass's house. A house that held all kinds of secrets that he may or may not know all about. She certainly didn't trust the guy, but did she have much choice in the matter? Who else would help her prepare for a fetish party?

She opened her mouth to object as Dane caught sight of her bandage. He leaned in, stepped up the stairs to meet her, and brushed his fingers into her hair, away from her temple. "What happened?"

Jess jerked away from his touch. She didn't know whether it was the fact that she was practically naked or maybe because he and Cass had some sort of mysterious history together—but she didn't want his hands on her.

She tugged her hair back down over the bandage. "It's nothing. I just had a little accident yesterday."

Dane seemed to get the message and pulled back from her, nodding. "But you're all right?"

"Yes, thank you."

His face contorted in concern. "You'll take it easy tonight." It wasn't a question, and Jess trembled at the gall of this guy.

Coming into her house, taking over a party she was hosting—well, Cass was supposed to be hosting, but whatever—and then bossing her around.

"It's a party." Jess threw her hands up. "How much easier do I need to take it?"

Dane's movements were slow and done with intent as he set his toolbox down. Did he always carry that thing with him? His gaze was heated as he moved past Jess and though she couldn't be sure, it looked as though his gaze dipped to her cleavage beneath the robe.

"I'll go get dressed," she said, pulling the robe tighter around her.

His breathing was labored and his nostrils flared as he licked his lips. "I'd say that's a damn good idea."

Jess didn't take long to throw on some jeans and a shirt. True to her messy form, she took a quick look around her guest room with a shrug—the closet door was left ajar, the top drawer where she put her underwear was flung open—a pair of leopard panties caught on the corner. *Note to self: Tidy up when home next. Especially if Sam is spending the night again.* Not that he would be . . . but just in case. She popped on some lip gloss and eyeliner and then ran back downstairs while tying her hair into a bun.

She tossed her camera bag around one shoulder, the weight of it strikingly heavy, and grabbed her purse as Dane entered the house, box in hand.

"You'll be here for a while?" Jess asked.

Items in the box clanked together as he set it down, a grunt bursting through his tight lips. "Sure thing. Will you be gone all day?" His clenched hands tightened their hold on his hips and he stared at the two boxes he carried in.

White knuckles. Lack of eye contact. What was that guy up to? Jess grabbed her sister's keys, slowly backing out of the house. "No. Not all day. Three hours probably," she said with every ounce of confidence that she could muster. If she told him three hours, she'd aim to be home in two . . . maybe she'd catch him in something. What, exactly? She had no clue.

"See you soon, Dane."

Jess made sure that her visit with the estate lawyer was quick. She dropped off the offer on the house and even as his eyes bugged out of his skull, Jess managed to keep a calm exterior. "I'll take a look," he said quietly, though there was a dryness to his voice that wasn't normally present.

She pulled into a spot outside of Cass's office building in South Portland. It was one of the larger buildings in the area. A coffee cart was situated outside, about thirty feet from the front entrance. Where Cass's master claimed the best coffee in Portland was. Jess rushed forward, pulling a five from her purse. "Hi," she said, smiling, and was met with a returned grin from the guy behind the counter. "Regular drip," she said. "Small."

Glancing around, she saw a handful of people zooming by, none stopping for the coffee. "Do you get a lot of regulars here?"

The guy gave her an odd look as he poured steaming ebony liquid into a cheap paper cup. "Uh, yeah. That's basically all we get. Pretty much everyone in that building." He gestured to the massive office building with his chin. "Milk?" he asked.

"Please. Half and half." She cleared her throat, scanning the courtyard once more. "Someone recommended this place to me, though. He said it was the best coffee in all of Portland."

The guy lit up at that comment. "Oh, yeah?"

Jess nodded. "Yeah. He and I met only briefly, but I can't remember his name. I didn't know if maybe you knew who your biggest supporter was?"

"What's he look like?"

Shit. "Um, you know. Pretty average dude. But with a commanding sort of vibe—" *Oh, Lord.* She sounded like a crazy person.

"Oh, for a second there, I thought you meant the guy who owned the building here. He loves this place. Comes every morning. Told me once it was the best coffee he'd ever had." The guy leaned forward, whispering as though he were about to reveal the secret to the universe. "It's chicory coffee. We have it shipped up from New Orleans," he said with a wink.

Jess nodded, taking a sip. Heat slid down her throat in creamy, spicy sweetness and her eyes lit up. "Holy shit—this *is* good." The guy tipped his hat. "So, the owner of the building— what's his name?"

The man shrugged. "Not sure. But you said the guy you talked to was average? This man is anything but average looking."

Energy buzzed through Jess's body and she wasn't sure if it was because she was getting close or because of the caffeine boost. Either way, she felt good. The owner of the building— that had to be easy to find out, right?

As Jess walked into the lobby, a list of various businesses and correlating floors caught her attention. Ninth floor: Holtz Health Sciences and Pharmaceuticals.

It took ages for her to be signed into the building. She handed them a photo ID, which they scanned into their systems. Then, they took her picture, printed a tag, and buzzed her through the electronic turnstile. You'd think by all these security measures that she was entering the friggin' Pentagon or something.

The building was fancy—for Portland, at least. It was no Fifth Avenue or Wall Street, of course. But it was pristine. The marble floors shined with a recent buff, the walls were painted a crisp white and adorned with simple but tasteful art.

As Jess entered the elevator, a man's footsteps pounded behind her. He wasn't running—it was the sort of heavy step that comes from a man in charge. His hand jutted out, stopping the elevator doors with a clunk, just as they began to close and as Jess punched the *door open* button.

As her eyes raked the man from head to toe, she severely regretted not putting something a little prettier on. Jeans and a top? What was she thinking? But this man in front of her—he was . . . wow. There were no words.

Jess's jaw slackened and though it was not overtly open and drooling, she was definitely gawking. She quickly snapped her jaw shut and directed her gaze at the elevator buttons. Something rolled in the back of her throat as she attempted to clear it. "What floor?"

"Top floor," he said. And that voice . . . it was raw. And deep. He was a scary man and he unnerved Jess to the core. Everything from his perfectly swooped black hair to his clean-shaven jaw to his polished patent leather shoes. Plenty of women would have swooned over him—in fact, Jess was certain they did. But she found him less sexy and more terrifying.

She pressed the button for the top floor and the ninth floor as well. As the circular number nine lit up with her touch, the man slowly turned his neck. His gaze assessed her in the same way that she had sized *him* up moments ago. As though he was trying to place her. "Holtz?" he asked simply, his brow creasing together.

Jess tilted her chin higher. "Yes," she answered. Why should he deserve more information than that? A simple answer to a simple question.

He searched her face, combing every minute detail from the top of her hairline to the tip of her chin, and the confidence she had answered him with earlier fizzled like an Alka-Seltzer dropped into a glass of water. Why the hell was he looking at her in that way?

"New employee?"

While looking at him face-to-face and not just stealing glances at his profile, she could see the razor-sharp angle of his nose and cheekbones. His eyes were striking and dark, but lined with red and framed by bluish circles. And for a second, this man who was clearly someone powerful, influential, looked fragile. Like all he needed was a hug and a pint of ice cream.

Jess shook her head. "No," she said, quieter this time. The muscles in her cheeks slackened along with his and her mouth tipped into a frown. "I'm here to collect my sister's things. She worked here."

Jess watched carefully as emotion flashed across his eyes, which glittered with recognition. His mouth tipped higher. Could this be him? The man from the e-mails? For a moment, Jess thought he might hug her. Or cry. There was something brittle in that expression. But like tempered glass, even if this man shattered, he would never break. He would self-destruct on the inside but the outside, the framework would still hold up. He reminded Jess of Sam in a lot of ways—the white-collar version.

As quickly as that expression was noticed, it was also gone. Faded back to the numb man beside her who simply stared ahead as the elevator climbed. "Good luck to you," he said quietly. But even as the doors opened and Jess stepped out into Holtz's lobby, she could feel the mysterious man's eyes locked onto her.

Jess turned, not sure what was coming over her. She made eye contact with him once more and just before the elevator doors closed, the word slipped beyond her lips. "Master?" she asked quietly.

Shock resonated across his face just as the doors closed.

# 19

One of the worst cards you can be dealt on a case is a hoarder. And thankfully, Dr. Richard Brown was anything but. His place was minimalist, lacking any sort of knickknacks. And it was quite clean for a bachelor. No crusted baked beans left on the stove. No empty beer cans scattered across the floor. Nope, this guy had it together. Either that, or he simply was never home enough to cause a mess. Knowing how demanding a doctor's schedule could be, Sam figured it was the latter.

A low, rumbling growl gurgled from deep within Sam's stomach and he tugged his phone out of his back pocket. Almost one o'clock. And they hadn't taken a lunch break yet. If he didn't eat—and soon—his belly would no doubt be screaming at him in no time.

A couple of crime-scene guys were sweeping the apartment with Sam and Matt—looking for the things that they wouldn't necessarily pick up on. Ideally, he would have had Jess there, too, to document the place, but he certainly wasn't dragging her out of bed for this. And he could only hope that these rumors of her party were just that. Rumors and nothing more.

And if they *weren't* just rumors, he needed to discover what the hell the entry ticket item was this time.

Sam wandered around the doctor's den, noting the black polished furniture and sparse art that decorated the walls. An entertainment center took up most of the wall across from the couch. On the shelves were four different types of gaming consoles.

When he tugged the latex glove higher onto his wrist, the rubber caught some of Sam's arm hair with a pull at the roots. A curse hissed through his teeth as he let go of the glove's edge and it snapped against his skin. Shaking it off, he opened the top two drawers under the television. Xbox games. PlayStation games. The third drawer down held movies. And other than *Animal House,* not good movies either. The side shelving unit consisted mostly of books: *Depression and Cardiovascular Surgery. Tort Reform in the United States. Heart Disease and Western Medicine Hurdles.* Wait—Sam snatched the book from the shelf, flipping through it. What the hell . . . why did he know this book? There was only one other person he knew who read this sort of shit and the realization slammed into him like a vial of frigid water being injected into his veins. Oh, no . . . Sam flipped through the pages, shaking the book to see if anything was tucked inside. The hope that flared within him came crashing back down when nothing was there. Could it be a coincidence? Both Cass and Dr. Brown *were* involved in medicine. It was more than possible that they would read the same books. It didn't necessarily mean anything. He handed the book to one of the crime-scene technicians. "Could you bag this and run it for prints . . . or DNA . . . really anything."

The girl nodded and slipped it into a bag before rushing to the other end of the room. On the next shelf over were a small handful of framed photographs. Richard with Marc, holding up beers and laughing. It looked like the yearly Oktoberfest they held in South Portland. Another from when he was a boy—

with maybe his parents? And another of a larger group . . . about seven or so people. It was sad, really—a man who had few friends, no family, no wife. Essentially no one except for his one remaining buddy and fellow doctor. Sam swallowed as the painful truth slammed into his chest. That was exactly his life. He had no one. No parents, no siblings. A few friends whom he could count on one hand . . . but that was it. If he died, who would be there to go through his stuff? To arrange his services? Jess's face flashed into his mind, but he squeezed his eyes shut, pinching his top and bottom lids so tightly together that little beaded stars flooded the darkness. He needed to get her out of here. Hell, she might not be safe in New York either, but at least there she didn't pose a threat to the fuckers responsible for Cass's murder.

His heart danced in his chest. When, and only when, he found the person heading up this drug ring, would Jess be safe. And maybe then, he could focus on getting her to forgive him, not that he was holding his breath for that. The knot that resided in his chest migrated to his throat and he coughed to clear it.

As he focused on the group picture, a toothy grin smiling back at him made that knot freeze and shatter. There, with Richard Brown's arm around her neck, was Cass Walters.

# 20

That was him. That *had* to have been him. Cass's master. Jess had to find a way to get another meeting with that man. A guy like that had secrets. And most likely answers, too.

It was easy enough for Jess to get into Cass's office. A girl sitting near the front buzzed her through when she said she was there to pick up Cass's things. Jess felt a knot the size of a walnut lodge in her throat as she walked in. Just what was in store for her to find here? Her sister wasn't possibly stupid enough to hide fake passports and stacks of money at her office, was she?

Jess scanned the area as the receptionist buzzed her through the glass doors. They were plexiglass; hard and nearly impossible to break through.

Her eyes followed the outline of the door's molding to a hefty alarm system and the receptionist was blocked with that same plexiglass from people as they stepped off the elevator. All guests had to be buzzed in or they needed a key card to get through. Unease skittered along Jess's skin like a chilled breeze. In fact, this would actually be the perfect place for Cass to hide something. Only hell—what else was there to hide? Stacks of money, dummy passports, skeleton keys . . . they were all in her floorboards at home. What else could she possibly be harboring?

*Some sort of relationship with our victim, for starters,* Jess thought.

"Jess." A quiet voice came from behind her, and when she slowly turned, she was met with Zooey's warm smile.

"Zooey, hey," Jess said.

Zooey tilted her head, her dark bob fanning out across her shoulder. "You never called."

Jess sighed. "I know, I'm sorry. Things here got crazy. Trying to clean out Cass's home and I just started this new job with the local police department. . . ."

Zooey scrunched her face. "Really? Does that mean you're sticking around for a while?"

"No—yeah . . . I don't know. Probably not, but I could really use some paychecks for the time I *am* here."

Jess shook the fog from her brain. "Anyway, I'd still love to grab coffee sometime. Maybe next week?"

The tension melted from Zooey's face as she nodded. "Yeah, I'd like that." Her red lips plumped with her smile. "So, what are you doing here?"

"I figured I should come collect the rest of Cass's things."

Zooey's smile drifted, sliding into a downward slope. "I could have done that for you," she offered quietly.

"I know, but I didn't have anything else to do today," Jess said with a shrug.

"Well, come on. I'll show you to her desk." Zooey led the way to a series of cubicles near the front desk, stopping in front of one and placing her hand on the corner particleboard. "Here you go. She didn't keep much here. Most days she was in her private lab. It's the first door on your left over there." Zooey pointed down a small hallway off a break area next to them. "And I'll be right over here if you need anything."

Jess did her best to return the smile. "Thank you," she said quietly. "It was nice seeing you again." Zooey nodded and made her way back over to her cubicle. One by one, Jess pulled the drawers open. Meticulously clean—as always with Cass's belongings. Flapping open a large tote bag Jess remembered to bring last minute, she emptied the top drawer inside. It basically consisted of a Rolodex, a couple of pens, and a Wite-Out stick. The next drawer had similar office supplies. For a girl who was neck deep into something scandalous that involved stacks of cash, her sister kept a pretty damn boring life. The final drawer held files. Not a huge stack—just one manila envelope a couple inches thick. Jess thumbed through the papers and one logo for Mercy Hospital caught her eye. Her entire body tensed as pins and needles coursed through her bloodstream. With a quick glance over her shoulder, Jess leaned into the paper. An invoice, it appeared. The short breath caught in Jess's throat and the paper wrinkled as her hold on it tightened. The signature at the bottom was *Dr. Richard Brown.*

*So, what?* she thought. So, her sister had paperwork with Dr. Brown's signature. They both worked in medicine. . . . That wasn't anything to bat an eye at.

Shoving the paper back into the file, she swept her gaze around the near-empty office once more before stuffing the file into her tote bag.

Pausing, she lifted up a small pen tray at the edge of the bottom drawer. There, underneath, was a plain business card. And even before she reached for it, Jess knew in the base of her soul it was something of importance. She carefully lifted it, and in the most basic font, with the Mercy Hospital logo, was Dr. Richard Brown's business card and information.

Jess's breath hitched, and she held her inhalation with expanded lungs as she flipped the card over. Scrolled in a messy cursive were the words "Call me."

A flash of tingly heat spread along Jess's body, and she

shoved the business card in her bag before she could pause too long to think about what she was doing.

The rest of the desk was empty, so she hiked the bag onto her shoulder and headed down the hall to Cass's lab.

The room was dark as Jess entered and the musky smell sat heavy in her chest. Almost as though this door had not been opened since Cass's passing; all the stagnant air just sat there with no circulation.

Jess forged into the room, being sure to leave the door cracked open slightly. On the off chance that someone came in.

There was a ton of counter space with various microscopes and sciencey-looking devices. In the center of the room was an island with a sink and several basins inside. *God, Cass was smart,* Jess thought as heat flushed her cheeks. Way smarter than she had ever been. Looking around the room, Jess barely knew what the hell any of these things were.

As she circled the small laboratory, she dragged a hand over the smooth counters. There was another stack of papers on the other end of the room, away from the sink, and Jess dove for them. Flipping through as quickly as she could, she paused, recognizing Cass's handwriting immediately. Drug trials, it looked like. Or something. Panic seized Jess's throat—was it illegal to take these? If she was caught, could she be arrested? Clenching her eyes shut, she shoved them into the tote bag. Maybe she could plead ignorance. All rational thought was out the window, and in the last couple of days, nothing was more important than finding the truth. Without the truth, Cass's whole existence would remain a mystery. And Jess would live on as the girl who knew nothing true about her own sister. She couldn't be that girl. Even if it was only after Cass's death, Jess had to *know*.

On a shelf above a series of petri dishes was a framed picture of Cass, Jess, and their parents. The picture was taken when she was five. The photographer came to the house with a whole caravan of tripods and lights and backdrops and even way back then, Jess was enchanted by the setup. It was magical; like their entire living room was transformed into a whole other space. Grief squeezed her lungs, and Jess clamped her eyes shut, tucking the frame gently into the bag. Beside that frame was a smaller one of Cass and Jess at her high school graduation and next to that one was a four-by-six frame of Cass with what looked like a group of friends. A group of friends that Jess had never seen before. She gripped the frame between her fingers. It wasn't the sort of group image that Jess had with her friends from college. It looked more formal than that; no hugging, no beers high in the air. She scanned the faces for any sign of someone she recognized.

"No." The word came out as a breathy whisper and despite the stuffy office, a chill ran down Jess's spine. Next to Cass was Dr. Brown. He had his arm draped over her shoulder and the other arm around Zooey's hip next to him. At the other end of the group was Dr. Moore. In the background, it looked like a lot of people were milling about—like a picnic. If Mercy Hospital was a client, it made sense that Cass would befriend some of the doctors, right? That wasn't so weird. Maybe she could even ask Zooey about it over coffee?

As Jess gulped, the knot stuck in the middle of her throat. Something felt off. Shaking the unease away, she tucked the frame into the bag and grabbed any other loose items she could find.

As Jess pushed the door open slowly, the hinges creaked like a warning to the world. She had every right to be here and collect her sister's things, Jess said to herself. Whatever this anxiety was, it had to be residual fear over what was in Cassandra's bedroom. Nothing more.

Jess hiked the bag higher, clutching her hand around the straps. A few more steps and she could be out of here and get home to make sure Dane wasn't going through her sister's stuff.

She turned the corner and yelped as she nearly ran into Gilles. As she placed a hand to her chest, her pounding heart thrummed against her palm in rhythm with each rapid beat. "Oh my God," she said to no one particular.

"So very sorry," he said quietly, the light accent flowing gently from his lips. "Ms. Walters—have you had time to consider my offer?"

Jess resisted the urge to step back beneath the man's gaze and, instead, smoothed her hair over the bandage on her head. It wasn't a large bandage, thank God. The absolute last thing she wanted a stranger to see was her vulnerability. Especially a stranger who made her cower like a puppy under a rolled-up newspaper. "Gilles, hello. I actually just dropped it off with the estate lawyer today. I'm sure you won't mind giving me a little time to discuss it with him, right?" Jess inclined her chin higher to match his gaze and shot him a smile that was friendly, but all business.

"Oh, of course."

"You're taking offers on Cass's house?" Zooey blurted out, her body stretched out from behind her cubicle.

"Um, well, initially no, but Gilles came to the house and insisted I take a look at his offer—"

"I would be interested in Cass's house, too," Zooey continued, and her voice pierced through the quiet office. She cleared her throat, bringing the volume down a couple notches. "Cass talked about selling it to me once already. She knew I was interested."

Jess eyed Gilles and then flickered back and forth between the two. "Um, okay. Well, I haven't made any decisions yet. So . . ." How well did she and Gilles know each other? They worked together, obviously. Did he know Zooey was interested in the house when he put his offer in?

Zooey beamed at this and stood straighter. Did she send a look to Gilles or was Jess totally imagining that? "Great! I'll get you an offer. Soon!"

Gilles snorted, rolled his eyes, and slid a hand slowly into his pocket, looking back to Jess. "Yes. And when you reject that offer, you and I will have lunch and iron out the details."

Jess gulped, heat flaring across her face. How the hell did she become the rope in this little tug-o-war match? "Well, I might not even sell. I might just keep the house—"

"That would be ridiculous," Gilles snapped. His eyes widened and an immediate look of regret softened his features. "I apologize. I've had a busy week. Take your time and go over my offer with your lawyer." He offered a final smile before turning and walking down the hall.

Jess offered Zooey a shrug and a half smile. "He made a really generous offer, Zooey," she said quietly.

Zooey's smirk climbed higher, crinkling bright eyes behind her glasses. "You'd be surprised at how generous I can be, too. There are hardly any large homes on the peninsula anymore. My grandmother always taught me that you can't go wrong investing in real estate."

But it didn't feel like Zooey was even talking to Jess at this point. Her gaze landed somewhere beyond her shoulder and her voice sounded far away, as though she were drowning in a sea of her own thoughts.

That hollow, uneasy feeling that had been planted in Jess's stomach the day Gilles came to her home was sprouting into a growing beast inside of her. Nothing about this felt right. That house was not worth the kind of money people kept throwing at her. "Okay, well, you know how to find me," Jess offered quietly, and with a final wave, she slipped out the door and onto the elevators.

The ride down to the lobby was several seconds of silent bliss and Jess relished every moment of it. As the doors slid open, a voice she recognized all too well echoed in the cavernous lobby. Sam. Panic slammed into her once more. If he was here, that meant he found something. Something that connected Cass to Dr. Brown.

"Which floor is it on?" he asked, in that rough, graveled voice of his.

Jess lunged for the staircase, slamming her shoulder into the door and ducking below the window. Jess's bag smacked against her hip with each movement. She cringed, a hiss sliding through her clenched teeth, hoping there wouldn't be a bruise there tomorrow.

Her thighs burned with the squat and as she heard two sets of footsteps approach, she lifted slightly higher, peeking through the window. Yep, it was Sam, all right. And Matt. And clutched tightly in Sam's fingers was a search warrant.

# 21

In the short time that Jess was gone, Dane had managed to carry in twelve large boxes that lined the foyer. He hovered over one box, nose buried deep inside as items clattered around. His carpenter jeans slid low on his muscled hips, revealing the sliver of a band from his underwear. Did that—holy shit, was he wearing Armani boxers? This guy knew how to wear some underwear.

Jess snapped her gaze away, finding the home's windows suddenly fascinating.

With a whistle, she shut the door behind her, assessing the various boxes. "What is all this?"

Even though Dane had yet to look up, he didn't seem startled or surprised to see her. A good sign; guilty people jump, right? "Party stuff," he answered, turning his head to look at her. "How was your questioning?"

Jess dropped the tote bag filled with Cass's things at the base of the stairs and flopped her weight onto the banister with a sigh. "Oh, it was fine." Using the tips of her fingers, she pulled back the cardboard flap of the box, finding yards and yards of black fabrics—some thick and heavy, others sheer and silky—inside. She peeked into the next box, which held silver serving platters. "What the—how—what am I supposed to do with all this?" Jess pulled out a sterling silver coffee carafe with one hand, holding up the fabric in the other.

Dane gently took the carafe from her and nestled it back into the box. "Don't touch that," he said quietly with a wink. "That's what I'm here for. The people who come to these parties expect a lot. You can't just throw some frozen appetizers in the oven and be done with it."

Jess opened another box and gasped. Paddles and whips and clamps and Lord knew what else sat in the box. She swallowed and looked up at Dane, who was watching her closely. His breathing deepened and Jess's eyes landed on his chest, which heaved with each exhale. "Will people be using these at the party?" Damn, her voice sounded small. Mousy.

"Of course," he answered.

She met his eyes once more. "Will *you* be using these at the party?"

"Perhaps." His lips tilted. "If I find someone to play with." His voice was barely above a whisper and it sent Jess's nerve endings on high alert.

"So, you don't have a . . . ?" Her mind swung to Cass. "Oh, right. Of course. Cass was—"

"No," Dane answered sharply. "Your sister and I . . . we never . . . she was not mine." His voice cracked with the admission and Jess narrowed her eyes at him.

"But you said—"

"I said we were good friends. That is all."

This guy was such a mystery. On the surface he seemed simple. A blue-collar worker who enjoyed a little kink. In actuality? Jess was learning daily that there were so many more layers to him. He wore Armani underwear, for Christ's sake. He knew about sterling silver and lobster puffs. A staggered sigh caught in Jess's chest. "But—why? It seems like you really cared about her . . ."

"We needed different things." Dane held her gaze and his eyes lit like fire. Not once did they waver from her, but yet she felt them all over her body.

He moved closer, taking the fabric from her hand and dropping it back into the box. His breath was hot as he looked down at Jess and she shivered at the way he made her feel. It took everything within her not to step back from his overpowering presence.

"Did you get my gift yesterday?"

She tilted her chin, making an effort to stand taller. "The dress? That was from you?"

He nodded. "You can't be the hostess without proper attire. No BDSM hostess ever arrived in jeans." His face transformed from heated to playful and as his hand extended, tugging on the hem of her shirt playfully, Jess's body tensed. She gave an inward sigh. Jesus, he unnerved her.

Jess shook her head. "I can't accept it. I could never afford Jimmy Choos and Vera Wang . . ." Her voice broke off. "I'll have to find something else."

"Consider it a housewarming gift." He bent back down and Jess was flashed the tightest ass—Jesus maybe even tighter than Sam's and that seemed nearly impossible. She averted her eyes to the ceiling instead, pretending to be suddenly fascinated with the ceiling fan.

"Tell me something," Jess said, leaning against the wall and folding her arms. "How does a plumber manage to afford such an expensive gown?"

"Sweetheart." He stood and looked at her through thick lashes. "I'm far from just a plumber. I own several construction businesses up and down Maine."

"But then why did you fix up this hou—"

"Cass was a friend. I took care of her personally."

"Because you liked her," Jess added quickly for him.

"Because I liked her," he nodded. Then, stalking toward Jess like a lion advancing on an antelope at the watering hole, he paused, inhaling deeply and hooking a finger under Jess's chin. "But she and I were never meant to be," he whispered. Tapping her chin, he pushed off the wall and moved back to the boxes. "Get your mind out of the gutter, kid," he added with a wink.

"I'm about to throw my first-ever kink party," Jess laughed. "My mind is trapped in the gutter for at least the next twelve hours."

Dane's eyes sparkled. "If I'm at all lucky, you'll like it there enough to stay a while."

"In the gutter?"

He nodded. "Oh, yeah. It's dirty—but the greatest treasures are found amidst the trash."

Jess cleared her throat and tugged on the edge of her shirt. "So, what are we serving at this fancy party?"

Dane's smirk twitched once more before he went about pulling out the various items and placing them on the coffee table. "The usual. Light fare, easy to eat and not too messy. Apples and brie, butternut squash soup shooters, lobster puffs, et cetera. The caterers should be here in about an hour to begin setting up. I typically lay all of the items out for them and they make good use of it all."

"Caterers?" Jess squeaked. "H-how much does this thing cost?" Jess had about three hundred bucks in her bank account and that had to last her until the first paycheck from the police department came in.

Dane paused, looking up at her beneath yards of sheer black fabric. "It's covered," he said quietly.

"Dane—I can't let you . . ."

"No, Jess. Not by me. Though I have been known to throw a few good parties of my own. They actually paid Cass rent for using the space for the parties. It's all covered. You'll get paid at the end of the night."

Unease slid over her damp skin. "Who are 'they' exactly?"

Dane's smirk slipped higher across his face. "It's so easy to forget what a newbie you are to the scene."

Jess gently picked up a serving platter from the box and walked it over to the coffee table. "I'm not a newbie to the scene. Because I don't plan on *joining* the scene."

Surprise flashed momentarily over Dane's face. "You don't? Then why the hell are you throwing this party? Cancel and be done with it." He paused what he was doing and, judging from the rigid way he was standing there, it seemed he expected Jess to stop as well.

"I told you—I wanted to meet some of Cass's friends."

"These people aren't her friends," he said quietly. Dane's smirk dropped and he held Jess's gaze until she was shifting in place. "Stop fidgeting," he demanded. "You're going to stick out immediately at this party." He shook his head and moved to one of the other boxes. "And if you're not looking to join the lifestyle, then the last thing you want to do is stand out."

"Why? Doesn't everyone come with a partner?"

Dane was in front of her in a second and Jess shivered as she looked up at him. It was the first time she felt just how massive he was before her. He was wide, muscular, and well over six feet tall. He hovered over her as though he *knew* how intimidating he was and she swore she saw a glimpse of a smile haunt his lips. "We don't arrive with partners. We arrive as masters. And we leave with submissives," he replied coolly.

*Masters.* There was that damn word again. It sat in her mind like cold, bitter coffee and Cass's e-mails flashed beside it.

"Does everyone? Leave with . . ." She couldn't bring herself to use the word.

". . . submissives. Say it, Jessica. It's not a bad word."

"Not everyone leaves with a submissive, do they?"

With an exhale, it appeared as though all tension melted from Dane's body. "I suppose not. But most do. If they haven't already fulfilled their needs at the party, that is."

"What? *Here?*"

"Oh, yes. I suggest you lock any rooms you don't want people to enter." He dragged a hand along the back of the leather sectional. "Though most people are not too shy about enjoying some pleasure out in the open."

"Oh God." Jess sank to the couch, lowering her head to her hands.

"I didn't think you'd be such a prude."

"Not wanting people fucking on my couch doesn't make me a prude! Jesus."

"It does in my world."

"Well, your world is fucked."

"Literally," he answered quietly.

Dane said nothing else, but when Jess managed a glance up from her hands, he actually seemed—what? Hurt? Something. His eyes never left her and she could feel that gaze searing into her like a laser.

"Why don't you get dressed, Jess. I'll finish with this until the caterers arrive and I'll send your makeup stylist upstairs when she gets here."

"Stylist?"

"Cass never held a party without professional hair and makeup."

Who was this woman? Certainly not her sister. Not the buttoned up molecular biologist whom Jess had to fight tooth and nail to even buy her first pair of heels. The girl who had never colored her hair until after college. Jess could barely remember a time that her sister wasn't in cardigans, slacks, and a ponytail. Christ, she was *born* a soccer mom. Or so Jess had thought.

"What time do you expect the stylist to arrive?" Jess asked quietly as she headed for the stairs.

His smile curved. And something in the victorious way he grinned set Jess's nerves on edge. "Sometime within the hour."

"Then shouldn't I wait to dress after my styling is done?"

He shrugged with a small twitch of his shoulder. "They typically prefer you to be dressed first. So that nothing gets smudged while putting the dress on. But, hey—it's your choice. You're a big girl."

Heat lashed through Jess's veins, burning like a shot of whiskey. *What a condescending asshat.* "I'll just put on a button-down shirt. Something that's easy to slip off." Her voice took on a husky lilt to it that was entirely unintentional. She peeked at him from under the dark feathers of her lashes to find him standing in the exact same position. He was controlling. Arrogant. And his strong mouth hinted at a smile.

"I approve of anything that's easy to slip off," he said, studying her for a moment that felt like it lasted an eternity.

Jess's throat was instantly dry as he dropped that bomb between them. It ticked with implication. And the air thickened with succulent, velvety sentience. Surely she was imagining it, she told herself. But as Dane's gaze dipped the length of her body, excitement raced in her veins. She could feel Wild Walters taking hold of her for the first time in years. No. She was not that self-destructive girl anymore. Not for ages. Fuck, what was it about this town? Did they put something in the water?

"I have a boyfriend," she blurted out, then cringed at the lie.

Dane looked taken aback for all of a moment before quickly gaining his composure again. "You do?" he said, and though Jess knew he had been surprised by the admission, his voice was still in complete control.

"Yes . . . no . . . well, sort of."

He sauntered over, leaning one hand onto the banister. "Well." He dipped his chin and though not once touching her, she could feel him on every part of her body. "When you figure out the answer to that, please let me know."

I almost walked out on you. When you ordered
me to undress, spread my legs, and drop my hands

to the floor . . . I literally almost walked out your door and never looked back. But then I stopped myself and explored what it was about your wanting to view my everything that I found so intimidating. What was so bad about one's master knowing my every curve? My every birthmark? Whether or not the stance was degrading was up to me and how I chose to do it.

I undressed slowly, keeping my chin high and my eyes on you. And for a few seconds at least, I felt confident. Like another woman entirely and it was as though I floated out of my body and was watching the experience from above. And as you circled me like a shark would circle its prey, that confidence flew away, like a bird out of a cracked-open window. My legs quivered as I stood there completely vulnerable. Naked to you. To the world. And all the emotion swelled inside of me. I didn't know why I did so, but I cried. My tears streamed from my eyes, pooling on the floor below me.

It felt good. Surprisingly amazing to allow myself to feel so exposed. You froze, staring with shocked eyes, but said nothing. I tried to swallow the tears at first—pretend it wasn't happening. But then, you scooped me into your arms and cradled me until every tear had drained from my body.

And the moments that followed—I don't know that I've known pleasure like that ever. In my entire life. The feather that trailed a path all over my body—down my back and over the area where I most needed your touch. I quaked with the gentlest brush and a shiver chased the feather.

And when you tied black silk around my eyes, though the world around me went dark, my soul had never been so light.

I still don't know that I am cut out for this, Master. And I doubt that any of your previous subs have cried when they stripped down for the first time . . . but I ask you to be patient with me. I'm not ready to give up yet.

—Your one and only, Cass

The door creaked open, and Jess's heart spring boarded off her chest, landing in her throat. She pushed the button, turning the iPad off, and shoved it beneath the cushion of Cass's reading chair. Dane's eyes followed to where her fingers nestled between her thigh and the cushion and he smirked in that annoyingly arrogant and yet gloriously beautiful way again.

"Ms. Walters." His voice rattled in the way one's does when you haven't spoken in a while. "Your stylist is here."

Jess rose from the chair; her long button-down shirt was almost a nightdress of sorts and covered the cutoff denim shorts she wore underneath. Dane's gaze swept her bare legs. Master sure sounded an awful lot like Dane, she thought, narrowing her gaze at the man before her.

"Send her up," Jess answered quietly.

Dane ignored her, entering the room with a glass of champagne and set it onto the mirrored nightstand. "To help you relax a bit. Drink up." His eyes locked on her, inexpressive. Though seemingly a nice act—something in the way he set it down in front of her and demanded her to drink caused her skin to crawl. It was polite to bring someone a drink, wasn't it? Then why did she feel as though taking a sip of that champagne would be accepting an invitation from Dane that she wasn't quite ready for.

The effervescent alcohol beckoned her and she desperately wanted to sip the sweet and bubbly beverage. Jess loved champagne—it reminded her of her parents' parties when she used to slip into the basement, grab a bottle of Verdi, and sneak out to Sam's. They would drink it straight from the bottle and lick it off each other's necks. It was even sweeter off his tongue.

"Thank you," Jess said, lifting the glass and raising it toward Dane. "Are you not going to share a drink with me? Isn't it customary to clink the hostess?" Jess swallowed, unsure of why exactly she was flirting with this man who exuded trouble.

Dane smirked and raised a bottle of beer. "I'm afraid I'm way ahead of you."

"I'm pretty good at playing catch-up." She tapped the edge of her champagne glass to his beer bottle. With a gulp, she swallowed almost the entire glass of champagne quickly. She had a feeling if she was to make it through the night, alcohol would be necessary. Pinching the edge of the glass, she handed it back to Dane, whose eyes widened. *Ha, take that, big man.* "Thanks for the drink," she said with a wink. "When you bring the stylist up, could you bring me a scotch instead?" She dismissed Dane with a little hand wave and spun back for the window.

She was dying to turn around and see his expression, but forced herself to remain focused. It was so much hotter to ignore him. A raspy chuckle came from the doorway. "Of course."

At least if Jess drank, it would be on *her* terms, not Dane's. If this world was all about control, then she sure as hell was going to maintain hers—at least when it came to Dane.

# 22

Jess blinked at her reflection. Jesus, who was that woman staring back at her? She looked elegant, refined. Chic. Her eyes flicked to the almost finished glass of Chivas on the nightstand and she desperately wanted to finish it off, but the fear of smearing her lipstick after Yves spent so long perfecting it won out. How was she expected to eat or drink anything tonight?

She paced the room, which was admittedly not the easiest thing to do in the form-fitting gown Dane had chosen for her. She ran a hand down the side seam and sighed. Jesus, it was beautiful and quite easily the sexiest thing she'd ever had on her body—and that included Sam.

It was a black Vera Wang backless lace illusion-styled gown that showed just enough skin in all the right places. The fact that underneath the dress Jess was wearing Victoria's Secret panties that were five for twenty bucks seemed to cheapen the whole damn ensemble. A dress like this deserved La Perla.

A wicked grin turned up her lips and when she caught another glance in the mirror, she didn't recognize herself. Again.

Wiggling out of her cotton thong, she tossed it into the small pile of clothes in Cass's closet. The idea of walking around this party commando beneath a five-thousand-dollar dress made Jess wet with excitement. It made her wish she could text Sam after the party.

Jess lifted the glass of scotch to her lips, then before she could take the sip, remembered her makeup and set it back down again.

"Go ahead, honey," Yves said, re-entering from the bathroom. "You're wearing the long-lasting lip color. You could polish chrome with your lips and still hold that rouge." She packed the rest of her supplies and slipped out with a final nod.

*Polish chrome.* Well, there was a visual. Jess snatched the glass, the ice clinking against her teeth as she finished the amber liquid in a gulp. It burned on the way down—burned in the best way and she inhaled through clenched teeth, enjoying the sting.

"Feels great, doesn't it?" a deep voice said from the doorway.

Jess swiveled to find Dane there. Again. Staring at her with a heated look. Jess cleared her throat, lowering the empty glass. "Nothing better than a scotch on the rocks."

Dane tilted his head back and forth. "I don't know if I can agree with that sentiment. I love all kinds of things—a crisp beer, a spicy wine, a piña colada—"

Jess's laugh erupted. Even if she wanted to, she wouldn't have been able to hold that one in. "Piña colada? I wouldn't have pegged you for an umbrella-in-the-drink kind of guy."

"That's what I'm trying to tell you. Everything is circumstantial—when I'm sitting on the beach in Playa del Carmen? There ain't nothing better than a piña colada in hand."

"You're a brave man to admit that," Jess said, arching her brow at him.

"Don't I know it." His voice drifted off and his eyes dipped the length of Jess's gown. "You look stunning," he added. "Just in case I don't get a chance to tell you later."

"Thanks. Though I guess you would know, considering you picked out the whole ensemble."

His lips tilted, though they didn't quite reach his eyes, and he gave a melancholy sigh. His gaze drifted over Jess's shoulder to Cass's reading corner. The room filled with a loaded silence that left unease crawling over Jess's recently buffed and exfoliated skin.

"Well," she said, adding a small cough to get his attention. "Is there anything I should expect for tonight?"

Dane snapped out of it quickly and looked back to Jess. "Yes," he replied. "Guests should start arriving any minute now. As the hostess, you should not come down until you've heard that doorbell chime at least five times."

"But as the hostess, shouldn't I gree—"

"Do you want my advice or not?" His voice sliced right through her like a blade and she snapped her mouth shut in response, nodding. "All right, then. Five doorbells. Come downstairs, greet everyone with the European double-cheek kiss. Don't offer to get anyone drinks—that's what the caterers are for. And the subs. You can differentiate the dominants in the room because their masks will match their scarves. If a dom is courting you, he—or she—will hand you a handkerchief. If you accept the offer—"

Jess snorted, and Dane's mouth snapped shut, clenched. His gaze bore into hers, and Jess felt her face flushing under his chastising glare. "If you accept the offer, you will take the handkerchief and dab the corners of his or her mouth, then put the scarf or handkerchief somewhere on your outfit. Somewhere visible. If you do not accept, dab your own mouth, graciously say thank you, and hand it back to him."

Jess chuckled. "Is this standard in the BDSM world? Hankie exchanges during masquerade balls?"

"It is more than standard actually. Typically, in the more

club-like environment, subs all wear dog collars and doms clip them with leashes."

Bile rose to Jess's throat. Up until that point, it had all been so silly. Suddenly, though, being chained like a dog didn't feel so frivolous.

The front doorbell chimed and Dane slipped his mask over his chiseled features. Turning to leave, he offered Jess a tiny dip of his head. She snatched onto his sleeve, tugging him closer. She didn't want to be left alone anymore. Safety in numbers, perhaps? Or maybe she trusted Dane even though all sense and rationality told her she shouldn't. "Wait—" she whispered, breathless. "I-is there anything else I should know?"

His lips turned at the corner and he placed a cool hand on top of hers. "You'll be fine," he answered. "You're a natural at this."

That's exactly what she was afraid of.

He slipped his arm from her grasp and held up his palm, with five fingers spread. "Five doorbells," he whispered.

Jess was left in Cass's room—living Cass's secret life and trembling. "This better be worth it," she said to no one.

She clicked off the bedside lamp, stealing a peek out the window. A couple walked up to her door—the woman in a floor-length red satin gown and the man in a tuxedo. Jess backed away from the window and ran a palm down her dress one more time. As if verifying that she was indeed here and a part of this game.

Jitters fluttered through her body. She hated the idea of all these people in Cass's house while she still had so many secrets to protect. Rushing for the door, she closed it as quietly as she could, locking herself inside the bedroom. She needed to split up the hidden items. That way if someone did come in here looking for anything, they wouldn't find a jackpot of everything. Rushing to the floorboard, she lifted the velvet bag out. The passport and some of the money could go in the air vent.

Digging to the bottom of the bag, she felt for the skeleton key, holding it up to the slice of moonlight coming in through the window. The silver was tarnished and dull. She slipped the key into her bra. This way at least *one* item would never be found.

The rest of the money could stay in the floorboards. The iPad was currently tucked under the seat cushion. Jess ran to the seat, unzipping the pillow cover. Shit. If anyone so much as felt the cushion, they'd know it was there immediately. Jess looked around the room.

On the edge of Cass's dresser was a sewing kit and she grabbed the little scissors from inside, running back to the seat. She unzipped the seat cover and sliced a gash into the center of the foam, making the cut large enough to slip the tablet into the actual foam of the cushion. Zipping the cover back up, Jess felt around and even sat on the chair. The only way someone would find it would be if they ripped the seat open. "Oh, jeez." There was an ink stain on one side of the cushion—how her sister ever lived with that stain was beyond Jess. The girl couldn't even leave a crumb on her counter, let alone a stain on her upholstery. Jess sighed to herself and flipped the cushion, so the stain-free side was faceup.

On the table beside the chair was the book Sam had been snooping at the other night. She completely forgot about it with all the craziness over the past week. Not to mention the fact that she avoided Cass's room as much as possible. Jess lifted it, opening the cover to get a glance at what he saw. Several photographs fluttered from the book into her lap. She lifted the five-by-seven black-and-white images and a cold hand seized her heart. The images were of *her.* Long-lens shots of her coming and going into her Brooklyn apartment. She flipped through them, throat closing more and more. Jess looked over each shoulder, feeling suddenly very aware of her surroundings. The third image was her in her bra, changing in front of her window—the curtains were almost closed, but there was a little opening in which you could just barely make out Jess's figure. Her hand trembled and she slammed the pictures back into the book, throwing it onto the table.

Who was following her? And *why?* Did Cass have surveillance put on Jess when she moved? That seemed doubtful. Cass sometimes played with the line of what was acceptable, but she never crossed it so blatantly. Jess's eyes wandered back to the closet. Sam must have seen these pictures the other night. Why would he keep it a secret?

Another doorbell chimed through the house. Shit, how many was that? Three, four? Minutes later, it chimed again. Jess stood on shaky knees. She'd figure out the pictures soon . . . get them analyzed down at the station for prints or anything that could help shed some light. Grabbing the book, she rushed to the closet, putting it on the highest shelf under some of Cass's shoes. And she would certainly be asking Sam about his knowledge of the images.

Her camera in the corner caught her eye and she felt that familiar tug; the itch to grab it and document this night . . . this masquerade. She was pretty sure that something like that would get her banned forever, though.

Another bell chimed and though Jess had lost count ages ago, it seemed as though enough people were here to justify her entering the party. Jess made her way down the stairs, careful with each step. She was used to wearing heels—especially back in her younger days. Though those heels were typically platform with chunky bases. Not the delicate extra three-and-a-half inches that Mr. Choo awarded her here.

A male caterer with long blond hair stood at the base of the steps. It was the sort of hair that beckoned you to run your fingers through it. It looked soft and silky and Jess gripped the banister harder simply by looking at him. Christ and he wasn't even one of the attendees at the party. *Get a fucking grip, Jess.*

The caterer turned toward her, holding out a hand for her to step down.

She swallowed, graciously taking it and offering him a small smile. "Thank you."

"Of course, Mademoiselle Pas Sûr," he replied, bowing his head. A bow? Seriously? Jess abstained from rolling her eyes. Jesus, what were they, in the Middle Ages? The "help" had to bow and curtsey at her entrance?

"Pas Sûr?" she repeated, looking behind her. She put her hand to her chest. "No, you're mistaken, I'm—"

"Mademoiselle," the man interrupted, "the party is anonymous. Monsieur Punir gave us your title for the evening." His French accent was beautiful even when he wasn't speaking in his native language.

She stilled and an icy chill replaced her blood. That frigid feeling flowed through her whole body, down to her toes. "Monsieur Punir?" Cass's e-mail flooded her mind—Master had mentioned a Monsieur Punir as the man who introduced him to Cass.

"Yes, miss," the man said, nodding toward Dane.

Jess's jaw clenched as her teeth gritted together. Not the master apparently, but the matchmaker.

"And, could you tell me—what does *pas sûr* mean?"

"*Pas sûr* est, ehm—foggy."

"Foggy?" Jess repeated. "Like—the weather? Misty?"

"Ehm, non, non. Foggy as in, uh, unsure."

Ahhhh. Unsure. Because her status was undecided here, perhaps? "And *Monsieur Punir*—what does that mean?"

"Punish. Discipline."

"Oui, merci," Jess said, offering the man a smile. She raised her gaze to Dane's. He met her eyes from the middle of the party, where he was sipping a glass of champagne with the couple she had seen enter earlier. He lifted his glass to her, those full lips curving into a smile from beneath his mask.

In the foyer, there was a small table set up and an elegant-looking woman in a little black dress. Nothing near as fancy as what Jess wore, but it was tailored to perfection and made of quality material. She had a clipboard in one hand and an ornately carved ebony box beside her.

Jess leaned over her shoulder. Inside the box were several pads. She lifted one out, studying it. "Prescription pads?"

"Yes, mademoiselle," the woman answered. "Today's entrance ticket." Jess nodded, dropping the prescription pad back into the box.

"Yes, of course." Jess lifted her chin as though she knew of the plan all along.

"As always, we will place the items in the basement after the party. Or if you would prefer them in the safe, we can do that, too."

Jess stilled. Cass had a safe? She vaguely remembered seeing one in the back corner on her first night in the house. "Um, the basement would be fine, thank you. So, then, you know the code for the safe? The one in the basement?"

The woman tilted her head at Jess, eyes narrowing just a touch before she offered a friendly smile. "Yes, in the basement. Monsieur Punir knows the codes; I'm sure he would be happy to help."

Dane knew about the safe? Well, she supposed that made sense since he was helping set up all these parties. After all, he knew the code to the keypad on the closet. An image of the skeleton key popped into her mind—could that be? It didn't seem likely. Didn't most safes have combination locks?

A group of three entered the door and Jess stepped back, lowering her chin. They each handed the woman a pad, which she noted on her clipboard, dropping them into the box. Jess looked around—the party was filling up. There were about fifteen people there. She looked into the box and there on top was a prescription pad with the name Dr. Richard Brown.

# 23

Jess gasped and the woman manning the front table slid her a sideways glance. Her lungs burned and Jess pressed her lips together so tightly that they drained of color despite the long lasting lip color Yves painted her with. Her gaze dropped to Dr. Brown's tablet and back to the three people who had just entered: a woman, a man, and a younger woman who looked to be just barely of drinking age. One of those three had given Dr. Brown's prescription pad as their entry. Could that be something worth killing for? "Do you know who the three who just entered are?" Jess whispered as they walked farther into the party.

"I'm sorry, Mademoiselle Pas Sûr," she said. "Even if I did, I'm not at liberty to talk about patrons of the masquerade. You could ask Monsieur Punir . . . he's the one signing our paychecks and he pretty much knows everyone here."

Jess's gaze darted up into the woman's deep-set brown eyes. "What did you say?" she whispered urgently, sneaking a glance over her shoulder at Dane across the room.

"I said, Monsieur Punir would probably know them."

"No, not that—he . . . he signs your paychecks?" The whisper came out even hoarser than before. A lump formed at the back of Jess's throat and she gulped it down. Dane had said he wasn't the one paying for these parties, that they were paid for by a private donor from the BDSM scene.

"Yeah, he does. Are you—are you okay?" The woman tightened her hold on the clipboard.

Jess gave her a strained smile, rolling her shoulders back. "Fine. Everything's fine." She walked briskly away from the table, pausing at Dane's side. "I heard a funny little rumor just now," Jess said, busying herself by adjusting her dress.

Dane looked momentarily taken aback as he glanced toward the door. "Oh?"

"Apparently, you are a little more involved in the funding of these parties than you let on. And considering you *write the checks,* can I assume you also arrange the entrance ticket?"

"Jess, what are you talking about? Yes, I sign the checks, but it's not my money that goes into this party. I have nothing to do with how to get into—"

Jess threw a hand up, walking away. "We can talk about it later. When you're showing me how to get into the safe."

She walked over to the group that came in with Dr. Brown's prescription pad and offered a welcoming smile. "Good evening, welcome. Thanks so much for coming tonight."

The man took Jess's hand, cradling it gently, and lowered his lips to her knuckles. He wore a *Phantom of the Opera*–style mask that covered half his face. A white scarf dangled from his lapel pocket, Jess noted. Did that mean he did not have a sub yet? If so, who were these women beside him? To his right was a woman in a full-on ball gown that poofed out in an 1800s way. On his other arm was the younger woman. A little mousier from what Jess could tell behind her mask. Shier. And plainer in dress.

"I'm Phantom. Whom do I have the pleasure of meeting?"

Jess allowed her hand to linger in his for all of a moment extra. Never hurts to butter a man up first, right? "I'm—" Shit. What was her name again? Madame something? No. Mademoiselle. "I'm Mademoiselle Pas Sûr," she remembered after mentally stumbling for a moment. "I'm hosting tonight."

Phantom looked momentarily stunned before he collected himself. "Where's Cece?"

The e-mail from earlier once again flashed in Jess's mind. Cece. Cass. Should she tell this man the truth? That Cece had suffered an unfortunate fate? Jess swallowed. No, it was better kept in the dark.

She managed a smile, though it didn't quite crinkle the eyes. "Oh, yes, Cece. She's . . . not around. I'll be filling in for her in the interim."

"Intriguing," he declared in a hushed tone, eyes drifting down to Jess's cleavage.

His gaze crawled over her skin like an ant infestation. "I'm sorry," Jess said, offering her hand to the ball-gown lady. "I didn't catch your name?"

"No," she stated with an icy reserve. "You didn't. I'm Lady Kennebunk."

"Oh! Are you from Kennebunk?"

The woman narrowed her eyes and regarded Jess as though she were a bug to be squashed. "You do not get to ask me that," she snapped. With two fingers, she stroked a scarf draped around her neck. It was silky and held the same brocade pattern as her hoop skirt. Ah, she was also a dominant. And since Jess wasn't wearing a scarf, she assumed Jess was a sub.

"I can ask whatever I want. It is your discretion whether you choose to answer or not."

Lady Kennebunk's mouth tightened like a lemon pucker and Phantom's eyes lit, ripe with challenge.

Through pressed lips, he hummed a noise that sounded slightly contented, and a smirk raised at one corner of his mouth.

"And this here is Lulu," he said, gesturing to the plainer girl beside him. "Lulu, offer Mademoiselle Pas Sûr your hand." She did as he instructed, though her eyes never left the floor.

Jess took the girl's hand, bending to meet her at eye level. "Hi, Lulu. Thank you for coming."

"Look at her, Lulu," he commanded, and her chin rose, gaze meeting Jess's. "It would be lovely for you to get acquainted."

She nodded an acknowledgment of Jess's greeting but said nothing more. A white silk handkerchief was tied around her elegant but simple ponytail, and Jess noted it was the exact same scarf Phantom had tucked into his pocket. Could he be in the market for another sub? Was that even allowed?

Jess didn't necessarily want to get to know these people, but they were somehow connected to her victim. And once they left this party, she had no way of finding out their identities. And there was something quite odd about the threesome—if you could even call them that.

She lifted a finger, gesturing for one of the waitstaff to come over. He placed a tray of champagne before her and she offered one to each of the guests before her. "Could I get a scotch on the rocks instead?" she asked the waiter.

He bowed. "Of course, Mademoiselle Pas Sûr."

"That sounds delightful," Phantom said with a smile. "Make it two."

Then, lifting one of the champagne glasses, he handed it to Lulu. "Pace yourself, love. Go get something to eat so that you don't get too tipsy."

She nodded and scurried off to the buffet of appetizers. Something deep in Jess's gut clenched. Seeing a woman ordered around, being told what to eat and how much to drink, was an awful sight. Even if it was her own choice to enter such a dysfunctional relationship, Jess didn't like it one bit.

She managed to bite her tongue. "And for you, Lady Kennebunk? Champagne? Wine?"

"I would like a cabernet sauvignon, please," she stated in a nasal voice. The waiter nodded in acknowledgment and ran to fetch the drinks.

Phantom couldn't seem to stop assessing Jess. He had dark, nearly black hair that curled around the nape of his neck. She wasn't sure if she were to touch it if it would be greasy or crunchy. Gelled or oiled? Goose pebbles shimmered down her arms. She definitely didn't want to find out either way.

"Is this your first time hosting one of our parties, mademoiselle?"

Jess noted how he shortened her name without her permission. A small but dominating characteristic. And not one she liked. Again, she gnashed her teeth and continued with grace.

"It is." She offered him her most demure smile. "How am I doing thus far?"

"It's a bit early to tell," Lady Kennebunk snipped.

Phantom laughed, the sound bellowing through her living room. "Come now, Lady Kennebunk," he chortled, a dimple forming to the right of his mouth. "I'd say she's doing a fine job." His eyes slid down her body once more. "A fine job, indeed," he added.

"I'm glad to hear it," Jess said, and her breasts hitched higher with her sharp inhalation. "Please let me know if I could possibly help you in any other way." She turned to greet her next guests. She needed this man to talk to her, to find out who brought Dr. Brown's prescription pad—and it was clear the Kennebunk hag wanted nothing to do with Jess. She'd find him again before the night was through. And she'd discover which of them brought Dr. Brown's prescription pad. Hell, maybe it was all of them.

Jess made her way to the door when panic slammed into her chest. He was in a tuxedo. And he had a black mask on, but she still recognized that stance, those shoulders, that body anywhere. Standing before her, next to a woman in leather from breasts to ankles, was Sam.

# 24

Sam's pulse raced, speeding to a level that he was certain he should be hospitalized for. Jesus, could she look any more gorgeous? She wasn't wearing anything super revealing or badass like Mary. She was elegant with a wild edge to the dress that made his pulse race. At first glance it appeared as though her dress was backless, but on closer inspection, it had a sheer, almost hose-like overlay with lace intricately sewn in strategic places. He narrowed his eyes, studying her from across the room. She was talking to that greasy-ass Phantom. The man wore a cape, for Christ's sake. *A cape*. Jesus. He remembered why he stopped coming to these parties in the first place. It was crawling with douchebags. And on the other side of the room was the king of the douchebags himself, Dane.

Jess spun, slowly strolling his way. Her gaze lifted and she froze, making eye contact with him. He grinned at her in a lazy way. In his breast pocket was his signature royal blue pocket scarf and tucked into his back pocket was a small gift box with a royal blue bow on it. His cock stiffened as he imagined tying Jessie's hands to the bedpost with that scarf. Fuck, she'd look hot like that. And she'd be his for the night.

Her neck muscles tightened as she walked over, her eyes flitting to Mary and back again to him. "Good evening."

He dipped his head. "Good evening."

"I don't recall you being on the list," Jess said.

His forehead wrinkled as he did his best to suppress the smirk itching at his lips. "Darling, I'm always on the list," he said quietly. "You, on the other hand, are new to the scene, are you not?"

She seemed momentarily taken aback and shifted her gaze around the room, brushing her hand over the tight curve of her hip. "Yes. Yes, I am. I'm Mademoiselle Pas Sûr." She offered her hand to Sam, which he took in both of his, cupping it possessively. He dropped his lips to her knuckles, momentarily letting his tongue travel over her salty skin. Hell, who knew when he'd have another chance to put his lips on her.

Envy burned in his guts, roiling like greasy takeout. He recognized Dane's role in naming her immediately and he hated that she had been branded by his Parisian theme. That fucker. There was no doubt in his mind now that it had been Dane's idea to continue the party as usual. "Mademoiselle Pas Sûr," he repeated, though the words rang tight in his own head. "I'm Private Dick."

She tutted on an exhale and rolled her eyes. Sam dove his teeth into his bottom lip to stop himself from saying something he'd regret. "You disapprove of my name?"

She pursed her lips in a way he knew to be unsatisfactory. He'd seen Jess that way many times in high school. "Nope," she snapped. "Not at all."

"Good," he said, then leaned in closer, placing a hand on her elbow. "If you were mine, I'd make sure you never rolled your eyes at me again," he whispered.

She shivered beneath his hand and he released her, letting his fingers linger on her forearm a moment longer. "Then it's a good thing I'm *not* yours," she said. But Sam inwardly smiled. She didn't back away; didn't wrench her arm from his hold. All good signs.

"And this," Sam added, holding a hand out to Mary, "is Epoly."

Jess's gaze shifted to his pocket where his scarf rested, then to Epoly—she had a purple scarf tied around her waist that matched her purple and black cat mask. Jess's shoulders relaxed. *That's right, baby,* Sam thought. *Epoly's not mine. She's no threat to you.*

Epoly glanced between the two and smiled, her mask shifting under the grin. "Pleasure to meet you. I didn't realize that you knew our new hostess, Dick."

Jess's gaze darkened and Sam inwardly chuckled. It was good to know he wasn't the only one unnerved when she received attention. She hissed like a cat protecting its meal. "*Dick* and I go way back," she said to Epoly.

The waiter interrupted, handing her a tumbler. As she sipped the scotch, the gold liquid caught in her eyes and matched their sparkling honey color. She stared at Sam over the edge of the glass as she swallowed. "Thank you," she said to the waiter. "Keep them coming, please."

The waiter bowed in acknowledgment and looked to Sam and Mary. "Anything for you?"

"Single malt scotch, please."

"Martini. Dry. Two olives," Epoly said. "Well, I'd love to hang out here, but it looks as though I'm in need of a slave tonight." She twiddled her fingers as a good-bye. "See you around," she added in a sing-song voice as she floated into the crowd.

Jess watched her disappear into the sea of people, then leaned in to Sam. "Your mask," she said. "It's crooked." Concern flashed in her eyes, and she glanced briefly toward the door, where some workers stood over the entry fees. Bending forward at the slightest angle, she acted as though she was straightening his mask, but whispered, her lips dangerously close to his ear, "Meet me in Cass's room. Ten minutes. Be discreet."

Blood thundered in Sam's ears and his cock jumped within his pants, going from flaccid to steel in seconds flat.

She turned, heading straight for Dane, and Sam's fists balled at his sides. Jesus. Did she do this shit simply to get under his skin? Sam's deep breath filled his lungs as he expelled the air slowly with a hiss. She wasn't his to tell who to stay away from. She wasn't his sub—fuck, she wasn't even his girlfriend. She'd made that more than clear the night before. And yet, he wanted more than anything to grasp her by those svelte shoulders and shake some sense into her. This whole damn party was a huge mistake—one that he hoped she didn't end up regretting by the end of the night.

The waiter brushed by, dropping off his scotch, and Sam sipped it, backing up against the banister leading upstairs. It was difficult to sneak up with no one noticing in a party like this. People expected you to have a fucking partner at your side if you slipped away. And they especially didn't expect it right when you first arrived. He made it to the third step up as though he was simply looking for a place to lean.

He studied the room—not a single eye seemed concerned with his crafty ascent up the stairs. However not even half of those who usually showed up was there yet. They had a long night ahead of them. Sam's eyes burned the back of Dane's head and he watched as his hand rested on Jess's lower back, right where the gown draped open, revealing soft skin above her lush ass.

Before he did something stupid, Sam slugged the rest of his scotch and turned up the stairs. If he simply looked as though he were supposed to be up there, it'd be fine. Do anything with authority and it's rare someone will question you. Besides—he *did* belong there. The home's owner had invited him up.

He slipped into Cass's bedroom, not daring to turn a light on. His eyes roamed the dark room. Had it only been two nights ago that he had been snooping?

He rushed to the table, feeling around for the book. *Shit; it isn't here anymore. What was the name of that one?* Heart Disease *and something...* Western Medicine? *Yeah, something like that.* He scanned the shelf running his finger over the bindings. *It isn't here ... why isn't it here!?*

He paced the room, scratching at the stubble poking through on his jaw. He only had a couple more minutes before Jess would come up—he might have no choice but to ask her about the book.

He tugged the box from his back pocket, placing it on the small table by the window, then dropped into the club chair beside it. Lifting one ankle over his knee, he leaned back, relaxing as much as his tensed body would allow. He didn't like the idea of Jess down there alone with all those vultures. Nope. Not one bit. She was a big girl though. And if he knew Jess at all, she had to do this alone or she would never forgive him for it.

Sam shifted in the chair as the corner of something pressed into his ass. He crossed the other leg instead, running his hand over the cushion. Nothing was there, though it felt sharp. His eyes scanned the shelf beside him once more. Maybe he had just missed the book before.

His gaze landed on the spine of a book—*FDA Approval and the Gritty Truth*. His knowledge of Cass's job was limited, though he knew she worked to find new medicines and she helped create medical trials for new medicines to the market. Every time he'd see her, the bags under her eyes would be larger, her hair flatter and her skin more sallow. It wasn't until he discovered her at one of the Portland masquerades that she seemed like the fun, vibrant big sister he had known back in the day.

He had avoided her most of the first evening. It wasn't until he needed to use the bathroom and the downstairs one was ... er ... occupied by a couple that he slipped upstairs to find a different one. He bumped into her; she was heatedly arguing with Dane, and Sam soon learned this wasn't just any party. It was *her* party. And her home. Sure, Sam knew Cass had bought a house in Portland—he just hadn't realized it was *this* one. The bright pink home was pretty notorious to the locals.

Sam swallowed. He honestly hadn't been attracted to Cass. She wasn't his type. The spark wasn't there—but that didn't mean he didn't care about her. She was his first love's older sister. Of course he cared for her. She and Jess were as different as two could be. But that night, he saw Cass in a whole new light—the potential for what she could be.

*Her dark hair was swept back in a low French twist and she wore a dress with a leather bodice and a black, flowing skirt. A gold sash had been tied around her waist and Dane had been gripping her arm with such force that Sam could see her flesh squeezed between his fingers.*

*"Are you sure about this? How do you know that this guy knows what he's talking about? You never even expressed any interest in being a dominant before," Dane grumbled, dragging his index finger down her jaw gently. "And just where is your teacher, huh? Isn't he supposed to be here with you?"*

*"I'm not ready to be a dominant yet, but I'm getting there. And he'll be here soon." Then, she added more quietly, "I trust him."*

*"Really?" Dane sneered. "You trust him? The man who trains subs as a hobby?" Dane snorted. "So, I guess if he says you're a dom, then you're a dom. No questions asked, huh?" Dane snorted, shaking his head. His voice broke and Sam thought for a moment his pain could be genuine. But then, he gripped the top of her arms, slamming her back into the door behind her. "No," he growled. "You owe me an explanation. I deserve at least that."*

*That was when Sam stumbled between the two, intentionally acting drunker than a Sox fan in Yankee Stadium. "Cassie?" he slurred. "Is that you, buddy?"*

*He stumbled closer, clamping a hand on Dane's shoulder. He was a large guy; Sam came just shy of his height by an inch or so.*

*Cass fidgeted, wringing her hands, and narrowed her eyes at Sam. "Sam? Sam Mc—"*

*"Shhhhh." Sam pressed his fingers against her lips. Jesus, she really was new at this.* No real names *was the number-one rule—especially last names. Sam had intentionally broken the rule, but it had been to help Cass out of what looked like a tense situation.*

*She pressed her lips together, immediately knowing her lapse in judgment. "I mean—um, Monsieur Punir, meet an old, um, friend—uh . . ."*

*"Private Dick." Sam gushed the silly name out in an exaggeratedly drunk voice.*

*Dane's lip curled as Sam held out a hand for him to take. "Charming," he grumbled. "I suppose I'll let you catch up with your* friend.*"*

*Dane stomped downstairs and as soon as he was out of sight and earshot, Sam stood straight, losing the drunk act immediately. Cass's mouth dropped as realization washed over her. "You're not—"*

*Sam pressed his palm to her mouth, pulling her into the empty room behind them. "You're not even drunk," Cass whispered once they were in the empty room.*

*Sam snorted. "Of course not." He tucked his hands into the front pockets of his tux. "You okay, Cass? That guy, he—"*

*"I'm fine," she snipped.*

*Sam's cheek flopped to his shoulder. "C'mon. I may not know you as intimately as I know Jess, but I still know you. And that guy seems like bad news."*

*Cass shook her head. "He's not. He's a friend and he feels betrayed." She shrugged as though the way Dane had had his hands clenched around her arms was normal. As though the redness and bruising forming there wasn't anything to be concerned about.*

*"Let me guess. He thought you were entering training for him? To be his submissive eventually? Only to discover you connect more with being a dom?"*

*Cass hissed a curse that was barely recognizable. If Sam had heard Cass ever use the word* fuck *in the past, he may have had a mini heart attack. "God, how long were you listening for?"*

*"Long enough to know he seems dangerous."*

*"He's not—"*

*"Cass—we're* all *dangerous," Sam added quietly.*

*She looked out the window, a sad tilt to the corners of her eyes. "That's not true. Not Dane. And not my master. They're both good to me."*

*Sam sighed. He knew the world and the types of people involved well enough to know nothing he said at the moment would change her mind. Though part of him had been surprised at the discovery of Cass as a dom, he had to admit, he shouldn't have been all that taken aback. There were times that people's personalities absolutely reflected their sexual preferences of dom or sub—then there were other times, like Cass's case, that you feel so out of control in life, you need the control in the bedroom to survive. If he had to guess, this was probably why she connected so strongly to being the one in charge. People saw her as weak—mousy, even. Shit, himself included. Even when she became the matriarch in Jess's life, it never felt natural to the community. People were always questioning her guardian practices—some even going so far as to try to get Jess placed in a different home.*

*Sam's mind wandered to Jessie. He hadn't talked to her in years. "Just be careful, Cass, okay? If you need me, don't hesitate to call." He reached into his back pocket and pulled out his card. "I could help, okay? Or if you're planning to attend one of these events and want a friend to join you . . . I can be a shoulder to lean on."*

*Cass took his card, eyebrows arching for all of a second. "De-tective, huh? Good for you."* She flipped open a book on the shelf and bookmarked a page with it, nodding. *"If it wasn't for Jess, I might have even taken you up on your offer."* She smiled, then added, *"As a friend only."*

The mention of Jess was like a branded knife sliding into his heart. *"How is she?"* he managed to ask without a single shake in his voice.

Cass shrugged. *"She's Jess. I only talk to her once in a while, but she seems to be okay. She's always . . . busy, you know?"*

*"Yeah,"* Sam rasped. *"I know."*

Cass's eyes narrowed and her gaze held to his face. *"Do you?"*

Sam shrugged. *"I know from high school days."*

*"So, you haven't called her?"*

Sam shook his head. *"Trust me. I'm the last person she wants to hear from."* He dove a hand through his hair and swiped at the beads of sweat gathering along his hairline.

*"Somehow, I doubt that, Sam."* Her gaze darted nervously about the room. *"Did you and Jess ever . . . I mean, this lifestyle—did you . . . with her?"*

*"No,"* Sam answered curtly. Probably too quickly. But Cass nodded all the same. Her sigh of relief was not one forgotten. She didn't want this for Jess either, it appeared. And it made Sam wonder even more just how deep Cass was.

Sam was snapped back to the present by a sharp edge poking his leg. He stood, flipping the cushion over and pressing against it with his palm. A zipper at the seam was partially opened and he pulled it back, reaching into a slice in the foam.

He flipped the iPad over in his hands. He swallowed, looking to the door—how much time did he have until Jessie came bursting into the room?

When he touched the screen, an e-mail lit up, dating from about a year and a half ago: And when you tied black silk around my eyes, though the world around me went dark, my soul had never been so light.

The end of the email was signed by Cass, and Sam gulped, clenching his eyes shut. God, he didn't want to hear these details about her love life. It felt so wrong. Did Cass hide the iPad here? Did Jess even know about this e-mail account? He clicked the iPad off, noting the account names in the correspondences. That would be easy enough to tap into down at the station. If it pertained to his case in any way, it was his job to read Cass's gritty, detailed life. But that sure as hell didn't make it any easier.

He shoved the iPad back into the cushion, zipping it up and placing it where he had found it. Then, he slid to the opposite chair. Just in the nick of time, too. The bedroom door creaked open, a sliver of light from the crack spreading wider into a spotlight. "Jess?" Sam pushed off the arms of the chair to his feet.

She spun, shutting the door quickly behind her and clicking on the bedside lamp. "Why are you sitting in the dark?" Though technically a question, nothing in her tone hinted that she was looking for an answer.

Sam strolled toward her, his eyes skimming the length of her body. He chuckled inwardly at her exclamation. He loved that she was so brazen with him. That she felt comfortable enough to constantly state what she thought, challenging him. "I wasn't sure how secretive we needed to be here."

Jess rolled her eyes. "God. Not *that* secretive." She walked to the chair and sat on the iPad, freezing momentarily, spine stiff before she relaxed into the seat.

Sam's pulse jumped. So she knew about it tucked into the seat. Why else would she react that way to the cushion?

She stared down, brow furrowing as she ran a hand across a small stain on the cushion.

Sam sat across from her, a small circular side table acting as a barrier between them. "So? What's this about, then?" His voice caused her attention to jerk back to him.

"Downstairs—the entry into the party, it's a prescription pad."

"I know. I got into the party, didn't I?"

Jess swallowed and Sam noted the gentle curve of her neck; the slight roping of her muscles there and the way her jaw ticked as she chewed the inside of her cheek. Sam's gaze was locked on those full, glossy lips of hers. "Yes. But, I saw a group of three come in. And though I didn't see who brought it, one of the prescription pads they handed over was from Dr. Brown."

Well, shit. That caught his attention. His gaze shot back to her eyes, tearing his focus away from that sexy mouth of hers, and his hold on the chair tightened. "What? Our vic?"

Jessie nodded. "I can point them out to you—introduce you. One was Phantom. The other two were Lady Kennebunk and Lulu."

"Shit," Sam whispered. "I know Phantom and Lady K well. Unfortunately. If we have to interview them, our covers will be blown."

"Covers?"

Sam cleared his throat. "Our anonymity. For the party scene."

"Um, Sam—I know this lifestyle choice is important to you, but Christ. This is murder we're talking about."

"Calm down," Sam growled. He didn't yell—he rarely ever yelled, but his voice held the punch of venom that a snake's single tooth held. Small and quiet, but deadly. Jess immediately stilled at the tone. Sam could feel his lips turning into a smile at her obedience, but he stilted it quickly as his cock twitched in his pants. "I'll figure something out. Matt could interview them."

"So . . . do you want me to introduce them to you?"

Sam thought a moment. "No . . . but point Lulu out to me if

you can. She's the only one I won't be able to recognize. When we go back down, find her—and send me a signal so that I'll know who she is."

"Send you a signal?" Jess snorted. "Like what? Tug my ear?"

Sam's gaze darkened and he leaned in, the smell of vanilla and cherry blossoms clouding his senses. "I was thinking something a little more sensual," he rasped. "Maybe find a way to stroke your own ass?"

Jessie gasped a tiny, hiccupped inhalation. "What? Sam, don't be ridiculous."

"What?" he asked innocently. "It's a sex party. You're telling me you're not comfortable enough to touch your own butt at a kinky masquerade?"

Jess rolled her shoulders back, sitting straighter. "That sounds like you're issuing me a challenge, Detective," she whispered, her voice tumbling over his body like silk.

"If you consider *that* a challenge then you are clearly nowhere near ready to handle me, baby."

There was a pause as they locked gazes. Grasping her bottom lip between her teeth, Jess nibbled and jerked her eyes away from his. Her focus settled somewhere outside Cass's bedroom window.

"Jess . . ." Sam started cautiously. Then, pushing to his feet, he scooped a hand behind her neck, cupping her silky skin in his palm. Her muscles flexed against his palm and he circled his thumb into the edge of her hair. "Talk to me, Jessie." Pressing his lips to her temple, he felt her sigh into his hold.

"I found stuff. Cass's stuff. And—and I think someone other than me should know about it." She paused, lifting her gaze to his, and shook her head. "Even though I *hate* that I have to rely on you for this. I think you're my best bet."

Every muscle in Sam's body knotted, but he forced himself to remain calm. "That's the smartest thing I've heard you say all week, Jess."

Her breath came out in short, sharp stretches. "Go wait in my room across the hall."

Suspicion pinged in his chest like movement on a radar screen. "Why?"

"Because." Jess gulped, avoiding looking him in the eye. "I don't want you to know this house's secrets."

Sam bristled at that. "This house's? Or yours?"

The silence was damn near suffocating and her lack of response was more than enough of an answer. Sam rolled his eyes, grabbed the gift from the table, and stalked into the guest room to wait. Because that's what he had to do when it came to Jessie, wasn't it? He had to wait and prove that she could trust him now. Wait for her to be safe once more. Wait for her to come back to him.

# 25

Jess ran to where the creepy photographs of her were and then pried open the floorboards and air ducts. Along with the photographs, she grabbed the fake passport, but left the skeleton key firmly in place within her bra. Rushing to the tote bag full of the things from Cass's office, she also grabbed the picture frame of Cass with Dr. Brown, pausing as her hand brushed the files. With a gulp, she left them behind as well as the stacks of money. What if someone came back for all that cash? She certainly didn't want to be in the position of having to say she had turned it over to the police. No, that was her bargaining chip if these sick fuckers came after her. After all, money *had* to have been the end goal here.

A tremor shook her body as she moved to the door. Scotch sloshed around in her belly and for the first time all night, Jess became all too aware of the fact that she had had hardly anything to eat all day. The flutter migrated from her stomach to her chest and she shook it away as the goose bumps flashed across her flesh. She rushed to the guest room, shutting the door behind her. "Here"—she shoved the items at Sam before she talked herself out of it—"I found some of these a couple days ago and others just today. But this whole story of Cass's death being a robbery gone wrong?" Jess shook her head and her voice broke as she tried to continue. Damn her emotions. If she didn't keep herself in check, there was no way Sam would let her continue with the crime-scene unit. "There was something bigger going on here. With Cass. But I think you already know that." She finished, fading off quietly.

Sam flipped through the items, jaw ticking with each new discovery. His body stiffened, hands gripping the pictures of Jess, and from beneath the collar of his dress shirt, his neck muscles visibly bunched.

"Those photos," Jess snapped, pointing at them in his hands. "You saw those. The other night in Cass's book. Why didn't you tell me?" Her voice cracked again and she hated that she had no control over the tightness in her throat. "Am I—am I in danger?" she whispered.

Sam lifted his eyes to her and in that one simple look, she saw it. Fear. And pity. "Oh God." Tunnel vision surrounded her eyes, blackening into an oval.

"Jess, baby, stay with me." Sam's arms were around her, one hand cupping the back of her neck. "Breathe. Deep breaths, come on."

She did as told and the prickles of stars became fewer and fewer as the oxygen filled her once more.

His jaw was tensed and a slight textured noise came from him as though he was grinding his teeth. "You're right," he finally said. "I saw these. I saw them a couple weeks ago, too. Cass showed them to me when she had received them. I was supposed to stage a time to pick them up from her, but—but she died before I could get to them. I think whoever ran you down with their car the other day . . . I think that was more of a message to me than you. A warning to get you out of here sooner than later."

"Why didn't you tell me?" Jess jumped as a lightbulb above them flickered before humming back to its normal state. Sam's expression was steel, but his eyes were warm and thoughtful. His fingers moved in little figure eights over the back of her neck and even though Jess didn't want to be enchanted by him, she was. Never before in her life had her chest hurt with such an indefinable ache.

"You knowing anything would just put you in more danger than you already are. I'm sorry, baby."

There was a slow burn behind her eyes. "Cass called me. The night she died—but, I didn't answer. And she left me the weirdest message. All she said was 'You're in the frame' . . . which, it's stupid, but it's something I'd always say to her if she was in my way." Jess gulped, a sob launching from the back of her throat. The tears singed her eyelids, threatening to spill out, and her throat felt tight like when you need a glass of water on a hot day. Sam opened his mouth to speak, but Jess cut him off, grasping his lapels with both fists. "I know," she whispered. "I know I sound crazy, but that message meant something. And it was really late when she left it, but it sounded like she was out-side. And then right after she left it, my phone went missing. I swear, I didn't lose it. I listened to the message, slid the phone back into my purse, and . . . and a bunch of waiters came over to help me because I knocked over a chair and as I was walking home, that's when I realized it was gone." She was babbling and she must have sounded like a madwoman. But it didn't matter. If anyone in this world would believe her, it would be Sam. He knew her. He knew when she was lying.

"Jess—" Sam's hands rested on her shoulders and the weight was comforting. His large fingers encompassed almost her en-tire arm and as her body started shaking, she knew there was no stopping the tears from there.

"Look at the passport. It's fake. A *good* fake. And the pictures of me . . . whoever did this might want to come after me next—"

"Jessica," Sam snapped, then quickly softened his voice once more. "You aren't crazy. You're right. And I believe you. Cass was involved in something—

"It's drugs, isn't it?" Jess whispered, cutting him off. She wasn't sure how she knew . . . it just made sense. All the money. The fake passport. What else could it possibly be?

It took Sam less than a moment to nod. "Yes. She was deep into some sort of drug ring." He winced with the admission and scooped his hand into Jess's hair. "I'm so sorry, Jessie. She never confided entirely in me, but I knew she was involved and I was trying to help her when she died."

Jess blinked, tears spilling down her cheeks as the truth slammed into her chest. The moisture was hot and salty as the tears careened over her lips and she licked them, wiping the remainders away with the back of her hand.

With his other hand, he brushed his palm up her arm, squeezing her shoulder. "We need the world to continue thinking it was a robbery gone wrong. We need the people responsible to think we're not onto them in the least bit." Sam hooked a finger under her chin and raised her wet eyes to his. "You understand, right?"

Jess nodded slowly, letting that information sink in. Cass was part of a drug ring. It made sense, given her job. Letting a final breath out slowly through her lips, Jess pushed the sadness aside. There would be time to grieve later, after they found the fuckers. After she was safe. Sniffling, she held out the picture of Cass with Dr. Brown. "They knew each other. That can't be coincidence, can it?"

Sam turned the photograph over, undoing the frame and pulling the back out. Behind the image, a small stack of stickered prescription labels fluttered to the ground.

They were the stickers you put onto pill bottles. A cry strangled in Jess's throat as she picked them up and clapped a hand over her mouth. The labels were from Cass's office. With Dane Murray's name printed multiple times on all of them. "Why would she be giving Dane medicine?"

Sam snorted, shaking his head. "I think the more important question is why did she feel the need to hide the labels? And look—she altered them so that her lab isn't listed anywhere on it."

"Does her company even give out prescriptions? I thought doctors did that?"

Sam's face sagged with a sigh and he raked a finger through his hair. "I have no idea. But I highly doubt that she was filling the bottle with Motrin 800. No one would go through this sort of trouble for a slightly higher dose of something you can buy over the counter," Sam whispered.

Jess scanned her bedroom as a frost settled over her body. "What the—" Zoning out, she moved past Sam to her closet, which was closed. Her dresser drawers, which she was certain she had left ajar this morning, were all perfectly lined up and shut. Before leaving for Cass's office hadn't she thought that she needed to tidy up?

She flung the closet door open but nothing looked askew. Well, no more than usual. But that door—she *knew* she left it open. She opened the top drawer on her dresser and her leopard underwear, which had been carelessly hanging over the edge that morning, sat rumpled on top of the pile. "I think someone was in here," she said quietly. "This place was way more disheveled earlier today."

"What? Why? Is anything missing?" Sam immediately looked around, taking inventory of the room. Typical of a detective.

"No, no," Jess said. "Nothing like that. It was just—I know I left this drawer open. And now it's closed."

"Anyone could have come up here during the party."

She nodded. "Yeah, I guess so. But the party just started. And I spent the first thirty minutes upstairs in Cass's room."

Sam's hands fell to his sides as his narrowed eyes swept the room.

Jess gulped, almost not wanting to say it aloud. "Dane was here. Almost all day. And he was alone for a while."

Sam's shoulders clenched to his ears. "You left that guy in your home all alone?"

With a shrug, Jess tried her best to act nonchalant. "He was Cass's friend. He spent a lot of time here. I didn't think it would be a big deal." It wasn't exactly a lie; Jess sort of suspected him of something, but she didn't think he was dangerous. Then again, she never thought Cass would be involved in a drug ring either. People surprise you. "Did you check out Dane? At the time of the murder?"

"Yeah, he was driving through a toll booth on Ninety-five South about twenty minutes before her death. I always thought he was involved somehow, but he didn't pull the trigger. Hell, there's not a single thing I can find that would link him to the drugs or the murder."

"Couldn't he have pulled off Ninety-five and still had time to get down to the wharf? Especially that late at night?"

Sam shook his head. "I don't think so. We would have seen his E-ZPass charged going the opposite way."

"But—there's back roads, right? There's ways around the toll—"

"Believe me, Jess. I wanted it to be Dane. But it just wasn't. The guy was on his way to Boston for a job. The hotel he stayed in confirmed his arrival at three-thirty a.m."

"Cass died at one a.m., right? That's two and a half hours . . . Boston is a two-hour drive if there's traffic. Where'd that extra thirty minutes come from?"

"He claimed he stopped to eat. He had a receipt and everything for the McDonald's off the highway."

"Did he pay for it with a credit card?"

Sam pursed his lips together, shaking his head. "No," he said quietly. "He paid cash. And no, the guy behind the register didn't remember seeing him. But they see a ton of people daily. The man's paperwork all checks out. But we have an eye on him. Like I said . . ."

"Yeah, yeah. If he's involved somehow, you'll find it," Jess said, finishing for him quietly.

Sam pinched the bridge of his nose, his eyes fluttering closed. "Wherever you were hiding these, keep them there for now. I'll get them when everyone leaves."

One delicate brow raised over her amber eye. "Does that mean you're staying the night, *Dick?*"

The tension knotted between his brows softened for the first time all night and a smile hinted upon those full lips of his. "I don't know. Does that mean I'm invited to stay?"

He still hadn't given her what she wanted—no, what she needed. The explanation. But, damn, did Jess want him there with her all night? Just went to show how fucked up she was. Something crackled in the air like static and the tense moment snapped between them. Jess moved first, reaching for him, and he was a mere fraction of a second behind. They came together in a searing kiss and his hands tangled into her hair, tugging and touching as she ran her nails up the inside of his coat across his back.

As the kiss ended, Jess pushed him to arm's length, rubbing her forehead with her free hand. "I can't think clearly around you. You make everything foggy."

He pulled back, searching her face through the sea of shadows in the low-lit room. Sliding a hand into his pocket, he pulled out a small box with a royal blue bow on it and placed it in Jess's hands. Shock washed over her and heat warmed her chest.

"For me?" she asked.

One side of his lips tugged toward his eyes in lieu of an answer. "It's an appropriate gift for the sort of party this is," he said.

She gently lifted the box, held it to her ear, and gave it a little shake. Then, popping the lid, she gasped as Sam's mouth lifted into a deliciously wicked smile. "You're so bad," she added, quietly lifting the lace panties from the box. "Oh!" Startled, she dropped them as they buzzed in her hands.

Sam grinned wide, holding up a remote from his pocket. "My challenge to you is to not come tonight," he whispered. "Do you accept, Mademoiselle Pas Sûr?"

Her breath hitched, causing her full breasts to heave with the sigh. She gave him an ultimatum. One that he still had not responded properly to. But God, she wanted him. She wanted this. She wanted to have fun. And if she was destined to die soon, she didn't want to die alone. "This doesn't mean I'm not still looking for answers about why you abandoned me. In fact, you should expect to have balls so blue, they'll be mistaken for blueberries. But I accept, Private Dick."

"Blueberries, huh?" His voice was just shy of a whisper and though he was stone-faced, there was the slightest trace of humor.

Jess flicked a glance to his impressive erection that strained against the material of his pants. One side of her mouth lifted. "Maybe plums," she said. Stretching, she rolled her hips, gathering the slinky dress from her ankles and dragging it above her waist. The silence between them was thick and Sam wet his lips as he lowered himself to sit on the edge of the bed. A breeze from the open window slipped between her legs, cooling the bare flesh and she turned, her tight ass facing him. Bending slowly—painfully slowly—she slipped her heeled feet into the panties and scraped the lace up her smooth calves and thighs. Sam groaned as she turned, dropping the gown back to the floor. Then, lowering her hands so that she was bent, her cleavage hung just below his chin, she swept her lips across his.

Before she could pull back from the kiss, his hand cupped the back of her neck, crushing her lips against his. A moan slipped over her tongue, vibrating into his mouth as he tugged her into his lap. Hiking the dress around her waist, she wrapped her legs behind his back, Sam's erection pressing against her damp sex. Trailing a line down her neck, Sam cupped a breast, squeezing it through the bodice. Her nipples strained against the stiff lace, begging to be touched.

Jess bucked against him, hitting the exact sweet spot above. Licking his thumb, Sam pulled back from her lips, holding her gaze steady before slowly slipping his wet finger into her panties. His touch glided over her damp skin, barely brushing her ultrasensitive clit. She hissed through her teeth, pumping her hips gently into his skilled hand. With little flicking movements, he brought her to the edge of climax. Jess bit down hard onto her bottom lip, curling her body away from his, and stood in front of Sam with her dress still around her waist. She smoothed the panties back in place and turned for him to get a view from behind. "Told you I had some superpower levels of self-control." Jess shot him a wry grin from over her shoulder.

Sam stood as well, moving in behind her. "I was just getting warmed up." His cock pierced forward despite the tuxedo pants tenting and pressed hard into her ass. Dragging his fingers gently down her bare arms, he clasped his fingers into hers and gently placed them palm down on her dresser. "Push that ass out for me, baby," he whispered.

"Or what?"

His stubble scraped against her jaw as he kissed a path up to her ear. His hand came down hard against her ass and she yelped, surprised at the sudden shift from gentle to rough.

"Do you even have to ask?" he growled in return.

Jess arched her back for Sam. The ache between her legs was growing with each passing moment. If she wasn't allowed to come until after midnight, then it was gonna be a long evening.

And yet, the thought of holding off until the witching hour sent frissons of excitement cascading down her spine.

Sam dropped to his knees behind her, nibbling the back of her knees, then the insides of her thighs and stopping at her ass. Jess groaned, pushing it out even farther, and gasped as his teeth came down hard between her legs. She yelped and yet despite the pain, she spread her legs wider.

The dresser pressed against her white-knuckled grasp. She would not come, she would not come . . . and yet, with each lap of his tongue, she could feel the tightness knotting low in her belly.

Sam pulled away, gathering her dress in his hands, and as he dropped it all the way down to her feet, Jess suppressed a whimper.

With false bravery, she turned, pushed off the dresser, and grasped Sam's lapel. Pulling him in flush against her body, she pulsed her hips over his erection. "See? You're going down, Detective."

He pressed the button and though the vibrator was silent, she buckled, falling into his chest with a cry. Sam smirked.

"We'll see about that."

# 26

Heat flooded Jess's cheeks as she descended the stairs back to the party. A couple she had never seen before was pressed together so tightly, she could barely make out where one person's mouth ended and the other's began. The stairway was narrow enough without two people taking up most of it. Jess turned to the side, averting her gaze from where his hand disappeared under the girl's dress. But, maneuvering around them was more difficult than she thought. Her panties buzzed sharp and quick and she slammed a hand onto the banister to steady her wobbly feet, sending her barreling into the man's back. Glancing over her shoulder, Sam stood on the top step grinning like a madman. Damn him. His whole look this evening made her clench between her legs, a river flowing from her pulsing sex. His unshaven scruff that peppered his strong jawline paired with well-styled dark hair and a tuxedo, all of which made for the perfect combination of shabby elegance.

"Oh! I'm—I'm so sorry," she said, her face burning. The man turned a head over his shoulder, sandy brown hair slicked back behind his ears. From behind his mask, his angry features softened as he looked Jess up and down.

He hummed an approving tone beside her as his gaze shifted down Jess's body. "You can bump into me anytime," he answered, his voice low as he chewed the inside of his cheek. The woman in front of him grasped his face, pulling attention back to her with a final scowl at Jess. Despite the awkward encounter, desire flared in her belly and Jess dropped her gaze to the floor before she rushed past the couple.

As she reached the bottom step, she scooped a champagne flute off a passing tray with the grace of a prima ballerina. The bubbles tickled the back of her throat and her nose as she sipped. Dipping a shoulder, she managed to weave seamlessly into the crowd, which was getting significantly thicker with every passing moment. On her sister's L-shaped sectional, the sight of a woman straddling a man she had never before seen, let alone even met, halted her in her steps. Holy crap. Dane had warned her this may happen and yet, a part of her didn't believe it to be true. But there the evidence was right in front of her face. The man had a grip on her upper thighs and the purple dress was inching higher and higher toward her hips with each thrust as his hands guided her over his body. Though he was on the bottom, he was clearly the one in control.

The buzz within her panties struck hard and fast and Jess let out a small yelp, clutching the mantel over the fireplace. Her knees knocked together with the sudden force of pressure against her clit and that combined with the heady scent of sex already in the air was almost too much to bear. Turning on her heels, Jess rushed for the other room. Anything to get away from the bodies crawling all over each other.

From the corner of her eye, she saw Sam hit the bottom step, straightening his cufflinks one by one. She didn't need to see him in order to sense his presence, though. And despite the calm exterior, he continued toying with her impending orgasm.

Moving into the dining room, she slammed into someone and as Jess reached out a hand to apologize, she was face-to-face with Lulu. The woman paled, her jaw dropping open, and a mousy voice was barely audible over the chatter of the party. "Oh my God. I'm so sorry. I'm so, so sorry," Lulu said.

For a moment, Jess was rendered speechless. Lulu was sorry? It was Jess who rammed into her, not the other way around. Lulu's eyes were still cast to the floor and Jess dipped, dropping into the line of her gaze. "Hey, it's okay. You can look at me, ya know. Lulu, right?"

Lulu nodded and through coal eyelashes, she raised her gaze to Jess's. As quickly as she made eye contact, she darted a glance around the room. Terror. The girl was absolutely petrified. This was more than the standard dom/sub dynamic. It was pure fear. And based on Jess's limited knowledge, that didn't seem to be the standard or the goal for any dom.

Jess rested her hands at the top of her hips and slowly ran her palms down her ass. God, she hoped Sam was watching. This was the girl he needed to break. She'd be the easiest to crack open of the threesome that came in, that was for sure. "Lulu," Jess said, "are you sure everything is okay?"

Her attention snapped up at that question and those brown eyes widened like marbles. "Yes. Fine. Why?"

Jess shrugged, doing her best to act innocent. "You just seem so jumpy."

This time, Lulu snuck a glance over each shoulder before sighing. Her svelte neck elongated like a turtle reaching for its dinner. "I'm not supposed to be talking to you," she whispered.

Jess forced a lighthearted chuckle at that. "Why not?"

Lulu gave that same one-sided shrug, pressing her bony shoulder into her earlobe. "Dunno. Those are my orders for tonight, though."

Jess allowed the tilt in her smile to grow. "Do you enjoy breaking the rules?" Then, dropping her voice, she leaned in, adding, "I know I do, sometimes."

Lulu's smile widened a fraction of an inch and it was the most emotion Jess had seen from the girl since she arrived. Other than fear, of course. "Sometimes, yeah. Other times, not so much. I guess it depends on his mood whether or not I want to risk it."

Jess's insides twisted into knots with Lulu's admission. "You know, I'm still new to the scene and all, but if you're not enjoying yourself, maybe you should find a dominant who will make it more . . . pleasurable for you. Isn't that the point?"

Lulu snorted quietly, the noise mimicking an irritated horse. "That's definitely not the point."

*Oh.* Well, that wasn't quite the answer Jess had expected. "What is the point, Lulu?"

Her spine straightened as Lulu bristled and pushed past Jess. "The point is that I'm not supposed to be talking to you," she murmured as she swept by.

Well, *that* could have gone better. Jess glanced over her shoulder to find Sam staring at her, leaning against the banister, his elbow cocked in a ninety-degree angle. Jess's blood turned to molten-hot lava as their eyes connected. His sweeping gaze caressed her body and with a final lick of his lips, he dipped a hand into his pocket.

"Oh!" Jess cried as the vibrations stimulated her. Her hand came down hard on the back of the chair and as gracefully as she could manage, she fell into it, sitting at the table. But the buzzing didn't stop this time. The tension coiled tighter and tighter and more than anything Jess wanted to dip a finger deep inside herself. She wanted to feel Sam's weight on her body, his cock pulsing with need deep inside her.

The lacquered wood was smooth against her fingers and she tightened her hold at the edges of the chair. Sam was still across the room, staring at her, blue eyes glistening like marbles below the water's surface. The vibrations sped up, becoming stronger and louder and as Jess ran her hand along the dinner table, she remembered how he feasted on her body in that exact spot just the other day.

Taking her bottom lip between her teeth, she bit down hard. *Too* hard—a coppery metallic taste trickled into her mouth. Yet, she couldn't stop. It felt too good, too damn good and she writhed, pushing her damp sex harder into the chair. She needed more. More pressure, more movement . . . more Sam.

It only took another moment before the release washed over her. Like jumping into a cold lake on a hot summer's day, the splash of pleasure slammed into her, momentarily shocking before dissolving into a pure state of bliss. Her body clenched and released in delicious pulses and she opened her eyes to find Dane on the other side of the room, watching.

# 27

The button was smooth beneath Sam's thumb. Smooth and so, so sensitive to his touch. Just the slightest slip of a finger and Jess was lurching into strangers to keep her balance.

The low chuckle rumbled through Sam's body as he took another sip of his drink and lowered into a club chair. Through the French doors, he watched as Jess tumbled into the nearest seat, gripping the table before her. Taut skin pulled against her strained muscles and her face twisted as she tried to hold on longer.

Pushing the lever, Sam increased the speed and pressure. Goddamn, he was hard. His cock strained against his pants, pushing toward her like a pup lunging for a bone. How angry would she be if he threw down and fucked her right here at the party? Hell, no. This was her fucking house, they had their pick of any bedroom they wanted, he thought as his grin widened. He wasn't sharing her with any of the bastards here. The stubble pierced his palm as he ran a hand along his jaw, scraping like sandpaper.

A wispy piece of brown hair fell from her updo and brushed

the tanned skin along the sinewy curve of her shoulder. Catching her bottom lip between her teeth, she closed her eyes, stretching her neck back. Black lashes fanned out across the top of her cheek and as her body shook in waves of pleasure, Sam watched as she rolled her hips deeper into the seat of her chair.

Fuck, yeah. The pink stain flushed across her face and down her neck to her cleavage as she gently brushed the stray hair off her neck. In that moment, it didn't matter that staying in Portland was dangerous for her. It didn't matter that they each had jobs to do and that his entailed catching her sister's murderer. All that mattered was the way his heart swelled at the sight of her. He wanted Jessica Walters. He wanted her forever in his arms.

With how loud his heart was beating, Sam was certain the whole damn party could hear his pulse and in the moment, he completely forgot that he had a job to do.

Fuck. He had a job to do. He wasn't at this party to get his rocks off. He was here to catch a fucking murderer. A murderer whose next target was right on Jess's fucking forehead. He did a mental shake, clearing his fogged mind. He loved Jessie. There was no doubt about that. But if he truly loved her, he had to get her the hell out of Portland. That didn't mean she couldn't come back once he had cleaned up this mess, but she sure as hell couldn't stay here. And Sam had to make sure of it.

On the other side of the room stood the willowy girl Jess had been talking to. Young, maybe in her early to mid-twenties. Lulu—the girl Jess had pointed out to him by stroking her ass. The leather groaned, mimicking Sam's own objections as he pushed off the club chair and headed toward her. She seemed to sense his presence immediately and her body seized, stiffer than a statue.

"Good evening," Sam said, lifting his drink to his lips. The liquid slid down smooth and despite the coolness of it, it warmed him the whole way to his stomach.

"Hello," she answered quietly. A chilly breeze from a nearby open window caught the sheer curtain, tossing it wildly against her side. With a shiver, goose bumps pebbled along her nearly translucent flesh.

"Can't believe they keep choosing to throw these parties at a damn pink house," he chuckled, leaning into Lulu and dropping his voice another notch. "I mean, not very inconspicuous, you know?"

A surge of air pushed through her nose and her pursed lips tilted into a small smile.

Sam's grin widened. "Was that a laugh?" He nudged her gently with an elbow, careful to offer only a gentle tap. The poor girl looked so fragile, he wondered if she was anemic. What dom in his right mind would let his submissive get so thin? It hardly seemed healthy.

"Almost," she whispered. Her eyes shimmered, the twinkling lights strung about the room catching in her irises and casting a golden hue.

"You been to one of these before?"

She nodded, playing with her master's scarf, running it between her fingers. Was it purposeful? Her shy way of reminding Sam that she was taken already?

"This one was a bitch to get into, huh? I mean, the whole fish last time? That was easy. But a prescription pad?" Sam rolled his eyes and exhaled a breath through gritted teeth, the sound reminiscent of a spraying water hose. "I had to call in some favors to get that."

Lulu peered around the room, her chin nearly touching her chest. "My brother's a doctor. Helped a lot."

Ah, now they were getting somewhere. "Wow, I bet. Where's he work? Over at Mercy?" Sam jerked a chin in the direction of the hospital that was a few blocks north.

"Um, yeah. Actually."

Sam slid his hands casually into his pockets and leaned back on the wall. His adrenaline kicked into gear, sending a surge of energy into his chest. Goddamn, he got off on leads. The thrill of questioning someone and finding the link? There was nothing quite like it. "No kidding? I probably know him. I know a bunch of guys over there."

Her sharp breath expanded her bony chest and for a second, she almost filled out the dress that hung on her body like a hanger. "We're not supposed to talk about our identities," she said quietly, avoiding Sam's eyes as though by making eye contact, he could read her thoughts. Hell, he was good, but he wasn't *that* good.

The girl was a natural sub; and she responded to dominant behavior. Even still, he couldn't bring himself to go completely dom on her ass. His grin softened, but one side still tilted into a smile. He leaned in, close enough that his elbow brushed against her forearm and he could smell a soft scent of sunflowers dabbed behind her ear. "Did I ask you his name?"

Her smile widened. It was subtle, but there. "No," she answered, her grin almost as sheepish as her voice.

"Then, I think your identity is safe." There was another silent pause and even though the room was roaring with chatter and music and laughter, all of that seemed to still as Lulu stared back at him. "Speaking of, do you have any idea who throws these parties? They can't be easy on the wallet." From a passing tray, Sam grabbed a lobster puff, popping it into his mouth and licking the crumbs off his thumb.

She eyed him suspiciously, not answering. Sam rolled his shoulders back, standing taller, towering over her. Grabbing another lobster puff, he held it to her lips. "Eat," he stated.

As she opened her mouth to object, he inhaled a sharp breath, both eyebrows shooting higher. "Are you arguing with me? I said *eat*."

A small gasp pushed through her parted lips as she opened

them wider. Sam placed the lobster puff gently on her tongue just before she closed her lips around the food, chewing slowly.

"Delicious, isn't it?" Sam asked, and she nodded, closing her eyes, relishing the flavor. Now that he had her literally eating out of his hands, he tried once more. "I know this is Maine and all, but lobster isn't cheap. Someone must be footing a hefty bill each month."

"Phantom has been trying to find out for years. He got close not too long ago. He found the guy who started it all, before the parties were even held in this house."

*Now we're getting somewhere,* he thought. "Long before you were old enough to sip that champagne legally, probably, huh?" Sam tossed a wink her way as he slugged the rest of his scotch.

The smile lit up her face more than he had seen since the conversation started. "Yeah, yeah, I look young, I know."

Sam bent his knees, lowering to her eye level, and leaned in so close that his chin damn near could have rested on her shoulder. "So, who is it? Who started these parties?" Sam whispered.

Lulu shrugged and a silent laugh bucked her body. "I don't know the guy. I think Phantom said he was a huge real estate tycoon in Portland. Owned a ton of properties . . . Elliot something, I think." Her gaze wandered over Sam's shoulder, landing somewhere beyond. "That guy knew him." She jerked her chin in the direction of the dining room. There was Dane, leaning dangerously close to Jess.

# 28

"I'd ask if you're having a good time, but I think I already know the answer," Dane said, and then assessed her for a long moment that sent ripples of awareness sizzling down her body. She wasn't sure if the tingly feeling was a result of having just come off an orgasm, the heated look in Dane's gaze, or the feeling of being watched.

Jess cleared her throat. "I just needed a minute," she said. "I was . . . having a panic attack." Not even Jess believed that lie, but Dane was kinder than he let on and allowed the moment to pass without further scrutiny.

Loosening her grip on the table, Jess pushed herself onto wobbly knees, standing to match Dane's assessing eyes. Why did he always have to look at her like that? Like . . . like . . . something to devour. Well, two could play that game.

"Here," he said, those crystal-blue eyes dipping to his outstretched hand. "This was waiting for you at the entry table."

Two sealed envelopes with *Jessica Walters* scrolled in clean, looped cursive were pinched between his thumb and forefinger knuckle. Jess took them cautiously, turning each envelope over in her hands. They weren't standard envelopes—they were smooth, nonporous, and almost silky in texture. On the back was an embossed lobster claw, but nothing else.

Digging a finger into the side crevice, Jess tore the first envelope open to find a simple navy-and-white blank note card. On the inside, in the same smooth cursive, was a concise note.

> *Ms. Walters,*
> *We hope you found your first masquerade*
> *quite pleasurable. Please leave the entry tickets*
> *in your safe until further instruction.*
> *Sincerely,*
> *The Party Planning Committee*

The gulp caught somewhere between Jess's throat and chest. It wasn't a threatening letter, but something about it left unease ringing through her body. "Who left this?"

Dane shrugged. "I don't know."

Jess clenched her eyes and ran her tongue across her teeth. "What do you *mean* you don't know? Don't you help these people plan this stupid event every month?"

"That doesn't mean I've ever met them or even know who they are."

Jess moved to open the second envelope, but Dane's hand darted out to stop her. "Open that one privately."

She narrowed her eyes. "Why?"

"Because," he whispered. "It's your compensation for tonight."

Jess peeked in the envelope, barely opening the slit. A wad of cash thicker than her fist was in there and she nearly dropped the damn thing before lifting her gaze to Dane's once more.

They held each other's stare. "Don't you pay all the workers here?"

Dane shrugged, his shoulders relaxing as they came back

down from his ears. "Look, I dunno what to tell you. Money appears in my account. I use it to put on the parties."

There was something in Dane's voice that made her believe him, though she couldn't put her finger on why. But it didn't change the fact that the man was hiding something. She just didn't know what, yet. "Why?" Jess's voice rose to a shrill tone and she quickly tamped her temper back down. "Why," she tried again, quieter. "Why would you do all this work for *nothing?*"

Dane held her gaze for another moment before a flutter of blinks caused him to glance at his shoes. "Because I enjoy these parties. If I didn't do it, they wouldn't happen. And I like the community."

His jaw ticked as he worked his molars over each other. He was lying. Or at the very least, not telling the whole truth.

"Fine," Jess said on a sigh. "Can you help me put away the prescription pads?" She waved the card in the air before dropping it to her thigh.

"Follow me," he grumbled, leading the way through the kitchen and into the basement.

Jess threw one last glance over her shoulder as Sam's stare burned right through her. He stood next to Lulu, but seemed completely uninterested in what she had to say.

The stairs creaked their warning as Jess followed Dane down into the cool basement. Cement surrounded them—the floors, the walls. It was like walking into a giant cinderblock and that chill immediately penetrated deep to her bones. She hadn't been back down here since her first day at the house and that same feeling of dread, of someone watching and waiting, crawled over her.

On the left was the washer/dryer unit and in front of her was the stack of prescription pads. Dane walked right past the stack of pads to the back wall.

Nostalgia slammed into Jess as her eyes fell to the boxes be-

hind Dane against the back wall. A stuffed Care Bear leaned
out of a dingy cardboard box. Jess lifted the bear, bringing it to
her nose, inhaling. He still held slight traces of strawberry scent
from when Jess decided he was hungry and could benefit from
fresh fruit. The fur was matted and dusty and Jess cradled the
bear as though it was buried treasure. What the hell else was in
these boxes? And why did Cass keep them for so long?

"Jess," Dane said quietly. His voice was soft, concerned
even, and it caught Jess off guard. "You okay?"

The musky basement air burned as she inhaled deeply. Or
maybe the burning came from the damn tears that tightened in
her chest. Either way, it hurt. It fucking hurt. Jess lowered the
bear back into the box, scooting it closer to the bookshelf that
sat behind. "Yeah," she said. "I'm fine."

Dane stayed silent as Jess collected herself, turning to where
he stood. Perpendicular to the boxes of memories sat a huge
steel safe. The massive hunk of steel nearly came to Jess's rib
cage. "Holy shit," she gushed. "What the hell do they usually
keep in there?"

Dane shrugged. "The tickets to the party vary greatly.
Sometimes they need the extra space."

Jess palmed the bodice of her dress, at the apex of her rib
cage. The skeleton key—she scanned the huge safe, and as Dane
crouched, his black dress pants creased around his thighs. Jess
ducked her gaze to the Care Bear again, diverting her eyes and
avoiding those inner thoughts as Dane bent over.

"Jessica, are you paying attention?" he snapped.

"Huh?"

"The code. To get into the safe. You're going to need it."

Shit. "Oh. Right, sorry. Isn't it oh-eight-one-five? Like
her—um, like the closet upstairs?"

"No. Not even close. Thirty-four, eleven, forty-four, two.
Can you remember that?"

"Uh . . ."

"Call me if you need it again. You've got my number in your phone, right?"

"Can't I just write it down—"

"No. Absolutely not," Dane grunted, shaking his head. "You never write down your code anywhere. What if someone found it?"

Right. She guessed that made sense. "Okay. I'll call you if I forget."

The door clicked and Dane opened it in a fluid motion. It was empty inside. Not even a piece of lint. "You want some help filling it?" he asked.

"Sure, thanks."

With both of them there to transport the items, the time passed quickly. Dane was able to stack the pads and with both Jess's and Dane's arms, they had the safe loaded within ten minutes. Jess looked over her shoulder before opening the envelope of cash and thumbing through the ridiculously large stack of money. From the corner of her eye she saw Dane slide one of the prescription pads into his back pocket. Jess's other hand clenched, wrinkling the envelope in her clutched fist. What the hell was he doing? Should she say something? Her throat was suddenly dry and with a cough, she tossed the envelope of money on top of the prescription pads. Dane shot her a funny look but said nothing, slamming the door closed. The hollow sound echoed into the cavernous basement.

"Well, that's that. They should send you some sort of notification when they're ready to pick them up."

Jess nodded, her attention wandering back to the box from her childhood. Beside it was another cardboard box with Cass's name scribbled in Sharpie.

"You comin'?" His voice sounded far away and when Jess finally looked up, Dane was standing at the base of the steps, one hand extended toward her. For a moment, those blue eyes were poisonous. As he smiled, the curve of his mouth erased any toxicity from his gaze and the chill warmed along with Jess's cheeks. Did she totally imagine that? The frigid moment crawled over her and lingered at the nape of her neck.

"Ya know, I'm gonna stay down here for a few. I didn't realize Cass had some of our boxes down here." Jess lifted the teddy bear once more, hugging it to her chest.

Dane's smile softened right along with his eyes as he nodded. "Take your time, Jess." He turned and his heavy footsteps pounded on the spiral wooden staircase.

"Dane," Jess called, neck tilted to catch him.

The steps quieted and there was a creak as he bent, turning to look at her. Their silence weighed heavy in the air and said more than Jess ever could.

"I don't trust you," she finally said. Her voice was so quiet, she wasn't even sure he had heard her. And maybe it would have been better if he hadn't.

His face remained stoic, completely unchanged by emotion. "Good," he returned, after a long pause. Turning, his steps back down the stairs were slower and, if possible, even heavier. His dress shoes pounded like a bass rhythm as he made his way over to her once more. The muscles in his neck and throat tensed as he swallowed hard.

Jess stretched, elongating her spine. Anything to appear taller and match him eye to eye. Though she opened her mouth to speak, words cracked at the back of her throat like a radio unable to find reception.

Dane's eyes searched her face and as he studied her, a hand lifted, cupping a fallen stray piece of hair that had been tickling the back of her neck. "You shouldn't trust me yet," he said quietly, his gaze finally settling on hers. "You shouldn't trust anyone blindly." His blue eyes were like water being thrown on coals and the steam billowed inside of her with one simple look. "Let me prove myself to you."

As he backed away, the silky hair slipped from his grasp, taking residency against her neck once more. Jess stared as he left her, walking slowly up the stairs, and she found herself wishing he'd look back once more. But he didn't. And when she was finally in the basement alone, the sense of loneliness was oppressive. Gripping her Care Bear, Jess backed up until she felt the cool cement of the wall on her back and slid down to the ground.

On her left was a bookshelf and she dropped her temple to it. Emotion swelled in her chest. God, she missed Cass. Why had she been such a shitty sister for all these years? Maybe if she had just answered that damn call two weeks ago, Cass would still be here. Maybe she could have gotten Cass the help she needed. Hell—maybe they could have run away together; escaped whatever the hell Cass was drowning in.

Jess curled against the bookshelf, inhaling the deep cedar scent. It smelled like home; like childhood. It was the same bookshelf that she and Cass shared when they had one bedroom between them. Jess had the bottom shelf, Cass had the top. It wasn't until her dad got promoted that they were able to move into a larger house. But even after Jess had her own bedroom, she used to sneak into Cass's bed night after night and curl up beside her. When you spend years sleeping in the same room as someone, a bedroom all to yourself can be the loneliest thing ever.

The shelf wobbled against Jess's weight and made a crashing sound as the entire unit nearly tipped over. Jess caught it, barely in time, and in doing so her elbow slammed into molding behind it.

"Son of a bitch," Jess muttered, rubbing her elbow. Tossing the Care Bear aside, she scooted the shelves out of the way. "What the hell—"

Hidden behind the shelves was a small door. The handle was cool against her grip and she gave it a tug. Nothing. She tugged once more—maybe it was stuck? The door rattled, but still didn't budge.

She ran a finger over the lock—old. Really old. The sort of lock that needed a skeleton key.

Pure adrenaline rushed through her blood and the high was unlike anything she'd ever felt as Jess scrambled to pull out the skeleton key from her bra. Her chest lurched with the staccato breaths and the key slid in effortlessly. She turned it to the right, and there was a click and then an even louder release. She didn't even need to turn the knob as the door creaked open, revealing a nearly black tunnel.

# 29

Sam watched carefully as Dane led Jess down to the basement. Outside, the wind caught one of the shutters, slamming it into the home's siding. The loud noise made several partygoers jump, but not Sam. He wasn't the type to be startled, especially not by something as simple as a loud noise.

A passing server knocked into Sam's shoulder, creating a clatter of plates and wineglasses nearly as loud as the shutter hitting the house. Sam put a steadying hand on the guy's shoulder as the server's cheeks turned to a dusky red.

"Sorry about that, sir." The boy mumbled his apology, eyes cast contritely to the ground.

"It's all right," Sam sighed. Hell, the kid could have spilled the whole bottle onto him and he wouldn't have given two shits. Not until Jess reappeared from the basement with Dane. He'd seen this back when Cass hosted. At some point in the night, Dane would help her carry the goods to the basement. Hell, he'd even snuck down there one night and had a look around. Nothing. He found absolutely nothing other than your typical basement things—a washer/dryer, storage boxes, gardening tools. The only thing that stood out at all was the safe, but he already knew that was probably where Cass had stored the party items until they were requested of her. Only Cass never trusted him enough to let him know when they were moving the drugs. That was the edge he finally had. Jessie knew him and though she didn't quite trust him yet, he only could hope they would get there.

Sam settled in for a long wait. Even though he rationally knew Jess would only be down there for a few minutes, it would without a doubt feel like a lifetime.

From across the room, Mary's chortle caught his attention. She was a demanding little thing—not only of her subs, but of the whole damn party. She sought attention like a spider seeks a fly: carefully and with an intricate plan that ends with its prey coming to her, not the other way around. Snuggled onto the couch with her was a man younger than Sam, but at least of post-college age. Mary dragged her scarf through her fingers and the edge snagged on her ring in doing so. The silk billowed as another breeze dragged through the window, catching it like an elegant dance. The man took it and dabbed Mary's mouth with it before sliding it into his breast pocket.

Sam narrowed his eyes, studying the newcomer. Only—he wasn't a newcomer. Sam knew that guy from somewhere. Even with the wolf mask that covered half his face, Sam recognized the wispy blondish hair, his rounded nose, and that faint scar that sliced down his chin.

It was more than possible that Mary might kick him in the nuts for this, but Sam put on his largest, falsest smile and trudged through the crowd. The sea of people nearly parted for him as he commanded his way between them. "Hey there."

Mary's catlike eyes narrowed and through her inky lashes, flashed brighter than an eclipsed moon. "What can we do for you, *Dick?*" Though her voice was steady and low, it slithered around him like the slow coil of a python. A little squeeze here and there and before you knew it, your neck was snapped; that was Mary.

Sam shrugged and flashed his pearly whites once more. "Can't a guy come say hi to his friend?"

She matched his saccharine smile and her heavily lined eyes creased with the faux grin. "Not at this party, *no.*"

Sam's laugh boomed throughout the room and nearly over the music. With a flippant hand gesture, he held a palm out to the guy—he needed a better look at his face. A voice to go with it—something to trigger his memory of where he knew this guy from. "How are ya, man? Enjoying the party?"

The guy nodded, his grin warming those apple cheeks and frat-boy nose. "Wild place."

Mary nearly eye-rolled herself into a coma before she sighed and fell back against the couch. "Mr. Fix-It, meet Private Dick." Her eyelids lowered as she said Sam's name, allowing her tongue to linger on her bottom lip when she finished speaking.

Mr. Fix-It? Hell, Sam wasn't one to judge. Not with a name like Private Dick. But nothing about this guy's name exuded sex and power. And on the opposite end of the spectrum, nothing about it proposed submissive and obedient behavior, either. "Nice to meet you," Sam said, grinning. "You ever been to something like this before?"

Fix-It barked a belly-rumbling laugh—if he even had a belly. Which, based on how his button-down shirt lay flat against his abdomen, Sam guessed not. This guy probably sported a washboard stomach. "Nah, never seen anything like it before. My boss invited me. He apparently comes, like, every ti—"

"Fix-It," Mary snapped, but her eyes remained on Sam. "That's enough. These parties are anonymous, remember."

He sent a sheepish smile to Mary. "Sorry," he said with a shrug.

Sam's smile slid like oil on tarmac along his face. Ah, yes—that's how he knew this kid. He was Dane's assistant. Mr. Fix-

It . . . cute. Real cute. Sam had met this kid briefly when they were questioning Dane.

"Where you from, Fix-It? Nothing specific, mind you," Sam added, darting a glance at Mary. She lifted a brow, seemingly pleased at his clarification. "Doesn't sound like a Mainer accent you got there."

"Naw, I'm from Boston originally. Folks still live down there."

Energy nearly jolted through Sam's body and his muscles stiffened as his detective senses tingled to life. "Boston. Great city. And it must be nice to not be too far from home, huh?"

Fix-It nodded. "Yeah. I was actually there a couple weeks ago."

"Oh, yeah? Just a quick trip home to visit the family?" Sam's grip on his glass had tightened so much, there was a moment he thought it might shatter in his hand. Instead, he set it on a passing tray. He needed to be more sober if this conversation was going to continue. The silky lining of his pockets slid against Sam's hands as he slipped them into his pockets. Mary cleared her throat beside Fix-It, nabbing Sam's attention once more. Her gaze had turned to absolute ice, and if looks could kill, Sam would've been a walking corpse. Yeah, yeah, he was commandeering her fuck buddy, but she'd get over it. This was way more important.

"Yes and no. Was there for a job." The kid rubbed a hand down his neck and scratched his clean-shaven jaw with dirty fingernails. His hands were calloused, filthy. The kind of hands you find on a hard worker.

"No kidding," Sam murmured. An ache settled at the back of his jaw, but he just couldn't stop grinding his teeth together. Sam nodded toward the guy's fingers. "Looks like you have a hands-on kind of job." Sam held up his own calloused fingers. "Me too."

Fix-It chuckled. He was a good-natured kid. Maybe not the sharpest knife in the cupboard, but nice. Goofy. "Yeah, you got me. I might be wearing black and white tonight, but my collar's royal blue."

Sam twitched a smile. A real one this time. "Yeah, I hear that. Must've been more than just you in Boston, then, for that job."

"Yeah. Just two of us, though."

"You know, the best rest stop? It's right outside of Mass Pike. It's got all my favorite things—Auntie Anne's, D'Angelo, Starbucks . . ."

"Is there a *point* to this?" Mary snapped.

"No, no," Fix-It chuckled. "He's right. It's the best damn stop on the route. I always grab some McDonald's there. My boss even gave me cash for the drive to get some food. He knows I love Mickey D's."

There was a *rap, tap, tap* as Mary's knee bounced, heel hitting the hardwood floor in rhythm with her impatient movements.

"Well," Sam said, backing away. "I'll, uh, let you get to it."

Mary snorted a response.

"Poor bastard," Sam whispered as he turned and yanked his cell from a back pocket. He pulled up Matt's number, and the ringing line crooned in his ear. If Dane traveled with this kid, they would have seen two people in that car with him on the toll booth surveillance videos. And if Dane brought his assistant to this job, why didn't he offer him up as an alibi when they asked for one? It made no sense. . . .

There was a grunt in lieu of a hello.

"Matt," Sam whispered, then slipped into the downstairs bathroom, shutting the door and locking it behind him. He threw open the shower curtain—at these parties, you never knew where couples may end up.

"Mmph," he grunted again.

"Mattie, wake up. I need you to research something for me, ASAP. Dane's alibi for the night Cass died."

"Alibi? Christ, Sam. It was a robbery."

"Yeah, I know, but I just have a hunch, okay? When we verified Dane's whereabouts, the traffic cam of the toll booth didn't reveal his face, right?"

"No. It was just a guy in his car with a baseball hat. But Sam—"

"Just listen. There's a stop along the route. It's a rest stop right off of Mass Pike. The lot is swarming with security cameras there. Pull the footage and check for Dane's face."

"Right now?"

"If you could give the rest area a call and get the ball rolling, I'll do the rest."

Matt sighed heavily and a faint cry from a baby filled the receiver. "Okay. Okay. I'll text you when I've got the paperwork in."

"Also, there's some sort of real estate guy in Portland. He apparently owns a ton of wealthy buildings. Elliot something. Sales records are public. Check in the morning to see if anyone by that name has been making large purchases in the area."

"What does *that* have to do with anything—"

"It's for the Brown case. I'll fill you in later when you're awake. And Matt?"

"Yeah?" he grunted.

"Thanks," he said quietly. Not waiting for a response, Sam hung up and slid the phone back into his pocket. It landed heavily, clacking against the remote for Jessie's panties. Sam smiled and the sight of her gripping the table while she came in front of all these people filled his mind. He always loved her adventurous side. But it was more than that. She was smart and the only person who was as hardworking and committed to what she loved as he was. Even in school, she gave everything to being the yearbook photographer. She would stay until the janitor kicked her out of the developing room.

As Sam exited the bathroom, he caught Dane coming upstairs from the basement. Spikes bristled against his back and he forced himself to calm down. Timing was everything in his line of work. Reveal your cards too soon and someone could easily cover their tracks, leaving you back at square one.

Dane caught Sam's gaze from across the room and his eyes narrowed. *Well, here goes nothing,* he thought as he passed by the dining table. There was a visible shift in Dane's expression as those cloudy eyes lifted into a moment of shock at Sam's approach.

"To what do I owe this pleasure, Dick?"

Sam rocked back on his heels, seemingly casual. A gait he had perfected through the years. In his line of work, you had to learn to keep a cool head. That false appearance that you're only making chitchat until *bam!* You catch the fucker in a lie and you can go bad cop all over his ass. Sam sighed inwardly. Maybe he'd been watching too many late night episodes of *Miami Vice.* "Can't a guy come over and say hi to another guy at a party?"

Dane snorted. "Not when one of those guys is you."

Sam smiled but it tasted bitter on his lips. Like accidentally biting into an orange rind. He brought his shoulders to his ears, and the tension rippled down his arms. Thank God for the monkey suit, otherwise that tension would easily have been visible to anyone watching. "Jess seems to like you. And I like Jess . . . therefore, I figure I should at least make an effort."

"That doesn't sound like the *Dick* I know."

Sam knew what he was doing when he chose his name. He just didn't realize how many people would take the obvious route to insult him. Did they not get irony? "Well, maybe she makes me want to be better than I am."

Dane and Sam stood silently in a showdown that Wyatt Earp would have envied. "I'd say you both have your work cut out for you, then." Dane swallowed, looking back to the door. Raking a palm down his neck, he sighed, lowering his voice. He almost sounded . . . defeated. "What is it you really want?"

"Who funds these parties?" Sam whispered, his jaw tightening. He didn't expect Dane to fall for his bullshit. Not for a second.

Dane snorted a laugh, shaking his head and looking to the ceiling. "Seriously? That's your question? I don't know. I have no fucking clue. Money is dropped into my account, I set things up, buy the food, pay the caterers. I have no idea who runs this."

"But you used to know. You knew the guy who started it all. Elliot-something, wasn't it?"

Dane's face turned so brittle that you could have flicked it and seen him crumble. A ghost of a smile trembled on his lips, more shaky than a Chihuahua in a ring of pit bulls. "You should probably go check on Jess," Dane said.

Sam's heart lurched, slamming into his chest at the mere mention of her name. "She okay?"

"I left her in the basement, but she seemed sad. There were boxes of stuff . . . probably Cass's. It looked like she needed a moment."

Sam charged the door, abandoning his line of questions. Dane's reaction was all the answer he needed. Elliot was definitely the guy's name. And how many entrepreneur millionaires could possibly exist in Portland by that name?

Sam made his way down the stairs, an eerie feeling washing over him. It was quiet down there—too quiet. Not even the faintest rustling or movement. "Jess?" he called out, immediately reaching for the gun tucked into his ankle holster. "Jessie?" he tried again, holding the gun with both hands. Anxiety dripped over his skin like sweat and an icy fear clamped onto his lungs.

As far as basements went, it was a fairly clean one. Boxes were stacked neatly along industrial metal shelves. A few small pieces of furniture—bookshelves, nightstands, old box springs—were lined against the back wall. In front of the bookshelf at the back was an open cardboard box with a teddy bear tossed carelessly aside.

Sam moved quickly, glancing around the basement a final time before he bent and lifted the bear. Had she gone back upstairs while he and Dane were talking? Could they have missed something as simple as her return to the party?

It was possible, but improbable. Sam scanned the area once more. This basement had no windows. No other entrances other than the one he came down. "Where the hell did you go, Jessie?" He flipped open his phone, dialing her number.

Pain slammed into the back of his skull and his knees planted onto the concrete floor as he fell. A black loafer kicked the gun and it skittered across the room. Sam shoved to his feet despite the pain that sliced through his temples and threw a fist as he spun to face his attacker. A meaty hand clamped behind his neck, shoving his face back to the ground as the other hand stopped his fist midswing.

The sharp curve of a bony knee speared his lower back and he clawed at the hands as they wrapped around his throat.

A gruff voice whispered in his ear, "Get her out of Portland."

Pinpricks of light flooded what little vision he had left and, in a final effort, he grabbed his keys from a pocket and slashed at the attacker's forearm as the world went dark.

# 30

About thirty feet into the tunnel, Jess was wildly regretting the choice to enter without a flashlight. The clip on her glittery clutch echoed in the damp tunnel as she popped it open, pulling out her phone. *Thank God for apps,* she thought as she turned on the flashlight feature of her new smartphone.

Seriously, maybe this was a bad idea. A tremble shimmied from her knees up the length of her body. She had no idea where this tunnel was going; no idea where it would spit her out. And yet, she couldn't stop putting one foot in front of the other. A force beyond her control beckoned her to see this through to the end. This tunnel was something important to Cass's operation—why else would she have hidden the skeleton key that accessed it?

A groove in the stone swallowed Jess's heel and she stumbled, losing her balance. Her palms slammed into the hard ground and she grunted, pushing herself back to her feet. Damn heels. Yanking it from the crack in the concrete, she took both shoes off, hanging them off her fingers before continuing on. The ground was cool under her feet and every now and then, cringing, she'd step on some moss or other weeds that managed to grow through the cracks.

After almost five minutes of cautious steps, Jess was ready to turn around. Maybe the tunnel led nowhere? Just a weird hideout; something kids used to sneak in and out of the house to break curfew? Or maybe it was made during Prohibition by bootleggers.

She was about to give up. Turn around and call it quits, but then the faintest sound reached her. The ocean. Jess froze, turning toward the soft waves, and inhaled deeply. The scent of salt effervesced on her tongue. Pushing on, she rushed forward, nearly jogging toward the end.

A sliver of bluish silver sliced through the darkness about fifty feet ahead and as Jess neared the arced hole, she slowed, getting her breathing back to normal. Her stomach flipped and her heart hummed like a hive of bees being threatened by a bear. It sounded like the ocean, but she didn't know what or who she would be walking up on—if anybody. The tunnel opened its mouth and Jess hovered at the exit, peering out.

Calm waves lapped at the shore's edge, gentle, like a kitten laving a saucer of milk. Jess stepped slowly onto the rocky ledge, moving onto the sandy strip, surveying the perimeter. No one appeared to be around, but then again, why would they? It was nearly midnight. A line of dampness stretched across the rocks and sand where high tide had recently pulled out and Jess noted that at its highest point, the water didn't quite reach the rocks. To the left of the tunnel were rickety wooden steps that led up to a dock above. A few blocks away the dim sign to Mary's Chowder House flickered, creating a low-cast light, which, other than the moon, was the only illumination in the area.

Setting her shoes down in the opening of the tunnel, Jess moved toward the steps to have a look at what was above. Popping onto the rocks, she skipped from one to the other. Sharp pain sliced into the pads of her foot and she yelped, grasping the foot in her hand. Scarlet blood flowed through her fingers and she hissed through clenched teeth, falling to a seated position.

"Fucking glass."

She picked at the tiny shard that had embedded itself below her big toe, digging it out carefully. A glimmer of light caught the glow of the moon from between the dry rocks. The corner of something pink and sparkly peeked through. Jess's heart stuttered in her chest. It couldn't be—no . . .

Leaning forward, she used a tissue to lift the item out of the rocks. A phone. A broken phone with a shattered screen and a custom pink bedazzled jewel case. Printed on the case was a picture of Cass and Jess, grinning on the beach with their parents. The image was over a decade old and pain spiraled through Jess's chest. *Cass's* phone. Jess dropped it carefully into her clutch, holding her own phone in hand and pointing the flashlight in the direction she found the item. No wonder the police never found Cass's phone—she had been killed almost six blocks away, closer to the docks.

With a glance over each shoulder, Jess yanked the panties over her thighs and ankles and wrapped them around the rock where she found Cass's phone. She needed to remember the exact spot it was in, but hell if she was going to risk leaving it here for even another few minutes.

As she took a few pictures of the area with her phone, it buzzed, sending vibrations up her arm. Sam's name blinked on the screen. Jess answered, pulling the phone to her ear. "Speak of the devil," she said. Silence buzzed on the other line. "Sam?"

Some muffled grunting echoed in her ear, and Jess's blood froze in her veins. "Sam," she cried again, rushing for the tunnel. Maybe she was overreacting. Maybe he only pocket-dialed her. Her foot throbbed with each step and she hobbled, grabbing her shoes as she ran back for the basement. One of her heels slipped from her fingers, clattering against the hard ground. Who needed shoes, anyway? She pushed forward, Sam's breathing still echoing from her phone as she hopped through the tunnel.

Jess screamed as a masked man nearly slammed into her. They both froze, locked in a stare-down. Twenty feet behind the man the door was slightly ajar. Jess took a quick inventory of what she had on her—a weapon or anything to defend herself. She had her phone and a high heel. That was it.

But if she was going to die, she wasn't going down without a fight.

Another moan came from the other end of the phone and the masked man's thin lips curved into a sadistic smile.

Jess lunged for the door, running beyond the man, and he took off, as well, running for the other end of the tunnel. She shoved the door open, and the wooden shelves fell forward. Cedar splintered across the floor, wooden shrapnel nipping at her ankles.

"Oh God." Jess's voice was barely more than a whisper at the sight of Sam facedown on her basement floor.

# 31

*No. God, no, no, no . . . he can't be dead.* He was no longer moaning. The thought of losing yet another person in her life was too much weight to bear. She was a curse to all she loved. A heavy rock that sank people to the ocean floor and flooded their lungs.

"Sam!" She brushed her hand over his neck and down the limp muscles of his back. "Sam!" she sobbed once more.

The muffled response was followed by a twitch. "Son of a bitch," he rasped, pulling himself to a seated position and rubbing the skin at his neck.

Tears streaked Jess's cheeks and she threw herself at him, wrapping her arms around his neck and burying her nose into his shoulder. His scent was her reward; woodsy, yet clean, and she inhaled a second hit of the intoxicating smell. "I thought you were—you were—"

She couldn't even say it, nor did she need to. Sam pressed his lips against hers, devouring her kiss. Taking what was his. And she didn't mind, not for one second. His tongue nudged her lips and she gladly opened herself to him.

"I'm okay, Jess," he said against her mouth. He could barely get the words out before Jess was tugging him against her once more.

"Are you sure?" Jess cupped each side of his face, trailing her gaze along his head and chest. "What happened? What did he do to you?"

"Someone was down here. They must have been hiding and they attacked me when I turned my back."

"Attacked you? Why?"

A wispy smile graced Sam's face, creating lines around his mouth and eyes. And despite the blood and bruises, he was breathtakingly beautiful. "Because I'm getting close. I don't know what exactly spooked them, but all I know is we must be on the right track."

A fleeting jolt burned through her. They were on the right track—but with who? With Dr. Brown's murder? Or Cass's? Or possibly both?

"You okay to stand?" Jess asked as she stumbled to her feet. "We need to get you to the hospital."

"No. Absolutely not. No hospitals."

"Sam, don't be ridiculous—"

"I'll be fine. It'll just be a little hard to talk for a couple days."

"Good," Jess joked. "That'll give us all a break for once." She winked, holding out a hand. Sam took it, however reluctantly, before he stood as well. "Come on, don't be stubborn. You need to see a doctor."

"Wait—" He grasped her hand, tugging her back to him. "I need to talk to you. I've been thinking and you're right. We should come clean with each other. Even if it means you never want to see me again." He exhaled deeply, momentarily closing his eyes before continuing. "In high school, the reason I ended our friendship—"

Jess's snort interrupted him as she shook her head. "It doesn't matter," she said quietly. "What a stupid, stupid thing to hold a grudge over. Whatever it was—it doesn't matter now. It's in the past. We were only fifteen, for God's sake."

"But, Jess—"

"No. Seriously, I don't want to know. What's the best-case scenario? I find out and forgive you? Worst case, I find out and it opens up old wounds. I'd rather just forgive and move on. Seeing you, lying there. Thinking you were . . . you were *gone.*" Tears sizzled against the back of her throat and she swallowed them down, ignoring that consistent burn. "I can't lose you again." Holding a grudge was like stabbing yourself in the gut and expecting the other person to bleed. And Jess was done bleeding. She was ready to be happy, complete again. "So, please, please . . . let's go to the hospital and make sure you're okay."

With the back of his knuckle he caressed the side of her face, lingering at the corner of her mouth. Pushing to her toes, Jess kissed him again. She kissed him hard, the way you kiss someone you think you'll never see again.

Jess hobbled over to where she had dropped her clutch with Cass's phone inside.

"Fuck, you're bleeding." Sam's hands curled gently around her ankle, lifting her foot. "What happened?"

"I'll explain in a minute. But here." She popped open her purse, handing Sam Cass's phone. "I found this outside of this tunnel." Suddenly reminded, she rushed to the door, shutting and locking it with the skeleton key.

"Cass's phone . . ." he whispered. "Jess, you have to take me through there." Sam moved to walk toward the door, but with the first step, he fell to the wall, clutching his head with a hissed curse.

Despite the shooting pain throbbing from her foot, Jess rushed over, to brace some of Sam's weight onto her shoulder. Her knees buckled under his nearly six-foot frame. "This isn't going to work," Jess said. "Sit here for a moment, okay? I'm going to get help."

"No," Sam snapped. "I'm fine."

"You're not fine. And Dane can help—"

"Dane?" Sam growled. "Are you fucking serious?"

Jess released a weary sigh, dropping her head. Frustrated, but not yet defeated. "Look . . . I know he's rough around the edges and we can't exactly trust him yet. But I need his help right now. *You* need his help right now."

"That guy's a snake, Jess. When Matt and I interviewed him, there was no doubt he was lying—"

Jess stilled. "Wait—you interviewed Dane? About Cass? When?"

Sam shrugged, bracing his weight on the wall. "The night of Cass's funeral. It was right when he got back into town. He was literally unpacking his truck."

"No." Jess shook her head, the deceit of it numbing her body, numbing the throbbing bleeding cut at her foot and the aching pain in her chest. "No, that can't be true."

"Why?"

"Because if that's true, then Dane lied to me."

"What?" Sam froze, squeezing her arm and dropping his voice to a whisper.

"He lied to me. When I first arrived at Cass's house, it was two days after her funeral. Dane was here and he claimed to be fixing pipes. When I told him about her death, he acted completely shocked, as if he had no clue."

"Now, why would he do that—"

"Unless he had something massive to hide," Jess finished for him.

# 32

A wave of nerves fluttered down her arms, and her fingers twitched involuntarily.

"We can't think about that yet. And right now Dane's the only person at this party who knows our identities," she said.

"And I'd like to keep it that way," Sam growled. "I hate that you're right." He rubbed the back of his head, stretching his hand out in front of his face; cherry-red blood stained the tips of his fingers.

"Oh my God," she whispered. "You're bleeding." Lunging for the steps, Sam gently tugged her back.

"Wait," he said, wrapping an arm around her waist. It felt firm against her soft lower back and her breasts pressed into a slab of muscle at his chest. Each breath pushed against her, growing more and more shallow. "Are we good?"

The corners of her mouth turned up as she brushed her lips along his jaw, stubble scraping her tender flesh. "We're better than good, Sam."

Emotion rippled in his blue eyes as his mouth came crashing down onto hers. She met his tongue stroke for stroke until she finally placed a palm on his chest and gently pushed him to arm's length.

"Stay here," Jess said, charging up the steps. "I'll be right back."

Rushing through the kitchen and into the foyer, Jess nearly tangled over her own feet when she saw Dane standing ten feet ahead. His back was to her. In a rare moment of clarity, Jess strolled over to Dane, placing her hand at his hip. "Hey," she said, offering him the warmest smile she could muster.

He yawned in response, stretching an arm overhead and landing it on her shoulders. "Well, hi there. Your boyfriend give you the okay to get cozy with me?" Dane grinned, looking down his broad nose at her. The foyer was particularly crowded, even for the party, and a tall, slender, masked woman knocked into Jess as she passed, shoving her harder into Dane's side. One of Jess's hands caught around his abdominals while the other landed somewhere midback.

"Dane." Jess pushed onto her toes, whispering as close to his ear as she could. "I have an emergency. I need your help." There was a hint of beer on Dane's breath and a slight sway to his body; as though he was hearing a song completely different from the upbeat swing the band was currently playing. How tipsy was he?

"Oh, yeah?" he responded, grinning. The swaying stopped entirely and the redness in his eyes was matched quickly in his cheeks.

"Yes," she said. "In the basement." Lacing her fingers into his, Jess pulled Dane in the right direction.

His head tilted, Dane's icy eyes narrowed, sliding the length of her body. "What's wrong?" He dug his heels in, refusing to move.

Jess licked her lips with a nervous glance around. "It's Sam," she whispered as quietly as possible. "I need your help getting him into my car and to the hospital."

Her gown billowed, sweeping the floor as she pulled Dane toward the basement once more, but this time, he didn't need much convincing. He was on her heels, following closely enough for her to smell the lingering aftershave on his jaw. "By the way," she said over her shoulder. "If you need a doctor's signature for that prescription pad you stole, I know some people at Cass's office who could help."

It was the first time she'd seen Dane's tanned skin pale to an almost anemic color.

"Jessica." His voice was a hoarse rasp, but she didn't stop as she rushed down the stairs back to Sam. "It isn't what you think."

"I don't want to hear it," she choked out through imminent tears. "Just help me carry him to the car." Sam was sitting on the floor, his head between his knees.

Without a moment's hesitation Dane scooped Sam's arm over his shoulder and lifted him to his feet. "We'll take my truck. It'll be easier to get him into."

And for once, Jess didn't argue.

# 33

"You should have come in immediately." The on-call doctor at Mercy dipped his chin, his eyes piercing Jess from over a pair of wired spectacles, before turning back toward Sam. "But you're a lucky man to have gotten here when you did."

Jess slid a glance to Dane, who sat in the corner of the hospital room on a small, metal stool.

Sam groaned, lying back in the temporary hospital bed. Beads of sweat dotted along his brow and into his dark hairline. "Can we dim the lights in here, Doc? My head is pounding."

Jess ran her hand down the length of his arm, lacing her fingers into his. This was bad. Worse than she thought. But Sam McCloskey would be fine . . . because he *had* to be.

The doctor dimmed the lights and clipped an X-ray of Sam's brain to a light box. "See this dark area here? That's where your brain has been hemorrhaging for the better part of an hour."

A gasp strangled in Jess's throat and she covered her mouth. "Oh my God!" Sam's hand tightened around hers and his thumb brushed over her knuckle. *He* was actually comforting her right now? A deep breath filled her lungs and the burst of oxygen was just what she needed. She needed to be Sam's rock right now, not the other way around. With steely resolve, she forced her knees to still and gripped his hand tightly, running her free fingers through his hair.

"Luckily," the doctor continued, "it looks like it has stabilized itself. However, with any head injury, we want to monitor it very carefully. We will likely have to keep you in here for a couple days, Mr. McCloskey."

Sam groaned, his head dropping dramatically to the pillow.

"Oh, c'mon." Jess managed to sound casual and unconcerned. "It won't be so bad. We'll watch movies, eat Jell-O. It'll be like a sleepover."

"Yeah," Sam grunted. "A sleepover without the fun stuff."

Jess met the old doctor's gray eyes once more. "Would it be at all possible for me to monitor him from home? So that he could get some rest?"

The doctor smiled, brows dipping in a way that implied he had known that question was coming. Everyone undoubtedly asked the same thing. "Unfortunately, no, we wouldn't recommend that. Head injuries can take a turn for the worse very quickly. We will keep him on monitors and if we have to relieve pressure, there's the potential for emergency surgery."

Sam winced, pinching his brow between two fingers as another apparent jolt of pain rocked through his body. He shivered, wiping the cold sweat with the back of his arm. A needling pain cramped in Jess's stomach at the sight of him pale, sweaty, and trembling with pain. Her gaze swept his body from head to toe—she'd never before seen Sam so vulnerable. Her body clenched and she caressed a path down his arm, excruciatingly aware of how dangerous Sam's situation was.

"Besides," the doctor continued, "if he stays here, he gets the good painkillers. If I send him home, he won't be able to get to a pharmacy for a prescription until tomorrow morning."

A smile twitched on Jess's lips. This doctor knew what he was doing. Those gray eyes twinkled as Sam's arm shot out.

"Hook me up, Doc. Give me the drugs."

It took about twenty minutes for the lovely cocktail of Valium and codeine to take effect. Sam was passed out, snoring like a trucker after a cross-country trip.

Dane and Jess slipped out of the room. Dane's lips pressed tightly together as he looked at the closed door. "He's gonna be okay." But Dane didn't know that. No one knew.

"Thanks for the help," she said quietly, unable to look him in the eyes. "I can't believe I'm gonna ask this, but would you mind going back to the house? Locking up and making sure everyone is out of there?"

Dane nodded. "Of course. Call if you need me." Pulling his keys out of his back pocket, he paused, turning to face Jess once more. "You know I would never do anything to intentionally hurt you. That prescription pad . . . I need it."

Jess clamped her eyes shut. "I don't care. Right now, you and your lies are the last thing on my mind."

A flash of pain resonated across his face, but it faded as quickly as it came. Dane nodded and walked away without another word.

Jess savored the extra moment of quiet in the hall, leaning on the wall. The bustling halls had finally stilled to a slow ripple of nurses and doctors. At the other end of the hall, the flash of a dark bob caught her attention.

Anticipation crashed over her body, landing at her toes like a lapping wave. "Rodriguez?" she said quietly to herself first, then again, out loud, calling to the officer. Pushing off the wall, Jess followed the curvy officer down the hall and through glass double doors.

She stayed far enough behind Laura that she wouldn't be seen or heard, but close enough to watch where she was going.

The halls were eerily quiet. Granted, it was well past two in the morning, but still. The only other time Jess had seen a hospital so still was the night her parents had died.

She shook the memory from her mind. Now was not the time to get sentimental. Instead, she crept along the wall, staying close as though it could shield her from being spotted.

Jess peeked around the corner just in time to see a blur of blue pants and black hair slip into room 304. What the hell was Rodriguez doing here so late? The door was slightly ajar; open. And on the inside, a small beam of light, a cool bluish-yellow hue was darting around the office.

Jess's heart pounded against her ribs and she could feel the rhythm pulsating in her blood. What the hell did she do now? Go to the authorities? No. No way. It was too late for that. By the time Matt or other officers arrived, Rodriguez would likely be gone. Jess was here, and chances were that both she and Laura had a decent argument that they had a legal right to see Dr. Brown's things.

Jess took a quick second to summon her courage before pushing through the door and clicking the light on.

There was a clatter as the person dropped their cell-phone flashlight and yelped.

Jess blinked into the flickering overhead light.

"Zooey?!"

# 34

"What are—what are you doing here, Zooey?" Jess recognized the petite, curvy brunette from Cass's office almost immediately.

"I-uh—I . . . wait, what are *you* doing here? Why are you in Rich's office?" Zooey challenged. But she wasn't as good at playing chicken as Jess was. She worried her bottom lip nervously between her teeth and her fingers clenched around her waist. Underneath her free arm was a stack of envelopes.

Jess folded her arms, lazily arching an eyebrow in Zooey's direction. "I have permission to be in here." Reaching behind her, she shut Dr. Brown's door as Zooey's gaze followed her own to the stack of papers she was hiding. "What's that?"

"N-nothing. It's nothing."

"If it's nothing, then let me see it." Jess held out a hand and Zooey recoiled as though Jess was going in to steal her lunch money. "Zooey, I'm working with the police on Dr. Brown's case—whatever you've got there, they're gonna find it."

Tears spilled from her eyes and her head dropped. "Please, don't," she pleaded, and her pale skin flushed red in blotchy circles.

"Talk to me," Jess offered gently, and cautiously lowered into a chair opposite Dr. Brown's desk. Gone was the competent office girl Jess had met only a few days before. In her place was a crying, shaking, nervous mess.

Zooey glanced over each shoulder, even though no one else was clearly in the tiny room, before she sank into Dr. Brown's chair. "Rich and I were in love," she said quietly, then on a sob, pulled in a breath through wet lips. "At least I thought we were. A friend introduced us at church one Sunday." The stack of letters she held in her hand dropped into her lap as she fiddled with the corners, pinching, tearing, and bending them. "I'm an idiot. I didn't realize he was sleeping with every woman he could get his hands on."

Jess reached over, placing a hand on top of Zooey's, squeezing harder as Zooey trembled beneath her touch. "That doesn't make you an idiot," she said quietly. "It makes you trusting."

Zooey sniffled and lifted the letters. "These were some of the notes I sent to Rich. Confessing my feelings." She rolled her eyes in spite of herself and swiped her finger under each of her eyes. "You know—I could have dealt with him sleeping around. That was just sex. But, when I saw that he liked your sister—"

Jess's heart skipped into her throat. "What?"

"Yeah. I can't believe it took me as long as it did to see it. He was always finding reasons to come to Holtz and, stupid me, I thought it was to see *me*. I thought they were just friends."

There were a lot of things Jess was learning about her sister, but Cass was not a cheater. And she would never deceive a friend like that. "Zooey, Cass wasn't seeing Rich. She was with someone else. Someone she really cared abou—"

"I know that," Zooey answered with a quiet shake of her head. "It was just the fact that Rich could keep me on the side while wishing he was with her. He was a player, but the way he looked at her? It was different. He really cared about her.

Maybe even loved her. And he didn't know she was seeing El-liot. Practically no one knew."

A rod of lightning shot through Jess's spine. "Elliot?"

"Yeah. Elliot Warner. He owns our building. Used to always come down and take Cass to lunch."

Oh God. Elliot Warner. The guy from the elevators with the shiny shoes and sad eyes. Jess did a mental shake to get her head back in the game. "Why don't you want anyone to find your letters?"

Her eyes widened from behind the plastic-rimmed glasses. "Jess . . . I did it," Zooey sobbed, the letters fluttering to the ground by her feet as she dropped her face into her hands.

Jess's heart ached, but she needed Zooey to say it. To say the actual words. "You did what, Zooey?" she asked gently.

Zooey swiped a hand under her nose, managing to speak through each hyperventilating hiccup. "I killed him. I didn't mean to. After he finished happy hour with Marc, I confronted him on his way home. We had a fight and I-I pushed him. He must have lost his footing and he hit his head."

Jess squeezed her eyes shut. "Zooey, why didn't you call someone?"

She scooped the letters off the ground and clutched them to her chest as big tears rolled down her cheeks. "I panicked. I put him on the bench and there was some random blanket there and I just—I just ran."

*Damn.* Jess liked Zooey. And this looked bad for Zooey from any angle. Involuntary manslaughter was one thing, but running from a crime scene? Placing and leaving a body, then being caught stealing evidence? Jess gulped, swallowing the sadness she felt in the pit of her stomach for Cass's friend and colleague. Not to mention, Zooey was the only prospective girlfriend Jess had in this town. "You know what I have to do, right?" Jess asked quietly. Moisture welled in her eyes as Zooey's tears spilled down her cheeks.

"I know," she whispered. "I'll come with you down to the station."

Zooey hesitated, clutching the envelopes in clenched fists. "Can I just—can I have a minute to read through them again? Before they go into evidence?"

Jess nodded, opening Dr. Brown's door. "You can read them on our way to the station."

As she turned to close the door behind her, Jess's gaze landed on Rich's desk. It was somewhere between messy and clean. Not quite as organized as Cass's, but also not altogether dirty like many of Jess's coworkers at the station.

Above his desk was a memo board with several Post-it notes tacked up there. Appointments and reminders scribbled in illegible cursive. On top of a pile of paperwork was a stack of blank notecards. The same navy-lobster-claw note card she had just received from the masquerade planner. "What the—" But it wasn't possible, was it? Brown had been dead for days when she got the note from Dane. No. No, it was just a coincidence. Every gift shop within a fifty-mile radius probably sold those exact same note cards. She shook the uneasy feeling away, closing the door and shutting off the lights. "Okay, Zooey. Let's get you down to the statio—son of a bitch!" The hallway was completely empty. Zooey and the love notes were gone.

# 35

Jess shouldered Sam's door open, speaking quietly into her phone. "Thanks, Matt. I think she'll be pretty easy to find. She wasn't expecting to be on the lam tonight." She thanked him one more time before hanging up and pressed the heel of her hand into her burning eyes. She was a photographer—not an officer. How was she expected to know arrest protocol? Still, guilt burrowed deeper into her belly.

Sam ran a hand down his face and his eyes fluttered open.

Sliding into the seat beside Sam's bed, she forced her tense muscles to relax. The last thing Sam needed right now was more stress. He needed rest and time to heal. Using her palm, she brushed her hand down his cheek, cradling his face. His cheeks were redder than before and she gave an inward sigh at the return of his coloring. "That was Matt on the phone," she said. "Zooey killed Richard Brown. Matt's sending officers out to find her now." Jess squeezed her eyes shut.

"Zooey?" Sam murmured, his head flopping to the opposite side of his pillow. "From Holtz Pharmaceuticals? No. No way . . . that girl's not a murderer."

Jess shrugged and linked her fingers through Sam's. "She didn't mean to. It was an accident."

Shifting his weight, Sam pushed himself to an upright seated position. "No. It doesn't fit—with his connection to Cass and his prescription pad showing up at tonight's party, Richard Brown's death cannot just be coincidence."

"Sam, I don't know what to tell you. Zooey's so sweet, it shocked me, too. But sometimes things are just coincidence. And trying to make sense out of them is futile."

The sound of his molars grinding mirrored the tightness in his jaw as he turned those sapphire eyes to Jess. "You need to leave Portland. The sooner the better."

Jess's first reaction was to laugh. He was kidding, right? "We just got back together. And you want me to leave again?"

"Look at us—in the last forty-eight hours, we've both landed in the hospital. It's a warning, Jessie. We were getting close and they were warning us to back the hell off. Who do you think attacked me in your basement? It sure as hell wasn't Zooey."

Their conversation was like a bucket of ice water being dumped over Jess's head. "There was a man in the tunnel. He let me go . . . but probably because he needed the time to escape." Jess gulped and despite the bottle of water she drank earlier, her throat was coated in sawdust. "I'm *not* leaving you here. You're gonna get yourself killed being a hero."

"I'm gonna get myself killed trying to keep you safe!"

His words stung and Jess pulled back as though he'd struck her across the face.

"I'm sorry," he whispered, reaching out a hand to hers once more. "What I meant was that if my focus is split between keeping us both out of danger it's harder to find the bastard who did this."

"I can take care of myself," Jess whispered, but even she didn't believe it.

Sam's mouth tightened into a line. "Jess—I didn't want to have to do this but I can't be with you if you stay here. I'm not going to sit around and watch you get yourself killed on some stupid fucking Nancy Drew mission."

Anger flared like fireworks within her. "That's what I am to you? Some amateur teenage sleuth?" She wrenched her hand from his, pulling it back to her lap. Counting to ten, Jess took a deep breath, releasing it slowly. "Besides," she said, "I don't think you mean that. I think you're trying to push me away so I'll leave you again. It's not going to work this time."

"Oh?" Sam's voice was deadly and sharp. "Then, how about I apologize? For lying to you."

Her blood went cold and she stilled. "You lied to me?"

"Yep." His eyes flashed an even brighter blue as the overhead lights flickered. If Jess narrowed her eyes just right she could almost see the stirrings of a tear in his eye. "I lied to you for years. I know who killed your parents, Jess."

Her parents? Jess's throat nearly closed up. What was he talking about? "Sam, you were out to dinner with your mom that night," she said, unable to keep the tremble in her voice controlled.

He shook his head. "That's just what she told me to say."

Even though Jess was nearly on the other side of the room, she took another step back. A flash of heat traveled through her body, beginning at the tips of her ears and rolling in a slow ripple through her limbs. The memories of that awful night in high school slammed into Jess with the impact of a cannonball. "Sam—what are you saying, exactly?"

"My mom was the drunk driver who killed your parents. And I helped her cover it up."

# 36

Sam watched as Jess's entire body shook with the impact of his confession. Her face twisted in an attempt to stay strong, to not crumble into an emotional fit. And more than anything Sam wanted to rush to her, hold her in his arms, and keep her there until there were no tears left to cry.

Only yet again he was the one to cause those tears. He was likely the last person in the world she'd want comforting her. Regret burned in his guts. But that was how he needed it. He needed Jess to hate him . . . and the truth was the best way he could think of to make that happen.

*Get her out of Portland.* His attacker's harsh, but clear words only came back to him once they got to the hospital. If they were both lucky, she'd leave this city and never look back. At least then she'd be safe. She may never be his again but at least she'd be alive.

Sam clenched a fist into the stiff blanket over his legs. "Jess . . . say something. Please."

"Your mom . . . killed my parents?" Something that resembled a half sob–half laugh escaped in a bubble. "And you knew?

All these years . . ." Jess's chin dropped to her chest and her head shook back and forth over and over again. "Sam, I can never forgive you for this."

That's what he was counting on. "I know."

Her attention snapped up along with her neck and the fire behind her eyes was unlike anything Sam had ever seen on Jess before. "That's what you *wanted*," she hissed. "You wanted me to end this. To leave. You were counting on me being so disgusted by your lying, deceiving face that I would go back to Brooklyn and never see you again."

With slow steps, Jess made her way over to Sam's side once more. "Well, guess what, Sam McCloskey? You can't get rid of me that easily. But you got one thing right," she added, pushing off the bed. "I never want to see your face again. Unfortunately for the both of us, we'll need to find a way to work together."

And on that final admission, Jess grabbed her purse from the side table and stormed out of his room. But not out of his life, as planned.

And even though he shouldn't be, Sam was happy that his plan hadn't worked.

# 37

Jess slid the key into her front door, the house eerily quiet in contrast to how she left it mere hours earlier. With Sam's admission, something inside of her had cracked. She couldn't bear to stand beside his bed for another moment. Couldn't stand the sight of him and everything else receded into the back of her mind. Nothing else mattered. Nothing else was important outside of the fact that his mother killed her parents. His mom was the reason hers had never helped her get ready for prom. The reason they had never seen her receive her diploma. All that she missed and all that she will miss moving forward slammed into her, the pain and loss freezing her heart with its icy grip.

That had been the last thing she would have expected to come from his mouth. All those years, all that time Jess had wasted wondering what she could have possibly done to deserve her best friend abandoning her during such a traumatic period—all the while, he was avoiding her out of guilt. Anger and heat raced through her and Jess felt the sudden need to hit something—namely Sam.

Dawn was cresting over the dark sky and the orange sun contrasted the navy outline. She needed time. And space. How the hell could she even remain colleagues with the man who helped cover up her parents' killer?

And yet, despite it all, more than anything Jess wanted to be in that hospital room, holding Sam's hand.

The door fumbled open and Jess dropped her keys and purse onto the nearest surface. The house was sparkling clean, she noted as her gown tangled around her ankles. Crazy how just a few hours before, she was relishing the feel of the soft lace swishing above her feet. Now . . . now, it was like shackles. Ratty and dirty with sand from the beach, sweat, and dirt from her basement.

Locking the door, Jess slid down the wooden column in the foyer, fighting the burn in her sinuses. Her body wanted to explode into a mess of tears and self-pity, but she'd be damned if she'd let that happen. She dropped her head into her hands, and a few silent sobs caused her shoulders to tremble.

Two seconds. That's all she would allow. Two seconds of tears for the man she thought she could have had a life with. After her seconds were up, Jess blindly pushed to her feet, barely able to see through the ripples of tears she wouldn't allow to fall.

A blue envelope sat on the front table, on top of a prescription pad. Jess reached for it, her fingers trembling—eager, but unsteady. The handwriting was bold, in all capitals with harsh strikes to each letter:

> **I'M SORRY. I PROMISE YOU, THERE WAS A GOOD REASON. BUT NO REASON IS SO GOOD TO PUT YOU AT RISK. PLEASE ACCEPT MY APOLOGY.**
> **—DANE**

Logic screamed inside of her head. Every ounce of her well-being was telling Jess to stay as far away from both Sam and Dane as possible. And yet, at the moment, she really needed a friend. Preferably one who wouldn't rip her heart clear out of her chest and do a little tap dance on it.

Exhaustion dragged through her body as Jess managed to make it up the stairs to her bedroom. She stripped her clothes off before curling into a ball on her bed. She was too tired to cry more. Too tired to think and dwell on what Sam's admission meant. Too exhausted to consider all the reasons that Dane would have stolen the prescription pad and the implications of him returning it with an apology. And maybe if she fell asleep, she'd wake up to find Cass making her famous heart-shaped chocolate chip pancakes, telling her this whole thing was just a nightmare.

Four hours later, Jess woke up to her phone going off. She grunted, reaching for it and startled to find Matt's name, not Sam's, lighting up her screen. "Hello," she croaked.

"Jessie." The way he said her name was like falling face first into a snow bank. She was sitting upright in seconds.

"What? Is it Sam? Is he okay?"

"Sam's okay. He's still sleeping."

A relieved breath pushed through her lips as she lifted her eyes to the ceiling. "Oh, thank God." Silence. "Matt?"

"Yeah, sorry. I'm here. That girl you called me about last night—Zooey."

"Yeah . . ."

"We found her."

Jess sighed, feeling a wave of relief rush over her body. Double good news in the course of thirty seconds. "That's great."

"No." Matt's voice cracked. "I'm so sorry, Jessie. She tried to kill herself. Left a note with the letters confessing to everything. She's down here at Mercy, but the doctors don't think she's going to make it."

"She confessed to everything?"

"Yes. Jessie . . ." Silence again.

"What?! Matt, whatever it is, just blurt it out—"

"She killed your sister. And Dr. Brown. They were apparently together behind her back and she went into a rage, killing them both."

Pins and needles pricked down her body. Oh God. No. "No—Matt, that's not possible. It's not what happened. . . ."

"It seems to be checking out, Jess. A witness puts her at both scenes. CS techs were at her apartment this morning and found the gun that killed Cass. We were wrong, it wasn't a robbery gone wrong. It was a crime of passion."

"Matt, seriously. I was getting to know Zooey. Why would she wait two weeks between killing two victims? If it was a crime of passion, she would have murdered both immediately!" Jess brushed her hands across her forehead. "Look . . . she confessed to me that she pushed Richard Brown and he fell, accidentally hitting his head. If she is guilty of anything, it is involuntary manslaughter—"

"His head wound was a decoy, Jessie. She poisoned him earlier in the night during happy hour. We found massive amounts of oxy in his system. It makes sense; she can get the drug from work. The bartender remembers seeing her during Brown's happy hour the night he died." They were each silent on the phone and white noise buzzed between them. "I'm sorry, Jess," Matt finally said.

Jess hung up, dropping the phone numbly at her side. Zooey was not Cass's murderer. And she wasn't Dr. Brown's murderer either. She was the fall guy.

And there was only one man out there who could help Jess prove it.

# 38

Monday morning, Jess pushed through the lobby and, after handing her ID to the security up front, slipped onto the elevator, hitting the top-floor button. It was midmorning and Jess held two piping hot coffees from the cart outside, dragging a rolling luggage behind her as well.

As the doors slid open, she moved gracefully toward the receptionist, her heels clicking against the marble tiles. She offered the woman her friendliest smile. "Good morning. Jessica Walters for Elliot Warner."

The woman tucked her nearly platinum-blond hair behind her ear and returned Jess's smile with an equally warm grin. "Do you have an appointment?"

"No, but I'm pretty sure he'll recognize me," she added.

"I'm sorry, Ms. Walters, but Mr. Warner doesn't take meetings without an appointment."

Jess set the coffees down gently on the counter and leaned onto the desktop. "I promise you, he will see me."

The receptionist studied Jess for a long moment before pushing out of her seat. "And what is this regarding?"

A quick smile flicked at Jess's mouth but didn't quite lift her cheeks. "If you could tell him that I've *mastered* Cass's secrets, that would be lovely."

A blank look washed along the receptionist's face, but she moved swiftly down the hallway, disappearing around a corner.

It only took a couple of minutes for the receptionist to come back and buzz Jess through the glass-and-pewter door. "Come on through," she said with a wobbly smile.

The inside of the office was adorned with crisp white walls and sleek gray-and-black furniture. Giant pieces of modern art lined the walls. The woman led Jess around the corner and to the end of a straight hallway. The office at the end of the hall had opaque doors with ornate pewter handles.

"Go on in, Ms. Walters." The receptionist gestured at the door before turning and heading back to her desk.

A shadow stirred from the other side of the large double doors. *Shit . . . if I can see his outline, then he can see mine as well.* "Here goes nothing," Jess whispered to herself before tugging the handle open while bracing the two coffees against her body.

She entered with her chin high and her shoulders back, taking assured steps over to his desk. The wheels on her luggage echoed softly against the slick marble floor. Sure enough, there he was—the red-eyed man from the elevators sitting behind a giant mahogany desk in a leather chair that likely cost him the equivalent of an average person's entire monthly rent. She set one coffee onto his desk before stepping back. "A little bird told me it was the best coffee in town," she said, lowering herself into a chair opposite him.

His razor-sharp eyes studied her and although he was only quiet for a second, it felt like a lifetime. Jess sat perfectly straight, her every movement solid and calculated. She would not fumble in front of this dom. She would not stutter or show any sign of submission.

"Ms. Walters," he finally said, his voice quiet and with the low rumble of a wolf's warning growl. His lips quirked, his eyes never once leaving hers.

"I've been expecting you."

Be sure not to miss Katana Collins's e-novella prequel

# WICKED SHOTS

Cassandra Walters has always followed the rules . . . until now. Introduced to the erotic pleasures of total submission, she spends her nights in the company of her master, doing as she's told and surrendering to exquisite ecstasy. But indulging in her newly discovered passion is a problem for Cass. She's caught in a drug-smuggling ring with no way out and nowhere to turn. Cass is not just running scared. She's running for her life. . . .

A Kensington e-novella on sale now!